S0-AWP-890

The
GUARDIAN ANGEL
Diary

To Sanchali,
Your Guardian Angel loves You!
All the best,

The
GUARDIAN ANGEL
Diary

Grant Schnarr

SWEDENBORG FOUNDATION PRESS
West Chester, Pennsylvania

© 2011 by the Swedenborg Foundation. All rights reserved. No part of this publication may be reproduced or transmitted in any form or by any means, electronic or mechanical, including photocopying, recording, or any information storage or retrieval system, without prior permission from the publisher.

Library of Congress Cataloging-in-Publication Data
Schnarr, Grant R.
  The guardian angel diary / Grant Schnarr.
    p. cm.
  ISBN 978-0-87785-335-0 (alk. paper)
 1. Teenage girls—Fiction. 2. Cancer—Patients—Fiction. 3. Angels—Fiction. 4. Diary fiction. 5. Domestic fiction. I. Title.
  PS3619.C44655G83 2011
  813'.6—dc22

                        2010042830

Edited by Morgan Beard
Design and typesetting by Karen Connor

Manufactured in the United States of America

Swedenborg Foundation Press
320 North Church Street
West Chester, PA 19380
www.swedenborg.com

*Thank you Ruthie, Steve, Skye, Lauren,
Lianne, Sue, Caroline, Randy, Pete, Mark,
Miriam, and all you anonymous angels.*

*As this goes to press, J, I love you more than
words can describe. "Arise, shine, for your light
has come, and the glory of the Lord rises upon
you." (Isaiah 60:1)*

Introduction

What can I say about Nicole? She was one of the brightest students I have ever had the privilege to teach. I found her intelligent, funny, wise beyond her years, and also as innocent as a little girl can be. She had to grow up quickly. Her mother died of lung cancer when she was only ten years old. Her father raised her and her younger brother as best as any father could, I suppose. But Nicole's greatest challenge came when she too was diagnosed with brain cancer at the age of sixteen.

Nicole gave this diary to me with the hope that I would be able to get it published. I don't plan to say much in the way of an introduction. It is a dialog between a brave young woman and her inner soul, a conversation with what she called her "guardian angel." As she searched for answers and tried to make peace with her life, and as she reached so high and deep to create meaning where there seemed to be none, her make-believe angel friend took on a reality all his own. Or perhaps he wasn't so make-believe after all?

This book is dedicated to Nicole and all like her who struggle to believe in something higher than themselves, and also to those special ones who help them and give them hope.

Although the original diary was in her own handwriting, I have put the angel's words in italics for clarity as to who is speaking.

 G. R. S.

Hi. I need some help from my guardian angel. Mr. Schnarr suggested I write to you. Maybe you'll answer me. I hear everyone has a guardian angel. I really need one.

I'm Nicole. My full name is Nicole Meredith Bealert. Yeah. I don't like my last name either. It sounds like some breed of dog. Like I'm a member of the Bealert family, kin to the Beagle, but also part of the Collie Clan. A mixed breed, I suppose. Anyway, what's your name?

Hmm. Yeah. No answer. I'll tell you more about myself. I'm sixteen. I live at home with my dad, Brent Bealert, and little brother, Luke. My mom died when I was ten. Now I'm in tenth grade. I hate school. But who doesn't? I'm getting good grades, always have. I don't like sports that much, but love music and drama. It's the usual for girls who don't like sports. I was in the *Wizard of Oz* last year. I played the Wicked Witch. It was so much fun being the loudest, scariest bitch I could be. Like all attitude, with permission! "I'll get you my pretty!" They said I looked like I was having too much fun playing the role. They were right. I never had so much fun!

Jenny got the part of Dorothy, which I think everyone knew would happen. She was born to be in the spotlight, probably had a white dress on when she came out, and ruby slippers. Yeah, I know. That's impossible. But why is it that the people who act like they SHOULD have everything GET everything? Why?

So let's talk about you. How is heaven? Do you have a house there? We live in a nice house, three bedrooms upstairs, but only one bathroom in the whole house. That's kind of a drag! I spend most of the time in my room or in our den, which is a new addition to the rest of the house. We have the usual kitchen, dining room, living room combo, much like most people's houses, I suppose. The sun shines through the tall, arched windows. Sometimes I sit on the cozy couch and write, or just stare out the window into our backyard. It used to have beautiful gardens in it, but now it's pretty much weeds.

You know, I was thinking, if you are my guardian angel, you've probably seen all this already, no need to describe it. Right? OK, well just in case you don't know, I live in the middle of nowhere, and the funny thing is that I'm in a sprawling neighborhood with a lot of other people living in the middle of nowhere. The closest town is Pottsville, which reminds me of an old mining town but believe me, I don't really know how that town got there. Everything here looks like it's in the middle of nowhere. The best thing about where I live is that there is a lake at the bottom of the street. It's not a huge lake, but it's big enough for people to bring their boats in the summer and water-ski and jet-ski, and fish and swim and have a lot of fun. I know it sounds like it, but it's not really a resort kind of lake like some. It's more like a lake in the middle of a housing development, which doesn't sound that appealing, but there are some really cool places to go and you can pretend you're in the wild, and except for the middle of the summer, it's not too noisy. I love watching the water, especially at sunset when the orange and red colors shimmer across the lake. Sometimes during the winter we can skate on the lake, but usually it's too rough because the snow mixes in with the ice and it's like skating on sandpaper. If we were a little more north in Pennsylvania it might be different, because the lake would freeze quickly and then the snow would just blow around on top of it, but a half-hour west of Allentown just isn't north enough. I don't care. I don't like the cold that much anyway. Do you like the cold? Does it get cold in heaven? I'm guessing it doesn't get really cold there.

Yeah. Mom died of cancer when I was only ten. And then Dad died. Not really. Dad didn't physically die like Mom. It seems that way sometimes though. He's kind of an ass. But we'll talk about that later. He's an engineer of some kind or another. I really don't know what that means, because I've never seen him work on engines before, but that's what they say he is. Duh. I know there are all kinds of engineers. But there is one thing I believe they all have in common. They are all in their heads. That's been my experience with all the people I meet from his work. My dad is a head case. He looks and dresses like one, too—short brown hair, dark-rimmed glasses, a lot of white permanent-press shirts and blah ties. He used to be less in his head before Mom died. He really disappoints me. He's never here. I don't mean he's never home. Even when he's home he's not here, if you know what

I mean. And that pisses me off because Luke needs him. Luke is only twelve. I asked him if he remembers Mom and he got mad and didn't answer me. When Mom died he seemed OK, but the older he gets the quieter he gets. I mean he doesn't talk at all. Sometimes he won't answer you when you ask him something point-blank. That's usually when you ask him something stupid. He decides it's too stupid to answer. He plays so much computer. He gets good grades though, and friends come over once in a while and play computer with him, so he's probably not in terrible shape. It would be better if Dad paid more attention to him though. Don't you think?

So, let's pretend you say, "Tell me about yourself, Nicole."

Sure. The most important thing for you to know about me is that I just got diagnosed with a brain tumor and I suppose I'm not exactly happy about that. I'm kind of scared. OK, I'm a lot scared. That's why I'm hoping you and I are going to get to know each other in this diary. But you should also know that I am pretty smart, and I think I'm a good person. I'm not ugly. I have long, golden-brown hair. Well, that's how I like to describe it. Some people say I have a mousy face. I don't know what that means except I will interpret it to mean I have petite features. I have hazel eyes, a small to medium build, about five feet six inches. I like flowers, world peace, and love. Ha ha ha. That was such a joke! I was pretending to be like a contestant on some stupid pageant show. You got that didn't you? Say yes. Hmmmm.

OK, I'm going to listen deep inside and if I hear an answer from you I'm going to write it down. OK? Hi there. I'm waiting. Maybe you don't understand. I'm going to talk to you and then listen deep inside and you are supposed to answer

me like in my thoughts, or whisper something for me to write
down. Get it? OK. Ready. Hi Guardian Angel. How are you?
Are you going to answer me, Guardian Angel? Hello?
Wow! I need to talk. I have a lot to talk about. It's really big
stuff. It could be life or death for me. I don't really want to
talk about it but I think I should. Don't you? It would probably make me feel better. I'm thinking I probably don't have
to tell you every detail of my entire life story because if you
are my guardian angel, you already know it. Don't you? Or
do you? Do guardian angels switch off and take turns watching over different people? I mean, have you been with me
from the beginning or did you get the teen shift? More like
the "teen shit," eh? Yeah. You're funny. You thought of that,
didn't you? You made me think that I came up with that.
Well, maybe not. I don't think angels are supposed to say
"shit." Are you allowed to swear? I know it's not a good habit,
but when I get really mad sometimes I can't help it. Hmmm.
Hell! I can't pretend to be a good girl with you, like Dorothy
in the Wizard of Oz. I'm no priss. I want a deep relationship.
I need to be myself with you. Or maybe even be worse than
myself and feel like you aren't going to judge me, or leave me.
     You get that, Guardian Angel? I'm listening. . . .
     Hell yeah!
     Yes! Your first words! I heard you say that. It was the first
thing that came to my mind and I wrote it down without
even thinking. I think it came from you! So it's the old "Hell
yeah." Cool. You're OK. Jeez. Hope there aren't any guardian devils, because I think I might be pushing it here. OK.
So, if anyone reads this someday, I really don't swear that
often. I just wanted to get real, and swearing is just words.

Right GA? Can I call you that? Seriously, you need a name. Or, you need to tell me your name sometime. OK? So, if I write something and then listen, will you answer me? If I hear something inside my head, like a thought, I mean, like if I hear anything I'll write it down like you said it. And then I'll read it later and I'm sure it will be very meaningful and all that. (Hint of sarcasm there. Did you get that, GA?) OK, let's talk. I will say something and you answer me. Um, like hi! And you say?

Hell yeah!

Oh you are a smart-ass! OK, if I say hi, you say? Hello? Hi there? Hmm. Not hearing anything this time. You there? I think you said something . . . but now I don't hear anything. Are you there????? I'm listening. I still don't hear anything. Why won't you answer me like you did before? Not answering me makes me sad. I really do need to talk to you. I'm not exactly in a good place. I might be coming to see you sooner than I wanted to. They say this tumor is "difficult" to remove. Um. Do you know my mom? Do you guys hang out with dead people or are they somewhere else? Can you believe I was only ten when she died? She didn't even make it to forty. Now I have it at sixteen. Guess that means it runs in the family. That doesn't seem fair. I feel sick.

This is hard. This is so incredibly hard. I'm so angry. Scared. Feel sick. I feel like I'm going to scream. And cry. You know that, I guess. Cry. You know I'm crying, don't you? Can you see me crying? Crap! OK, time to go get something to eat! BRB (That means "be right back" in case you didn't know.)

※   ※   ※

Back. Got some V8 and a piece of cheese. It's hot out.
A hot day in September! Sounds like a book, or the beginning of a novel. "It was a hot day in September. Nicole had
been crying, because she was dying from a brain toomer.
HAHAHA. I MEAN TUMOR! And she opened her journal
to write to her angel friend. But he was not there! So she ate
cheese and cried, and though it was early September, somehow to her it seemed like a winter's day. Even though the
heat of August still hung in the air, the chill of death breathed
down her spine." Pretty good, eh? Ha!

Hell yeah!

Yes! You're speaking to me again! I heard that. You are so
funny! You are a funny angel. Don't say it. Don't you dare
say it!

Hell . . .

Don't!

OK.

Thanks. We need to move on. Something deeper. They
say I'm smart and have a good head on my shoulders. My
drama teacher says I'm wise for my years. My school counselor says I'm an "old soul." An oooooold soooooul. She's
sort of a flake. But I like that "old soul" feeling. Ooooold
soooooooul. What does that exactly mean? It must mean I'm
reincarnated from some old woman, maybe a sage? Why do
most people believe they were royalty in past lives? There
just weren't that many kings and queens in history for everyone to have been one. Do you believe in reincarnation? Ha
ha, that's so funny, because I think you probably know more
about all those things than anyone down here, hmmm? Anyway, I don't believe in it. I think that whole thing is just wish-

ful thinking. The old concept of reincarnation was about not coming back here. I mean, coming back was really sort of a sentence, to learn something, because you didn't quite make it in the past life. Isn't that right? I think most people today think that it's some divine gift to come back. I think people don't want to leave. So if they have to leave, they make up something of a belief that says they can come back. Interesting. I never thought about it before. It's a return ticket, like, round trip. People made up that death is a round trip. That's so pathetic. Yeah. If I go I just don't think I'm coming back.

Well, I could do this forever. But if I'm going to spend most of these pages just talking to myself with a few "hell yeahs" thrown in, that doesn't seem very useful. I need more than a diary. I need a conversation. I need answers. Maybe answered prayers. My teacher said there are answers when we pray. He says prayers are answered in quiet ways. They come in small voices, or quiet feelings, or like whispers deep inside. Talking to you is like prayer isn't it? You can answer me quietly, inside me. I'll listen. Am I going to die?

I don't hear anything again. Well, I hear silence. That's worse than nothing. I'm not coming back, am I? No more answers from you today? It's a sunny day out my window. Literally, the sun is coming right in here now. It's bright. Hot! And very sunny. Ha ha. Time to go. It's time for dinner and no Dad. What's new? I'm not hungry anyway. You hungry?

"Angels don't get hungry." Is that what you said? No. I think you get hungry.

Yeah, we get hungry!

OK, so I made you say that. Whatever! Thanks for answering me. Do you have McDonald's up there?

No.

Good answer. That was a trick question anyway. If you'd have said yes I'd know you were a fake! Did you see that movie where that guy ate all that fast food and almost died? Whatever! I'm going to do homework and watch TV 'til Dad gets home. See you tonight.

Labor Day, September 3
11:35 p.m.

Hi. I'm back. It's late. I wanted to check in before bed though. I hate homework, especially when they give it to you over a holiday weekend. It seems like school is just a bad idea. They take you out of your home, fill you full of ideas you really don't need to live your life, or make a living, and they use fear tactics to get you to do things, like homework. Grades are stupid! It's demoralizing. School is demoralizing! I think it must have something to do with the Industrial Revolution. When they made all the workers leave the fields and head to the factories, they needed to do something with the kids.

Children also worked in factories.

Yeah, I know. But when it became illegal for kids to work in factories, they made kid factories. Schools! BTW (that means "by the way" in case you didn't know), I heard something inside tell me that kids worked in factories, so I wrote it as if you said it to me. Did you? I took a shower, and I love this new soap I bought. It's orange. It smells like orange, feels like orange, and yes, it looks orange.

Did you taste it?

No. I knew you'd ask that. You already know I didn't taste it. It smelled so good I wanted to. Lathering up in this soap is like a citrus bath. Refreshing! My skin smells so good. My sheets are washed. Wearing my favorite purple T-shirt! It's a cool breeze now, through the window, nice. I love getting into a clean bed. I like clean sheets. I like clean everything! I bet you do too! Angels are clean, aren't they? I mean REALLY clean! Don't answer. I know the answer. Mom was a cleaning nut! Mostly I remember following behind her as she scooped up the dirty wash from every room. Luke likes to leave stuff around, like a dog leaving his scent, marking his territory. You know, like a good Bealert pup! He's claiming space as his. Problem is, he claims the whole house. Of course, I'd kill him if he came in my room.

Ha ha!

I knew I'd get you to laugh. Well, it's true. And Mom used to ask me to follow her, and pick up anything she dropped on the way to the washing machine. I don't know why she didn't use a basket. Funny thing. I'd usually end up picking up a sock and somebody's tighty-whities—very gross. I remember her mostly just cleaning, vacuuming, dusting, doing the dishes, putting stuff away. That's what she did. My friend Tammy's house is a pigsty. One time when I went overnight we slept on a sofa bed in what I think was a family room. It was filled with stuff, like a storage closet. I remember feeling something sticky on my calf when I rolled over. We lifted the sheets and there it was. Part of a jelly sandwich! They have like fifteen kids. They're Italian.

(Smile)

Yeah. You're nice. You're very quiet, but I haven't really given you much time to talk, have I? I imagine you have a nice smile, warm, calming, a little devilish, even if you are an angel. I feel sick about going to school. It just gets me in the pit of the stomach. Grades. Peer pressure. Teachers with attitudes! Three more years of this? It seems like eternity. I suppose I'll live. Well, maybe I won't live!

You'll live.

No. I don't mean survive school. I mean LIVE! Like NOT DIE!

I knew that.

Oh you are such a smart-ass! I like it when you talk. Or when I let you talk. Or when I pretend you talk. No. You do talk. Because some of these thoughts are from me and some of these thoughts, or rather, responses, are not from me. At least that's what it feels like. Am I on to something?

Hell yeah!

I knew you'd say that. It's not even really funny anymore. I think if you were to really talk you'd say something like this: "We don't have to curse in heaven. We feel it. I mean, swear words are used by you mortals to embody a lot of emotions. Like so many expressions, words are only a container for your thoughts. But we are beyond thoughts, or can think many thoughts at once, and feel many things deeply. We are beyond words. Angel language is like thunder and also like a whisper at the same time. It encompasses all, and holds all thoughts and emotions simultaneously. Our language is at once simple and at once complex. We angels are pretty cool."

LOL (That means "laugh out loud" if you didn't know.) I think that was a great imitation. I feel like an angel COULD have said that, and really, when I was writing it, I didn't know what I was going to say. It just came out, and sounds plausible, maybe even . . . wise. LOL

Hell yeah!

Exactly! And I know that your "Hell yeah!" has so much more meaning than we mortals could ever grasp or feel. You angels are cool!

AMEN SISTA!

Hell yeah! Thank you, Angel. Thank you. I'm looking for our relationship to develop into something really awesome. I'm hoping we'll be able to talk together often and explore the world, the universe! I feel like I need to do this because I may not have the time most people get to learn about life and love and God and the universe and all that. I need to know more, to feel more, to understand. I know you'll help me do that. Maybe you could even throw in a miracle or two, but I'm sure that's asking a lot. You and I could be secret friends. I mean I have friends but they aren't very deep. I guess that's part of being sixteen? But I can't afford to be shallow. OK, I never liked small talk or gossip or "Oh my goshes," or "toootally rude-ass cool" language anyway. We'd better be secret for now. Who would understand? You OK with that angel?

Yes.

Excellent! Fare thee well then!

And thee.

Oh. I love you already! Goodnight. I want to cry again. Oh, maybe just a flush of tears to the eyes. I like to cry. It's cleansing.

Like the citrus soap?

Better. Even more pure.

Like you?

You are sweet. Goodnight.

'Night.

THE GUARDIAN ANGEL DIARY   13

Wait!!!!!!!!!
What?
Will you stay with me when I sleep? Do angels do that? I think they do. I think angels don't need to sleep. At least GUARDIAN angels don't sleep. They sit there, or maybe at night, they lie there, and watch. They just watch all night, don't they? They quietly watch, with their sparkling amber eyes. And you might even pat my hair, or stroke it quietly as you protect me from danger with your watchful eyes while I sleep. I like that idea. Except I don't want to be patted like I'm a damned dog! JK (That means "just kidding" if you didn't know.)

Stay with me tonight. I know you will.
I will.
'Night.

Tuesday, September 4
A Gloomy Afternoon

This is only the second week of school and it's driving me crazy! The long weekend made me realize how much I already miss the summer. I find school pointless and intimidating. Today I walked several blocks to school, down a crowded hallway and into the homeroom without anyone saying hello or even looking at me! I feel invisible and I'm not that unpopular. I have friends but people seem to be in some kind of state of unconsciousness when they first get to school. Even my friends don't say hi. We're all being hypnotized! JK. On the other hand, I'm not sure I want everyone looking at me and saying hello. I don't want the attention. I've heard terrible things about chemo and radiation and I'm not looking forward to having my hair fall out in front of everyone. The first chemo is coming up Friday. I don't look sick right now. Maybe I won't get sick. Duh. I'm going to get sick like everyone who has that stuff. Why am I even thinking about that?

I need to get serious. I want to tell you how lonely I feel. I said I'm not that unpopular, but I'm not one of those people who has a lot of friends hanging around all the time. I don't even really have any good friends. My dad says, "Well, you don't have to be Miss Popularity." He says you only need one good friend. I wonder why he says that. He doesn't have any friends. I suppose his coworkers are his friends. Do people only need one good friend? Tammy is my best friend, but I'm not sure how close we really are. I don't think I have a truly good friend like most people. Sometimes Tammy and I talk, and we've been together as long as I can remember. We used to play at her house a lot, but now we just sort of hang out at the school or sit at a picnic table at the park and wait for boys to show up. She does all the talking and I just listen. I guess Lauren and Skye are friends too, mainly at school, and I like Emily a lot, but she is so popular I always feel like I'm wasting her time when we're together, like I'm taking her away from her real friends. I don't know. I sometimes feel like the loneliest person in the world. Even if I was in a stadium full of friends, I don't think I'd feel any less lonely. It's a cold feeling, in my bones. It's depressing.

Why don't you do something about it?

I knew you were going to say that. As soon as you started saying it I knew what you were going to say. My answer is: no time. I have no time. If I'm going to die, why bother? It's too much work, or risk, for such a short-term gain. That sounds like economics class. No short-term returns. Long-term gains won't help me, in this case. There may be no long term. It's like some guy working so hard to save for retirement, and then having a heart attack and dying at fifty. Oops—looks like that was a waste of effort.

Really. Get back to the subject.

OK. If I close my eyes and feel, it feels very alone in here. I think about Mom. I think about Dad. I think I am very angry at both of them. I know Mom didn't mean to go. But she did go. Right? So, whether that makes sense or not, to a ten-year-old, that seemed like the meanest thing anyone could ever do. Or the most horrible thing! I'm sorry, Mom. Tell her I'm sorry. I didn't mean that.

She knows.

I know. It just felt so bad and I didn't really get it. What can you understand when you're ten years old? I hate Mother's Day. It was such a downer when other kids in elementary school were writing cards and making gifts for their moms on Mother's Day. The teachers usually wouldn't even acknowledge that my mother was dead. There was one, though. She said I could write my card to Mom in her new home in heaven. I liked that. But it was still hard to know that all the other kids could go home and give their cards to their moms and see a big smile and get a hug and maybe some cookies. My cards ended up in the trash. I didn't want to do anything special with them because that would feel even worse. So I just threw them out. I feel sick thinking about it. Never mind.

And your dad?

Not much to say. He's not really here. No time for me. No time for Luke. No time for the damned dog!

Bealert?

You are funny! No. Reggie. Reggie is a mixed breed. He's half Bealert and half German shepherd.
You're funny!
Thank you. Yeah. Dad. Before Mom died, Dad was still a nerd, but he was a happy nerd. He used to play all sorts of silly games with us, like pretend he was a sleeping troll and we'd pass by and he'd wake up and grab us. Mom and he would take turns getting us into our beds at night. He would always make a game out of it, like pretend he was a pirate who would threaten to capture us if we weren't in bed. I would sometimes let him capture me because then he'd carry me to bed. I liked that.

He has always liked his beer, but he got really drunk when Mom died and he drank a lot every night for a long time after that. He never did anything bad or abusive when he drank. He would come home from work and drink and watch television and seem preoccupied with his world, and would occasionally raise his head and ask if I had done my homework yet and if I knew where Luke was. That was before Luke started staying in his room. Then Dad started drinking less about a year ago, and that was a relief to me because I didn't realize it but I felt like I had to be the one who needed to take care of everything, like Luke, and the house, and worry about all those things Dad wasn't worrying about. When Dad started drinking less this sense of relief came over me. I didn't know how stressed out I was before that until I could finally relax. But then he seemed to put even more time into work, coming home even later, getting on the cell phone after dinner, then crashing in front of the TV. He still didn't pay much attention to us. I think he should have taken some time off when Mom died. He never stops working. He's like the Energizer Bunny. He keeps . . .

Going and going and going.

Oh, are you going to start finishing my sentences now? Actually, I appreciate you being there. Or, if it's only me pretending to be you, it's fun. But I don't believe that. I believe you are real. In fact, I'm going to write you a poem right now. Remember when I asked you to stay with me? I could feel that you were there last night. It was one of the first good night's sleeps I have gotten since I found out about the tumor. I really feel like you are there, and that helps a lot. You just being there and caring about me really helps. Here's a poem about that, just for you.

My Guardian

I asked you to stay last night
And you did.
You sat by my sleeping body,
Breathing in the citrus air,
Calming me,
Caressing my hair,
As you surveyed the horizon.
Vigilant are you,
My guardian.
Loving are you,
My angel.
I awaken from my deep slumber:
A gift to live.

N. M. B.

Yeah, deep, even maybe for you angels. But it means a lot to me. I love poetry. Did you know that? You know everything. I love to write poetry. It's therapy for me. Anything that might be on my mind can be made a bit easier through words, images, and poems. If you take something, a problem, a care, a hurt, and make it art, it changes. It becomes more than it was, and less than it was. It loses its power over me, and makes me think about higher things. Anyway. It's good therapy for me—poetry. Any kind of writing, actually. Hence . . .

This journal?

There you go finishing my sentences again! Yeah. Hence this journal, this diary to my angel. It does feel good to write these things down. I must confess though, I just went back and reread what I wrote, and I have to say I sound like a dork. You know how you write something and it's for you, but at the same time you imagine someone else reading it someday? I just hope they can forgive me.

Forgive you for what?

For being such a dork!

A d-o-r-k?

Yeah, that.

They will.

I suppose, if they read it. I hope Dad doesn't find it. He'd probably throw it out. Hmm. I'll give it to Mr. Schnarr. He suggested I try this diary because I really needed some focus to lift me out of feeling so bad and cut off from everything, especially from anything having to do with God, because we kind of had a falling out when I got this cancer, me and God did, that is. The idea is that if I journal with you about all this I might feel more connected and get some answers. I can see that's already true. I will give this journal to Mr. S. before I go in for the operation and if I die he can keep it. He's a minister. He'll know what it is and understand. If I live, I'll get it back and you and I can continue our conversations together. That seems like a good plan, doesn't it? But we'll see how things go, with the sickness, you know.

Are you going to tell me more about it? I really want to hear, and help you by being a good listener, and I can comfort you. That's what angels are for.

Not yet. Not now. Just can't. . . .

❊   ❊   ❊

OK, so I've been sitting here for ten minutes staring at the wall. There's this picture on the wall of an old abandoned beach house. Why would anyone buy a picture like that? Dad is so creepy sometimes. It looks haunted. It's just this isolated, old, broken-down house sitting on a dune with nothing around it except sand. It makes me feel bad to look at it. Can you see it?

Yeah.

It's scary. Isn't it?

Yep.

Do you think Dad bought it because that's how he feels inside? All abandoned and broken down? Hmmm.

It's very possible.

Did you like the poem I wrote you?

I did.

I know it's really about me. But it's . . .

Therapy.

OK. DON'T FINISH MY SENTENCES! Yeah. Therapy.

Thank you for the poem. I like it.
You're welcome.
Going to do your homework now, like a good girl?
Don't patronize me. But yes. I am going to do that now.
Check in with you tonight. OK?
OK. If you need any help let me know.
Do you know anything about geometry?
No. I don't know anything about it.
Some angel you are! See ya.

Tuesday, September 4
10:00 p.m.

Back again. I can't put it off any longer. It is time to really talk. I often get sad when I start writing to you. I have so much to say, and it seems like I don't have time. I want to capture so much of what I've experienced, even if it's been a short life for me, but I can't get it all out. Worse yet, what I'm trying to express is being taken away from me. I can feel it. Oh GOD! Jesus! Help me! Yeah, tears, blah blah blah. This thing in my head! What a terrible feeling, like my words are being sucked out of my brain with an invisible vacuum cleaner. One by one they just can't cling on anymore and release their tiny hands and slip away into the black hose. OMG! (I won't tell you what that means.) OMG I'm dying!
Nicole.
I'm dying.
Nicole!
I can't do this!
Nicole!!!!!!!!!

What??????????

Breathe!

Tears tears tears tears. . . . Breathe. Breathe. . . . Breathe.
. . . OK. What?

*We've got time. You and me. Talk to me. Tell me. Tell me
anything. Tell me everything. Breathe!*

Ahhhhh. I'll try. . . . Trying . . . OK. That feels good. I can
feel your hand gently touching me, stroking my hair, the back
of my neck. That's so soothing. I need to relax and be calm.
You do help me so much. Thank you. I'm breathing again.

You're calming down. That's good. Can you talk to me?

What do you want me to tell you?

*I know you want to tell me all about your life and what
you've learned, and I want to talk to you, and tell you
whatever you need to hear. But maybe, since it's on your
mind, you should tell me what happened with your tumor.
What's going on? I know it's hard. You can make it short. I
think it would be good for you to tell me.*

Oh. I feel sick. I really do feel sick, like dizzy sick. It's
partly just the thought of everything, but it's also part of IT.
When I think about it I start crying. So, this might take a
while. This page is going be soaked by the time I'm done.

That's cool.

Think so?

Yeah. Now tell me.

OK. Let me go get something to drink first. BRB.

❈   ❈   ❈

Back!

Let me guess? V8?

Apple juice on ice.
Nice!
I know. Oops. Now I have to go to the bathroom.

❅　　❅　　❅

Sorry. I'm back now. OMG, Luke is such a pig!
What do you mean?
He's gross. He does this on purpose! Whatever! How does somebody forget to flush? It's just beyond my comprehension. But now to the story.
Good.
I was at a swim meet on August 22. It was a Tuesday, because that's when meets are scheduled at the community pool. It was late morning, but really hot for that time of day in late August. I came there to watch the competition. I'm not on the team. Skye asked me to come. She's a big jock! She asked me and Tammy, and some other friends were there. I had eaten one of those new Mounds bars with extra-dark chocolate, and was sipping a Dew. I felt really nauseous, and at first thought it was the candy or being in the sun for too long. Then it miraculously went away. I felt really light. I remember about five or ten minutes later everything shifted. I was with everyone next to the pool, and the concrete surface below me just seemed to tilt. Suddenly, it was like gravity shifted sideways. I had no balance. The earth seemed to tilt. I fell down. I tried to get up again, but kept falling. I think it was Lianne's mom who got me to one of those fold-down chairs in the shade. I was shaking. Someone gave me water. It was OK. I felt better but was still shaking, and then I felt I was going to black out. It felt like a switch in my head was loose, and some electrical impulse was disconnecting and

then reconnecting over and over again. I felt like something was going OFF-ON-OFF-ON-OFF-ON. Very stressful!

I can imagine.

So, anyway, I didn't know it but they said my face was twitching. I felt numbness in my hands, or maybe like a tingling. People thought I must have had some heat exposure thing. See? I can't think! A heat . . . What do they call it? Well, whatever! They called Dad and he took me home. Dad got me dinner and rented a movie, and I felt better after eating and lying around watching television. Dad said it must have been the heat, and that sounded right to me. Everything seemed fine until the next day.

What?

I woke up at 7:30, which is really early considering I didn't need to get up at all, because I had quit my summer cleaning job since there was only one week left before school started and I wanted a break. So I could have slept in but it was good that I didn't.

Why?

If I had gotten up later, then Dad would have already left for work when I fell down the stairs. As it was, I fell down right before he walked out the door. I just remember losing my balance and heading toward the first floor. The only thing I remember about being at the bottom of the stairs was that I was upside down and that I hurt all over my body. Dad just looked at me with a dumb look and asked, "Are you OK?" I mean that's dumb, isn't it?

Maybe.

I started crying and saying, "Oww. Oww." Actually I was screaming, "OWW! OWW!" He got the message. He said, "Can you walk?" I said, "I don't know." Blah blah blah. I finally did walk to the car and he took me to the emergency room. By the time we got there I wasn't crying anymore and the only thing that really hurt was the back of my neck. I had bruises on my elbows and right hip and my face felt funny. At the emergency room they put me on a bed and got me to wear one of those crazy gowns that open in the back. Really embarrassing, but I could get under the sheet which was good. Then we had to wait for an age for anyone to come in at all and even say hello. But then one by one people would come in and ask me the same questions, like my name and address, and insurance, and why I was there, and yada yada, and then someone else would come in and ask the same thing again. Finally, a nurse came in and asked lots of questions like whether I had been having headaches or convulsions before, or felt anything in my muscles. Then the doctor came in and asked the same questions again. I had said that I hadn't felt any of those things to the nurse, but when the doctor came and asked me, then I remembered the incident at the pool, and also that I did feel weak in my upper arms and shoulders, and had more headaches than usual. I just thought all of that was normal.

It could have been. But wasn't your dad there? Did he say anything?

He came in and spent some time with me, but then kept going down the hall and making phone calls, probably work related. He helped give them information about insurance and stuff but he wasn't there when the nurse asked the questions about headaches and dizziness and stuff. But he was there when the doctor came in and yeah, he sort of reminded me of the pool thing. The doctor looked over my whole body, which was really embarrassing and they brought a nurse in at the same time, so two of them were looking me over. Thank goodness Dad left for that! And then they said that everything looked good besides some bruises and that I was going to be fine.

It's a blessing you weren't seriously hurt. Right?

I guess that's true. But then they did say that they wanted to do some tests to make sure, like some X-rays and stuff. They took an X-ray and then they did an MRI, or whatever those scans are called. It was after lunch by that time. Dad got me a tuna sandwich at the cafeteria after the tests. He could have gotten me anything in there, like a chicken Caesar salad or a burger or something really good, but no, he got me a tuna sandwich because I'm sure that was the easiest thing he could grab and bring to me. But I do admit it was good, because I was really hungry by then.

We stayed there 'til about 3:30 or 4:00 p.m. when the doctor finally came to talk to us. Then a nice-looking young doctor with dark hair and a stethoscope came into the little stall they had me in at the ER where I waited all this time, and said, "Well, the good news is you didn't break anything. The bad news is you have a tumor in your brain." He actually said that was sort of good news.

What do you mean?

He said if I hadn't fallen down the stairs they wouldn't have done the scan and discovered it. He said I was actually lucky because it would most certainly have killed me if no one knew about it. But now they can work on removing it.

That's great!

Yeah. He said that maybe, maybe, HEY! He said maybe my guardian angel had saved my life by giving me a little shove down the stairs. OK! Did you?

(Smile)
Come on!
I'll never tell. Let's just say you have friends "upstairs."
Oh, boo! What a terrible pun! I think you did it.
Nah. We don't work that way.
Yes you do.
No comment. Let's move on. So, what happened?
It was strange. After that they said I could get dressed
and go home. It was weird to come home around supper like
nothing ever happened. Dad got us Taco Bell on the way
home which was good. But that night it felt so strange to
do normal things, like homework and stuff, and at the same
time know that I had something wrong with me that had to
be fixed. I called Tammy to tell her and she was really upset,
which scared me. But then she started talking about her life
and went on and on and that helped me to not think about
what had just happened to me. Aunt Ellen came over and she
was kind of over-the-top emotional too. She's Dad's sister. I
guess he called her. She was really caring and put her arms
around me and cried and wanted to talk about it. . . . I didn't
want to think about it any more. Dad was on the phone with
Dr. Silverman, our family doctor, and also had a conversation with Aunt Melinda, Mom's sister. She didn't come over,
thank God. I hate her. But she did have some good things
to say, because she's a nurse and she knows a lot about the
subject. Dad spent a lot of time with his ear to the phone
and this sour look on his face as he listened to her. And then
he gave the phone to me. She told me that they would have
to do more tests, and that there would be an operation, and
that lots of people get tumors and have them removed and I

shouldn't worry. I appreciated that, but didn't know if she was just trying to make me feel better. She's like that, like she'll make things up. I don't trust her at all. After that everyone calmed down and Aunt Ellen left, and I went to bed.

What about Luke?

Oh. Yeah. He looked really surprised, and then he went into his room to play computer games. I didn't want to think about how he was doing. I was so overwhelmed. I was glad he could go and play and not have to listen to everyone talk about it.

Makes sense.

So, to everyone's surprise, something showed up. The tumor, I mean. It's interesting that now that I'm talking about it I don't feel anything. I don't feel sad right now, or afraid. I just feel, I don't know if it is numb, or just empty.

Interesting.

Yes. It is. So, the doctor explained they have to shrink it. Then they are going in and get it. Dr. Silverman has a way of making everything seem like it's going to be fine. The new doctors. All the specialists? They're less friendly, or I guess just more professional-sounding because they don't know you like your family doctor. They were more serious and said that the tumor was up against something, and truthfully I didn't understand a lot of what they said, but I got the message that it wasn't going to be easy. What I got from our conversations is that because it's pressing against some vital area in the back of my brain, they need to try to shrink it and then operate. They didn't exactly say this but it sounded like they don't want to unnecessarily kill me unless it's inevitable that I'm going to die anyway. Basically, I think they are just stalling so that when they kill me I would have died one way or the other. Then my dad can't sue them. When I think about it, it doesn't make any sense. If the tumor is life threatening, which of course it is, why not take it out right away? Why wait? Especially if it's in a dangerous area? I don't know.

Sounds like if they can shrink it then it will be easier to remove it.

Yeah, I think that's it. Sooo, then the tests and stuff started that Friday and have never stopped, it seems. Too much for me to talk about right now. Hospitals, tubes . . . ucky, ucky. It was all a dream when it happened. I suppose it was more like a nightmare. But I managed to stay caught up in school because the teachers were nice and gave me some breaks, or took special time to help me with the homework the first week.

Do they know about the sickness?

Yes. Dad talked to Mrs. Fischer, the principal, and I also think Aunt Ellen told everyone too, because she has a hard time not sharing her feelings with people. So all the teachers know, everyone Aunt Ellen knows knows, but only a few of my friends know, for now. Tammy's been very open with me about it but my other friends don't seem to know how to handle it, like they don't get it. I look fine so they don't really understand. Most people don't know I'm sick. It's a little weird, but it's not as weird as when I'm doing the tests.

What do you mean?

The tests continue to be a very strange experience. Most of the tests take place in the basement of the hospital, and it's creepy. It looks the same, like how the waiting room looks like a waiting room in the doctor's office, but there are no windows down there. It feels claustrophobic. Is that how you spell it? Some of that feeling might be from just knowing I'm in the "Cancer Unit" which just makes me feel ucky all on its own.

Ucky? What does that mean, anyway?

I know that "ucky" sounds stupid. But "ucky" is exactly how it feels to be down there. So, yes, it is an "ucky" place. The people who do the tests have been really nice. I think because I'm so young, so they try extra special to pretend like I'm going to be just fine, though they don't say that. They smile and ask, "How are you?" That's a weird question when they know you have cancer. But it's OK because what else are they going to say? The good news, I suppose, is that they can't find anything else wrong with me. There are no tumors anywhere else on my body, and believe me, they looked EVERYWHERE!

How has that been for you? You speak very matter-of-factly about the last few weeks, but it must have been rough.

Please don't act like one of the technicians with "How are you?" or "How are you feeling?" Because I just want to bark back at you, "How the effing hell do you think I feel?"

Effing?

Yes. Effing. Don't worry. You don't need to understand that one. But please understand that I am happy not to have cancer all over my body, and that really is good news. The one thing, though, which I think may be the hardest part of all, is that the closest person to my age I've seen in there being tested has got to be over fifty! I really feel so out of place in there that I keep thinking I've got to be one of the unluckiest people in the world. Why me? That's one thing that I keep asking myself during the tests. I feel embarrassed to be there, like I want to apologize, "I'm sorry. I'm sorry for being so young. Yes, I am in the right place. I do have cancer. I promise." It's a drag.

An effing drag, I suppose.

Definitely.

So Friday is your first day of chemotherapy.

Yeah. Thanks for reminding me. I know for some people it's not that bad. My mom had it and she said it wasn't as bad as she thought it would be. She didn't get that sick. I'm hoping the same thing will happen for me. Maybe when God made us susceptible to cancer he also gave us some of the right chemistry to handle it. I hope so. But I'm not going to think about it 'til it happens. I don't know why but I'm not frightened of it. I saw Mom go through it. I can too. They might do other things though.

Like?

Radiation. I hear that's bad.

Possibly. But you want to live don't you?

If I were a ninety-year-old woman I'd just say let me die. Maybe if I were seventy I'd say that too. Maybe even in my sixties. I suppose at my age it's immoral to say something like that. I don't want to die, but if I do have to die, I'd rather not be tortured before I die. I'd rather not be humiliated before I die, like hair falling out, and teeth and stuff, or whatever falls out. So, why don't you just spare me the pain? Tell me. If I am going to die, then maybe I can just tell them to leave me alone. If all this stuff is going to work, OK, I'll do it. But if not, what the hell?

Sounds like you're only willing to work toward retirement if you know you won't have a heart attack at fifty. Don't you think it's worth putting up a fight to get better?

What are you saying? Are you trying to say, "Keep your chin up no matter what?" Why should I go through all this if I might end up dying anyway? Or, are you saying it's worth it to let them do all this either way, whether I live or die? Why not just tell me if I am going to die or not? That seems easier.

I don't know if you are going to die. If we guardian angels knew things like that ahead of time we'd lose faith. Knowing the outcome of everything not only takes the incentive out of life but the mystery. Why bother doing anything if you know the outcome before you even begin? I hope you live. I really do. I also have every faith that you are going to be fine. How's this? Even if you die, you are going to be OK. So . . .

So, what? Relax? It's better to burn out than fade away or rust out or something? I think the chemo/radiation combo does all of that to you! So, what are you telling me? What am I supposed to do? If I'm going to go, I should go out kicking and screaming?

No. Go out with class! Live! Even if you are going to die, LIVE!

Yeah. Live. If I can. It makes me tired to think about it. I do get tired. They want me to stay in school as long as I can and want to. If I lose my hair I am NOT going!

Got it. What's next?

Um. All kinds of stuff. It's all leading up to brain surgery. When that will happen is up to how quickly they can shrink the tumor and feel comfortable working on it. I don't want to spend my time telling you every day how sick I'm getting. I'll keep you posted, but that's not the kind of journal I want to write. If you want me to LIVE then I want to have our time together be quality. I want to talk life. LIFE! I want to talk about good things, and maybe even hard things, and deep things, and have fun too, and I'm sure I'll cry. And, OK, maybe I'll talk about how sick I feel once in a while, just so you know.

Oh, I already know.

I thought so. So let's accentuate the positive and . . . um, how does that saying go?

Never heard it.

Yes you have! Something, something the negative and accentuate the positive. My brain! It sucks. Diminish? Um. Shrink the negative? Thesaurus! Oh, there are a million antonyms for "accentuate" and none of them are the right one. If I was on the computer I'd look the saying up on the Internet. But, whatever. I am so confused. Oh, who cares?

It's OK. Just let it go.

Breathe? That's nice. I have one final question. If I lose my mind completely, will you still stay with me? I mean if all the words go away, and we have nothing to talk about anymore, will you stay?

Hey. A lot of people can't talk, can't walk, can't think, or can't even move. Some people are kept alive by machines, and they can't even breathe on their own. We guardian angels don't leave them. That's when they need us the most. We're there to comfort them, hold them, to love them, even if they don't know it.

But they do know it, don't they? I mean inside they know.

They do know. You are a smart little girl.

I like it when you call me a little girl. Somehow that brings me comfort, fills an empty place inside me.

I know.

I can't believe it's already 11:40!!!! It was a great conversation, but it's soooo late! 'Nite! I look forward to some more head patting tonight. Don't forget.

I won't. Goodnight.

Wednesday, September 5
A Brief Note

Hi Nicole!

Hi.

Guess what?

What?

I found the quote you were looking for.

What quote?

This one. It goes like this: "You've got to accentuate the positive. Eliminate the negative."

Where did you find that?

I looked it up on the Internet.

No you didn't! *I did!*

Shhhhhh.

Wednesday, September 5
Evening

"Despite all my rage I'm still just a rat in a cage." I love that line.

A poem?

In a way. It's a song by The Smashing Pumpkins.

Smashing . . .

It's a rock group.

I knew that. What made you think of that song?
Several things.

Tell me.

First, Luke had it on his iPod. I know because when I went over to him to tell him to get off the computer and get a life I could hear it in his headphones. The song was apropos, if that's the right word, to the whole scenario because he's such a prisoner to his computer! I told him he should go outside and get a life.

And?

He told me to shut up and go away. It's the same old thing. It never changes. Then he said, "I'll kill you." I think that's a joke when he says that. He doesn't seem mad, more like he just wants me to stop disturbing him so he can play his game. I needed to give him grief and then leave. It's his life. But the real thing I want to share with you is that I'm really not that different than Luke. He's just trying to cope and the computer is his way of coping with the harsh realities of this world. Luke has his computer. Dad has his work, football, and Budweiser. Yes, he still drinks a few beers every night. But he's not an alcoholic. I knew you were going to ask me that so I thought I'd tell you before you asked me.

I'm here for you, Nicole. How are you doing? What do you do to cope?

Lately, the way I cope is to come home and be alone. Tammy and Rick asked me if I wanted to hang out after school. I like both of them, but I just wanted to come home. Truth is, I've had a crush on Rick for a long time. I was sort of a third wheel in their relationship last spring. They'd ask me to tag along when they went bowling, or to a movie, or just hanging out. They decided just to be friends this summer. Not sure what happened. So Rick is Tammy's ex-boyfriend, but we all still hang out. Yeah, he's really over her, believe me! I've always liked him because when the three of us are together Tammy usually takes up all the space. She has opinions about everything and doesn't do much pausing between expressing them. Rick would always ask me how I felt about whatever we were talking about. Or if Tammy wanted to do something Rick would always ask me if I wanted to do that or something else. I think he always liked me better. But she's more aggressive than I am. So now the two of them are just friends, and he's still showing me a lot of interest. I think he really likes me a lot.

That's great. Isn't it? Isn't that wonderful?

I told them I didn't want to hang out. The reason I told them that is because I'm afraid I might cry if he asks me how I am, or wants to hear about my, um, health issues. I think if I'm honest with myself I'm also scared to start a relationship right now. A part of me is shutting down. I don't want to start something new. I don't want to enjoy myself and later get depressed because of my disease. What if we start going out and my looks start changing? I couldn't take it if he left me because I got ugly. He's so good-looking too. He's tall, blond, with hair over his blue eyes half the time. And he's NICE. Good-looking and nice—that's rare for guys and stuck-up girls.

You'll be pleased to know that angels are all good-looking and nice as well. And they will listen to you as long as you want to talk. They don't get caught up in things like time and space, or feeling caught in a cage.

Truthfully, rats don't have it so bad. We used to have rats. I mean pet rats. People think rats are dirty animals that crawl in sewers. Well, I guess they ARE. But our pet rats were smart. They seemed more human than dogs sometimes, the way they wanted to play with you. Really, rats aren't so bad. The neat thing about our rats was that you could let them out of the cage, and they'd just sit there playing with you. They wouldn't run away. Well, sometimes they'd run somewhere, like under the bed, or find some boxes to hide under in the closet. But when you called to them—this is the truth—they'd come!

Really?

Yeah. Most of the time. And the really surprising thing is that when you opened the cage door to get them to go back in, they'd just walk into the cage themselves. It wasn't like they didn't want to go back in. They didn't care. There's a lesson there. I can feel it.

Rats like their cages?

There's more truth to that comment than you might think. They are so content no matter where they are. I know that for me to want to come home isn't all bad. To be content with being alone is a good thing, don't you think? Tammy can never be alone. I like being alone. I'm sad I can't really start anything with Rick right now. But don't you think this is because of the circumstances? There's nothing wrong with me is there, just because I want to be alone?

Of course there is nothing wrong with you, Nicole. You need to do what feels right to you. And that might be different at different times. Maybe the memory of the pet rats being so content is a message for you to be content? I have to admit, after what you've been sharing with me about your rats I must say I'm more impressed with rats than I was an hour ago. I suppose angels and rats have a lot in common, now that I think of it.

Ha ha. Really?

Neither puts a lot of stock in time and space. They just are. So, the sewer would be hell to most of us, but it can be a rat's heaven. However, a nice, clean cage, with two loving kids as owners, feeding and caring for them, and letting them run around the house, may be heaven too. So, heaven is really what you make it.

Yeah. You've got it, GA!

So, one question, Nicole.

Go ahead.

If angels and rats are similar, which I realize is stretching it a little, why aren't there rats in heaven? I've never seen one. I've seen lots of church mice on earth, but no rodents in heaven. Tell me, what's up with that?

Oh . . . . GA! I've got it! They don't need to GO to heaven. They're in heaven already. These simple little dirty creatures are having a blast here on earth. If they are in heaven, they probably look different, anyway. Evolved! And, if we keep true to the premise, even if the rats go to hell, it's heaven to them. They can't lose.

Got it. I think. Or, like you'd say, "Whatever!"

You smarty! I'm glad I have a funny guardian angel.

Do you really know anything about rats?

Not really. Do you really NOT know anything about rats?

I know a lot about everything.

I thought so. And I get it that you aren't going to recite some angelic encyclopedia to me. I wouldn't like that. It would be too much like school. Wow. It's late. Now I can't help but think about all kinds of rodents hiding under my bed. So, let's change the subject before I go to sleep. What do you want to talk about?

What do YOU want to talk about?

You sound like my counselor, if I had one.

Maybe I am.

Dad would be happy with that.

Why?

Because you're free. He's a cheapskate. So, let's see. I do feel like talking some more about life and stuff. Um. Let me go back and reread this entry. Maybe I forgot something. . . . OK, done. I realized that I am not at all content with life. Let's continue the rat analogy. If I were a rat, I feel like the kids taking care of me forgot about me. They forgot to open the cage door, or to feed me. It's hard to be content when I am dying in here. I used to look out through the bars and wait for them to come home from school to play with me, but the girl left and never came back, and the boy likes his toy guns and the cat more than his rat. I don't look out the bars anymore. I don't even play on the little wheelie thing either. I just stare into the empty water basin, and . . . and just wait.

For what?

For nothing. For death, I suppose.

That's depressing, even for an angel.

I know.

So you're in the cage. Now what? What do you want to do?

Nothing.

You just want to sit there and fade away?

If I did, the boy would maybe someday see my dead rat body here and feel bad that he killed me. I want him to feel bad but he'd probably just throw me out, or give me to the cat as a plaything. Gross!

Is there nothing you want to do?

Not really.

What if anything was possible? I mean anything.

Anything? Like my guardian angel would grant me a wish or something?

Well, what if you found that you could suddenly do anything you wished? What would you do?

I'd transform into a magical being and break through the bars. I'd become a beautiful bird and fly to a different land where people cared, and every living being had a place, and there would be plenty of food, company, and things to do. That's what I would do. I'd fly away. But I'm just a rat.

Hey rat!

Yeah?

See those bars?

Uh-huh.

Start chewing.

What do you mean? You mean chew my way out?

If that's what it takes. Yeah. And then, I dare you to fly to that place you dream of. You can do it.

If I were a bird.

Who made you a rat? I mean you came up with the analogy. Change it. You can make it different. You are going to eat through those bars and then fly away. What kind of bird are you going to become?

A golden eagle.

Fly, golden eagle!
Oh, you are so positive! A bit unrealistic too. But I guess that's how angels are. Is flying fun?

It's better than anything you could ever imagine.

I suppose it feels freeing and refreshing. All that air and stuff. Ha ha . . . . I can't think anymore, too tired.

Go to sleep. Maybe you will fly in your dreams tonight. I'll be here.

I know. Thanks GA. It's so late. Goodnight.

Thursday, September 6
Morning

Dear Guardian Angel,

You gave me that dream last night, didn't you? It was a gift from you. If that's what being an angel is like I'm not afraid to die. I know you are real, because you held me in your strong arms and carried me into the sky. I saw you. Words can't describe it, but I'm going to write you a poem anyway.

A Ride into Heaven

I saw your face,
The face of my angel.
You have a wide face
To fit your smile, I suppose.
Your deep eyes sparkle
With life and love.
You have golden hair,
Flowing in the wind,
And man, are you buff! (sorry)
I stood on the top of a grassy hill

As the storm darkened and approached.
As the first drops of rain began to fall
You called my name.
I've never heard my name spoken
With so much love.
When I turned you were there,
Behind me,
Already shielding me
From whatever the storm would bring.

You did not speak another word,
Yet somehow you asked for my consent
To be held in your arms
And lifted up from this empty ground.
No one has ever asked me before,
Not like that.
My "Yes!" was in my smile,
My delight,
My seven-year-old giggle—
A child once again.

As we lifted from the ground
I felt no pull from above,
But rather support from below,
Or all around.
Your power pushed us effortlessly
Into flight.

You surprised me
As we headed into the flashing storm.
I thought you might have taken me away.

Yet I understood the genius of your navigation,
And felt no fear
With you surrounding me.
We dashed into the raging clouds
Faster than anything I can describe.
It felt that somehow by your angelic strength
You pierced the night.
Cutting through the torrent
We broke into the light.
Above all,
Where all is calm, always.
And the higher we flew,
The more I could see
How little this storm really was.
A tiny swirl in a still sea.
A muddy droplet in the glassy deep.
That thing down there wasn't me.
On the top of it all
It seems there was a place
Called heaven.
We found ourselves standing
On solid ground.
And you turned me toward you.
Lost in your breast,
Found in your heart.
So in your control,
Yet so free!
I know what it means to be whole,
Within the "shelter of your wings."

N. M. B.

I know the poem's not that good but it's just impossible to describe something so beautiful and heavenly in earthly language. Maybe in angel language I could just look at you and burp some noise and you'd get it all. Perhaps more appropriately, I could sing something, and you'd understand all I was trying to say? That last part is a quote from the Bible. I thought you'd like that. Don't bother answering me, GA. Shhhhh. Let me touch your lips. Silence. I have to go.

Love,
Nicole

Thursday, September 6
Afternoon Excursion

Dear Guardian Angel,

It's a beautiful day. I have seen many days. Maybe I'm looking more closely or something, because this is beautiful! The sky is a deeper blue than I've seen, with scattered cumulus clouds hanging pretty low, and some clouds moving in very lightly over top of them. The sun is very bright, and is giving everything a heavenly glow! A breeze is blowing through the house. The trees are making extra sounds, because the leaves are starting to lose their vitality, and it won't be that long until they turn all sorts of colors, and drop gently to the earth.

I went down to the lake. Often there are many people there in the summertime. It was so quiet today. As I reached the end of our road and the lake opened up before me, I saw two children playing on the beach by a dock, running in and out of the shallow water, laughing, talking intently about their game they seemed to make up as they went along. I took a right at the shore and headed to one of several favorite spots on the lake. This one is along the shore, where the land is still undeveloped, a few lots strung together, still up for sale, or perhaps the owner hasn't decided what to build yet. I hope they never build there. Along that shore the shallow water has a floor of mainly pebbles of all sizes mixed with sand. The water laps up against a small, one-foot ledge of rock, earth, and grass and right there at the water's edge the trees shoot up with their branches hanging over the water. There are two old logs under the water where I suppose the trees reached too far from the shore and fell into the lake long ago. The fish gather there around the logs, and often old men in their small electric motorboats stop there and drop their lines. Sometimes they talk to me as I stand nearby on the shore. One in particular smokes a pipe, and long after he has gone the sweet aroma of that pipe smoke still hangs in the air just under the tree branches.

I took off my shoes and left them on a large rock in the usual place. Walking ankle deep into the water made me feel so alive this time, more than any other time before. The cool water created a tingling sensation that shot up my calves, thighs, through my body into my shoulders and down my arms, like a faint electrical current of energy and aliveness. Listening to little waves rhythmically lap against the shore, as a very gentle wind off the water brushed my face, I thought for a moment that whatever people said about my condition must be wrong. I was fine, healthy, and all was right in the world. And you know, even though while I stood there I could feel that smoldering pain in the back of my upper neck, which reminded me of my sickness, I felt for a moment everything would be just fine. And at that moment it seemed that I knew I would be fine. Some minnows swam up to me and poked my feet and toes with their little mouths, and I wiggled my toes as if waving hello. I didn't spend that long there, because as it approached dinnertime more boats appeared on the lake—locals coming home from work getting a little more recreation in before summer left completely and winter demanded they put their boats away for a season. I left because I didn't want to see anyone I knew, because I didn't want to be asked how I was feeling or doing. I didn't want to have to perform for anyone, and that's how it would have felt. I just wanted to be myself, with me and the lake, and the little children's voices so happy and free of worry and of pain. I came home through the woods, crossing the street and a few backyards without running into anyone. And I must say that I was happy. I was able to take a part of the lake with me, the water, the wind, the trees, the little fishes' kisses, the children's laughs, the sun, and that feeling. There is something underneath all of this, just under the surface, something quiet, steady, beautiful, and so peaceful. It tells me everything is alright. Everything is fine.

Now that I've written this down, and have had a few minutes here on the couch looking out the window, I can still see a portion of the lake down there. It's not that far away. But it's funny. It's so funny. Now I feel bad. When I started this entry I was high as a, um, um. Duh. Just really naturally high. Now I feel like I crashed, all in about five minutes. Well, don't bother answering me.

Nicole

Hi Nicole!

Hi GA!

I read what you wrote about this afternoon. It's very beautiful. I'm sorry you started to feel bad again. How are you now?

I really do feel better right now. Dad actually made dinner tonight—meatloaf and potatoes. It was really good, and he and Luke seemed unusually talkative tonight at dinner.

Do they talk about what's happening with you?

Not really. I'm glad. I don't want to talk about me. I like that the three of us don't have to be gloomy all the time and act like something huge is going on. If there is something to say then Dad will talk about it, but mostly we just talk about ordinary things and not very dramatic things. I like that. But I do like talking to you about everything, and that's because I know you can take it, and I can talk to you on my terms, about what I want to talk about. I hope you understand.

I think I do. I do understand.

Tonight I feel good. This afternoon at the lake was a very special time for me, and I can still feel some of that sense of peace. Right now homework is done. Dad and Luke are watching TV together. I'm comfortably relaxed on my bed with a glass of apple juice on ice. I have time to relax and breathe. I think I want to tell you something about my life. I want to share more of myself with you.

I'd like that. So, what do you want to talk about?

I want to talk about good things. Probably do some free association. Doesn't that mean just go where your thoughts are taking you? What I want is to remember all the good things. Maybe not remember ALL of them, but the really good ones. Imagine I'm on a pirate's ship and we're being hunted down, soon to be sunk by a British Navy vessel. I'm dragging out the old chest in the hold, dragging it to my room, opening it up, and pulling out the best of the treasures, the gems, the gold, the old maps I never got to follow, the memories of places I've been or seen. I'm like dumping all the good stuff on the bed and telling you about some of it. I know what you are thinking! There are no girl pirates. But there are!

I know. I saw the movie.

No. Historically there were girl pirates. Like usual, I can't remember their names, but YOU can look it up on the Internet this time.

I believe you. I think I saw some show about girl pirates on the Discovery Channel.

You don't really watch TV, do you?

We do whatever we have to do to keep current. It's all part of the job.

Ha! OK. So, now I think that's a stupid picture. I don't want to be a pirate. But the image of a chest of treasures being looked over one more time before the ship sinks is a good one. That's all. I want to look at some things and show them to you before the ship sinks.

Before the battle?

Yeah.

Because it is quite possible that you will win the battle. Your ship may not go down.

I know. But it might. So let's look at some of this stuff before the British catch up to us.

Aye, aye, Captain!

Oh, no. I'm not the captain. I'm the captain's girlfriend!

I should have known. A pretty one at that.

Adorable!

Aye! She be a good looker! She be—

Stop!!!!!!!!

Sorry. I got carried away with the whole pirate thing.

No problem. Let's begin.

Show me something.

I will. Let's see. I have a memory of Luke being born. I know people doubt that, because I was only four years old. I have this distinct memory of Dad bringing Mom home, and the baby was in her arms. I remember how much Mom beamed. She seemed a bit unkempt, really not the usual perfect look she always had. Mom and Dad were both so nice to me. They took such care with me, knowing, I suppose, that it would be hard for me to have another center of the universe in the house. I just remember snippets, like short reels of film, a foot long or so. But the most vivid and beautiful memory was looking into Luke's face. Mom set me on the couch and let me hold him (while she sat next to me). He wasn't looking directly at me, but over my shoulder. His eyes reflected this vast space. They were deep, dark, so empty and at the same time so full. He looked wise. His stare over my shoulder was so focused, like he was looking at something. He smiled in a way that made me think he was seeing . . .

THE GUARDIAN ANGEL DIARY 49

Angels?

Yeah. Angels.

Can I butt in now?

Yeah.

That was me.

No it wasn't!

It WAS!

Get serious!

It was me! He was looking over YOUR shoulder at ME, YOUR GUARDIAN ANGEL!

Seriously?

Of course. I'm not going to lie to you. Angels can't lie. Well, they're not very good at it when they try. But I wouldn't lie to you about a thing like this. Angels are with people all the time. They are especially around babies. You can feel them. They protect babies from, let's say, unfriendly influences. And they hang around their moms as well. Babies look wise because they are so connected to the wisest and most powerful angels. That angel-wisdom shines through. That blank little mind isn't full of so many delusions and misconceptions that block out the angels' influence. The angels aren't pushed away. The baby is just a baby, but it is totally receptive to the feelings the angels bring—peace, innocence, love, and all that stuff.

So, you have been with me from the beginning?

Yes. And before I forget let me also say that angels are with old people in something of the same way. As people get really old they turn back into little children, for the most part. That's hard for some people to see, because these old folks can be cranky, and they look like they are adults, but they're becoming children again. You come into this world as a child and you leave as a child. You have angels with you coming in and angels with you going out.

And angels with you the whole time you are here too! I mean, basically, angels are just always there!

Yeah. But in a special way during those times of life.

Is that true with me too, even if I die young?

Absolutely. But let's not dwell on that. I'm sorry I took so much of your time to share, but I got excited when you started talking about your little brother and I knew it was me. Small world, huh?

LOL. You are such a comedian! But one more thing. I always picture you as being like, well, this is embarrassing . . .

Like a young man?

Yeah. A very good-looking, buff young man. Very masculine too. Not that there aren't, I suppose, girl angels, but are you really like ten thousand years old or something? Don't say, "Girl, I'm old enough to be your father." That would ruin my day.

I am really laughing. LOL. You are so cute. Well, let me say that angels are timeless and ageless. I know that's hard to comprehend, but that's the truth. Think about love. How old is love? It's at least several thousands of years old, ever since people have been around. I will tell you that love has been around longer than people, than creation itself. And when will love just stop being, and fade into nothing? It won't. It will go on forever. It keeps . . .

Going and going and going.

Nicole, DON'T FINISH MY SENTENCES! Just kidding!

That's JK for short if you don't remember.

I do, but thanks anyway. So, let me finish. How old are you? Sixteen? Let's say that all you think, love, feel, is the real you. Pretend your body is just a container of the real you. It's like a space suit. When that space suit wears out and drops off, and you become like me, how old are you? How old is your love? How old is your thought? It may be immature, and can grow forever, but it is ageless. You are ageless inside.

That's deep. But I guess I've always felt that if there is some sort of afterlife that we'd all be in perfect health at a perfect age, beautiful and all that. Right?

Exactly, Nicole. So, most people/angels/associates/ whatever think of me as being in my early twenties or even younger. That's the way I like it. Twenty years? Decades? Centuries? Light years? Who cares? I'm just me.

And I will be just me.

Yes. Just as you are now, on the inside. Exactly. Now, sorry for the interruption. What else did you want to say?

No need to apologize. That was fun. I couldn't agree more, and frankly, couldn't have said it better myself.

No. I probably said it better than you could have. That's why I'm the angel and you're asking me the questions. But go on.

Well, I wanted to say that the memory of my little brother's face is one of the most beautiful memories I have in this treasure chest. When I think of the way he looked, it reminds me how much wonder I can have about life, about nature, grass, trees, bugs, sky, air, water, people's faces, and people's lives. I can almost just turn it on.

Turn what on?

Turn on this switch that says, "Look at the world like he did." Then I put on this baby face (on the inside) and look. I simply look.

And what do you see?

I'd say I see everything. In some ways that may be true, like everything is there, all the possibilities, all the dreams, all the tiny microcosms or whatever they call those things, and yet I know I don't think about all of these things at the same time. I just know they are there. When you really LOOK, like a baby looks, everything becomes brighter, alive! I love going down to the lake and looking at everything through those baby brother eyes. I see the water waving to me as it plays with the children, and the sky is like a changing banner. The clouds tell a different story every few moments as they change shapes and fly overhead. The sky is like God's movie. It has a thousand plots, dramas, and sub-dramas a day.

Maybe a million.

Yeah. A million or more.

So, that way of looking at the world is a gift your brother gave you. He didn't even know it. You see the world a lot like I do. There is so much to see. Some people live such flat lives, only seeing one dimension, one story, one very B movie!

Like most of my friends!

I wasn't going to be mean, but yes. And there are many ignorant adults who think they can just run all over others, and plow over nature for a few dollars, yet believe they are doing no harm. Oh, no. Now you've got me going. I'd better stop right now. I don't want my wings to fall off.

Do they do that?

No. JK.

But there are people like you describe. They're wrong.

Everyone is wrong to one degree or another. Or rather, everyone makes mistakes. No one sees the whole picture. It's human nature not to see. It's actually a very spiritual person who sees more than what is there for the human eye.

Then how do you get to see more? Was I lucky? I don't feel that spiritual.

For some people it's a gift. For some they have to work hard for that kind of sight. And you can't force people to see more than they want to see. You can invite them to see more. You can inspire them. You can even give them a hard time about it. But they have to see for themselves. It's like that old saying which has nothing to do with seeing, but it works here. You can lead a horse to water . . .

But you can't make him drink.

No. I was going to say, you can lead a horse to water, but if there isn't any water there anymore the horse is going to die, and so will you if you don't wake up and get with it!

You weren't going to say that, but as long as you can make me laugh the way you do, I'll forgive you.

So, what now?

Bedtime?

Oh. Sorry about the time. I got carried away.

Me too. I loved it.

[Note: A half-finished sketch appears on the page of this entry. It is an infant's face gazing upward, smiling. **G.R.S.**]

Friday, September 7
Chemo Day

Hi, GA. Today is Chemo Day. The appointment is later this morning so I didn't have to go to school. I thought I'd write to you early because I feel like I want to continue our wonderful discussion from yesterday, and I have time right now. Later on I know it's possible I won't feel good. So, can we talk?

I'm ready to talk. I also really enjoyed our conversation yesterday. It's not that often that a guardian angel actually gets to talk with the people they are looking after. I feel like this is a real blessing for me. You are so very much fun to talk with, and I love hearing about your life. It's an honor.

Thank you. I'm glad to know that you also feel like this time together is special. I never thought that this might be a gift for you like it is for me. Wow. I think what we've been talking about has been so cool. I'm surprised about what I wrote. It feels so good, like I really have something to say that people might like to read.

Yes. It's true. But don't think about that. It would be better for you to write down the things you need to talk to me about for your own sake. It's your therapy. It will help you even if no one reads this. If you think about people reading this, you won't be able to be yourself as much as you want. I won't be able to be myself either.

You're right. I'm having a good time writing this diary whether it is read by someone or not. In fact, I love talking to you. I think I'm becoming something of a homebody because I want to stay here and write to you all the time lately. Probably that's why I'm hesitant to go over to Tammy's. My make-believe angel friend is getting to be more fun!

Ha ha. Why do I doubt that?

Uh. 'Cause you have low self esteem? Or maybe 'cause you know Tammy? LOL

What do you want to share with me this morning?

When I was telling you about that special time with Luke, I was remembering some other special times with Mom before she got sick. There was this one time I just have to tell you about, because it's how I want to feel again someday, when I get better. Speaking of no inhibitions, I want to share another one of those earliest memories with you. It helps me appreciate life so much when I do that, and feel like I've had a good and meaningful life.

Go ahead. Let's hear about it.

My mom was a nap taker. She took a nap every afternoon. When I was little, and I really don't know how old, I'm thinking I was like five or six, maybe a bit older, she'd make me lie down beside her and take a nap with her. We'd climb under the covers of her queen-size bed and cuddle up to each other. I look back now and wish I had enjoyed that more. I mean I'd give practically anything to be able to snuggle up against her body again. I can smell her now. It was a good smell. A slight hint of Chanel Number 5, or whatever it's called. Ha ha. But she also had this human smell, a little pungent.

Oh?

No. It wasn't bad. It was her body. Everybody has a body that smells like something. It doesn't mean it was bad. I think the smell of her is always accompanied by the heat of her body when I think of it. I'd lay there right in her arms as we first slept. And it would only take a few minutes before she fell asleep. I knew she was only going to be holding onto me while she fell asleep, and that when she was actually asleep she would move her arm or even roll over. Wait . . .

What?

I'm getting a rush of dizziness. It just happens sometimes. I'll be back.

OK.

❖   ❖   ❖

Back. My stomach is so screwed up! I'm eating fruit now.
I think that might help. It's one of those plastic plates of fruit
you can get in the produce section. So. OK. So I really didn't
want to take a nap. I don't think I took any naps. She thought
I did, but I didn't. She'd fall asleep and then roll over. And
then? Yep. I would so slowly, so stealthily, so "mindfully" as
much as you can do that as a kid, slip out of the bed and onto
the floor. Once on the floor I would crawl out of her bed-
room like a snake. I actually crawled out of the room on my
belly, with big eyes watching for movement in the bed.

Did she ever wake up?

Never!

Not even once?

Not once. I'd get to the hallway and get up and bolt to
the back door. I'd open the door, walk out onto the patio,
strip off all my clothes, and run across all the backyards on
my street.

Naked?

Totally naked! Free! I loved it! I don't have much more
to say about it. It was a really good memory of escaping and
running naked and free around town.

*Well, I certainly don't have anything to say about it
either! So. How did you get back without getting caught?*

Usually I came back and got dressed and then went and
played inside. Mom thought I had just gotten up early from
the nap and had been such a good girl keeping myself occu-
pied with my dolls until she woke up.

Dolls?

Yeah. Doesn't everyone play with dolls at that age? Anyway, I did get caught several times after the initial escape.
Some neighbors would hunt me down and take me home.

Mrs. Adams, Mom's best friend, knew that I wasn't supposed to be out there. I think the naked thing gave that away. She'd call from her window. I'd go over there, and she'd walk me home. Other people would call Mom and say, "Your naked daughter is at it again." I don't remember getting punished. I do think they finally solved it somehow. Whether they tied me to the bedpost or glued me to the sheets, I don't remember. But it did stop.

So, what's the lesson? Why was it important to tell me that story?

I don't think there's a lesson in this story. I wanted to share with you about sleeping with Mom, and I knew you would understand the running naked and free part of my story. It was such an adventurous thing for me to do at that age, and so freeing! I love the image. So innocent, so uninhibited, just running, naked through the world! Today, I think I probably would have been abducted.

You mean if you went out today? I think you'd be arrested.

No. Duh. I mean if I were a kid. A little kid. A baby!

OK. Good story. Thanks for sharing.

Don't tell me you've never gotten naked and run around!

Nicole. We angels do some pretty crazy things. But this is not about me. Nor is this the time to divulge all the naked-angel stories I've been dying to share for centuries. This time is for and about YOU.

That's a cop-out.

Yep. So, it must be nice to remember sleeping in your mother's arms.

Way to change the subject. Of course it was nice. Actually, like I said, back then I didn't want to sleep in her arms or smell her pungent body odor. But things change. I dream about her occasionally, and lately my dreams have been vivid. All of them. Most of the time I dream that she never died. She's just there, doing her thing. One time we were walking on the path by the elementary school together. We were having a great conversation, though I couldn't remember what it was about when I woke up. I do remember as we approached our house looking at her and realizing that she wasn't supposed to be alive. I asked her why she wasn't dead. It slipped out that way. "Hey! You're supposed to be dead! What's happening?" She looked concerned, like she had found herself outside running around naked or something. In fact, she looked a bit embarrassed. Then she shrugged her shoulders and said, "I don't know." I left her on the path, crossed the street, and went into our house. Then I woke up. That's the dream.

Do you know why you left her there or why she didn't follow?

I think now, I mean right now, I wonder whether there wasn't a message there for me. Oh, jeez. Not going to cry. It was like she was clearly saying that she is alive. OR someone was pointing that out to both of us, like God or something, that we are both alive. We were having a real conversation, and the idea that we couldn't do that kind of got in the way. It was like, if I hadn't known that we couldn't talk because she was dead and me alive, we could have kept on talking. I think the reason she looked embarrassed is because . . . hmmmm. I don't know. Do you?

Maybe because she knew she was kind of giving away the whole life after death secret thingy?

You are as bad as me with words! No! Now that I think of it, it could have been my unconscious logical self saying, "Stop pretending. She is dead."

Wow. That's sad. And that doesn't sound like you.

I don't know what it means. But I think I left her there on the other side of the street because on some level I knew that where she was I couldn't remain, and where I was going, like back to being awake, she couldn't be. Not fully anyway.

And maybe, Nicole, it was an opportunity for her to say, "Hello. I'm alive! You are too! Isn't it great? Oh. Oops! Can't make this too real! You know, can't take away people's freedom to disbelieve and all that! See you when you get here! Love ya!" Is it possible she was saying that?

Yeah. Someday we will run hand in hand, as children, naked children in the backyards of heaven! Hell yeah!

Yes. And someday you will sleep in her arms again.

This time I think I'll stay there for a while.

I know you will.

Oh, you always make me cry. Goodbye.

Friday, September 7
Evening

I'm alive. That's probably all I can write before I get sick.

Chemo Day!

Yep. It's a liquid they put in your blood with an IV. Almost as soon as it started I felt sick. There was this funny taste in my mouth, like I had been sucking on a handful of old pennies. I can't even think about eating. I tried an apple at dinner and it tasted bitter. I thought something was wrong with it so I asked Dad to taste it. He said it was fine. I don't know . . .

That's too bad. Hopefully you'll feel better tomorrow. It's part of the side effects of the treatment.

I know but it is weird that they have to drip something into you that makes you sick, like you have to drink poison in order to get better.

That is strange.

When it was time for me to get it they took me to this room and put me in this type of lounge chair, and like there were several other lounge chairs in this part of the hospital. Three old ladies were in the other chairs, and it looked like they arranged it so we could see each other and have a tea party while getting the chemo.

No. Really?

I'm sure that's not what they had in mind, because the thought of tea makes me want to puke, and you can't eat or drink while you're getting this stuff because I'm sure you'd puke it all over everyone. They must have put us close together so we can talk, but only one lady said anything and it made me feel sick even before they put the needle in my arm. She said, "Poor girl."

Oh. That must have been hard to hear that.

She was just pointing out the obvious. Wait. I have to go to the bathroom.

❊ ❊ ❊

Back. That's the other thing. Everything wants to come out both ends. Like I can see that this stuff is hardcore that they put in me because nothing wants to stick around inside me when it's in there. I didn't throw up until I got out of the car on the way home. I thought that was an accomplishment. And diarrhea is also a common side effect. Looks like I won't have to worry about my weight for a while. Guys like thin girls, don't they?

Guys like all types of girls. That's what I think.
When that lady said, "Poor girl," I smiled politely but didn't say anything back to her. I did feel like I got invited to some retirement meeting or old ladies' auxiliary tea. I just kept thinking, "What am I doing here?" I'm not an old lady, not that there is anything wrong with old ladies, but I'm not one. You know?

I know. I think that's what the woman was saying. She was saying that she was sorry you had to be there with them.
I may have to continue this journal in the bathroom. Got to go.

❊   ❊   ❊

Back. People have no idea what chemo patients go through. I had no idea what Mom had to deal with. She said she was fine. I never saw or heard that she threw up, but she wouldn't have told me about the diarrhea anyway. She seemed happy though, like when she said that she didn't get sick she looked relieved. I think she did handle it better than most, I suppose. I hope I can learn to do that. The doctor is checking up on me to see how I do with it. They told me that they can work with the medicine and add things to help with the sickness. I don't have to go back again for a week.

Tell the doctor exactly how you're feeling. He can help you feel better, I'm sure.
I don't want to go to school. If I keep feeling sick I won't be able to go. Wow. Everything is changing so fast. Before, I knew I was sick, but now I'm feeling simply awful.

This nausea will pass. Give it time.
I have no choice. Do I? Done for tonight! I'm exhausted.

Hello Angel. I felt sick when I first got up, but now I'm doing better. I made pancakes for Dad and Luke, but I couldn't eat them. I had coffee, which also tasted really bad. They said my taste buds might be all screwed up for a while. Luke ate my share of pancakes. I'm glad for him. Turned out Dad slept in 'til almost lunch so he didn't eat his either. I ended up making myself scrambled eggs, and I could eat them with lots of salt and pepper. They were OK. Figure that one out! I am so very glad it's Saturday. I can rest and get ahold of myself. I'll check in a little later.

❖   ❖   ❖

Hi GA. I'm feeling better this afternoon. I think I can explain a little more about what's going on with me without getting sick. Do you want to hear it?

If you want to tell it, I want to hear it.

If I can bring both worlds together, my sickness and the help I feel when talking to you, I think I will feel better. They call it anaplastic astrocytoma, which means, as far as I can tell, a tumor in the brain. It's a level three, which means it is more dangerous than a level two, but not as dangerous as a level four. I love how helpful these simple explanations are for patients. Really tells me a lot! The tumor is located near my cerebellum, which is the part of the brain at the base of my skull, and quite close to the spinal cord. They say this is malignant, which doesn't necessarily mean that it is full of bad cancerous cells. Apparently it can also be called malignant if it is pushing against things that it could be hurting. This tumor can cause a lot of different things to happen to me. As the doctor says, the brain controls the body, so if something happens to the brain, it will affect the body. When things go wrong with my body he tells me not to worry or get scared, but that's easy for him to say.

The doctor said that where my tumor is located, the temporal lobe, is why I am having problems with my speech and memory. Oh? What a, um, a thing that happens that you didn't expect? What is that? Oh yeah, what a surprise! Or is it a prize? Sur-prize? Or should I say, uh, "wah uh suweez." I hope I never talk like that. I'm not trying to be funny. GA, just kill me if I start talking like that. It's not really affected my speech too much actually. But you know about my memory, and there is also a balance problem, which hasn't really gotten worse since the day you pushed me down the stairs.

I didn't push you. However, getting to the point, I know you feel nausea from the chemo and you mentioned a sore neck. Are you still having headaches?

Yeah, mostly headaches, bouts of dizziness, feeling like puking, actually puking, diarrhea, sometimes feeling numb in places but that comes and goes. Strange feelings in my head. The little people in my head are trying to burrow into my skull so that they don't get sucked out by the big black vacuum. It feels funny when they dig their tunnels. No, but seriously. No, but seriously. No, but seriously. Oh sorry. No, but seriously. Aches and pains. Tired. Some of this is the treatment. No, but seriously.

Enough!

After various CTs, PETs, DSAs, MRIs and stuff, they have, as I said, decided to treat me to a variety of treatments, including chemo and surgery. Radio therapy may also be used. And I don't think that kind of radio has anything to do with the top ten.

Top ten?

Never mind. They say this is the only way to shrink the tumor before the operation, and it will be less likely to get messy and kill me. OK, they didn't say it exactly like that, but that's what they meant. How are you today, GA?

I'm fine. Angels are always fine.

How boring.

Angels never get bored. Do you know why?

No. Do tell. Is this going to be some one-liner?

A joke? No. Not at all. Angels never get bored because they keep busy. They do good and useful things for people, and for each other. When you love people you want to help them, and when you help them, it feels really good. Sometimes the work is hard, but most of the time everything we do feels like play. I think you could learn a thing or two from this.

Like what?

Like lightening up a little, and going outside and hanging out with your friends.

I'm not going to fight you this time. I think you have a point. I need to lighten up, even if it's just for a day. Life's too short to be serious all the time. When I hear all these big words about my physical condition, and all the other big words about how they are going to try to help me, I get tired. I feel like crawling inside my head, and perhaps even under my bed, and giving up. But that won't work. I know that will only make me feel worse. I need to lighten up. I need to continue to be a child in some way or another, to play, to dream, to wonder about the universe and ask all those questions that children ask. I need to do that. No. I want to do that. I will try. Or I will not try? I will try not to try so hard. Oh, bother. You know what I mean!

Sunday, September 9
Evening

You will be proud of me.

I'm always proud of you, but tell me why.

I hung out with Tammy and Rick today!

That's great!

It really helped me forget about everything and just have fun. I didn't feel like doing a lot of walking so we went to see the new Harry Potter movie. It was good, but not as good as the last one.

I love those kids.

Have you seen the movies?

I've read all the books. And I've seen every movie you've ever seen, since I get to accompany you places.

I wondered, but I never see you with me.

True. Angels are never supposed to be obtrusive. Think about it. If you did see me all the time you'd probably get freaked out and want me to go away.

Are you ALWAYS there? Um . . .

Look, for the sake of your own sense of privacy, the answer is no. I don't see everything, listen to every conversation, watch every little move you make . . . It's more like I'm waiting in the wings, right next to your mind or consciousness, and if you call, I'm there. If you are in need, I'm there. If you are stressing out, I bring comfort, or if you're angry I try to bring peace. And when you're attacked in temptation by what you might call "the enemy," then I'm there to fight for you, provide alternatives, and whisper to you the truth when they tell you the lies. But your privacy is protected by order of the Supreme Being.

You mean, God.

Sure, if that's the name you use. Only God gets to be with you all the time, in you, around you, everywhere at once and forever.

OK, so did you see the movie with me?

Yes. I confess I really wanted to see it. I kind of relate to Sirius Black. He's cool.

I think you're more like Hagrid.

Ha ha! I'm not that hairy. I can tell you're trying to pick a fight with me.

Perhaps. I must say, the person I most identified with in that movie was the villain, Lord Voldemort.

In what way?

He looks like he's been undergoing chemo for several years. I kept thinking, "This is how I am going to end up." I'm noticing a little more hair in my brush lately. If more comes out I suppose I'll wear a scarf or a hat or something. But that's all I could think about during the movie.

Uh, that's not exactly true.

What do you mean?

Well, I couldn't help but notice that Rick sat between you two.

You weren't listening in on my thoughts were you?

If they weren't so loud I may not have heard them, but sometimes your thoughts were louder than the movie, as far as thought language goes.

Oh, great! You stay out of my thoughts!

I tried not to pay attention. I was rather caught up in the movie, but I was happy to see that you were having such a good time.

How dare you!

Look, I got up and went for popcorn when it got really steamy. How steamy did it get?

Nothing happened. Nothing at all. We shared an arm rest. That's all. And when it got scary I grabbed his arm a little, that's all.

Yes. But I couldn't help but notice he was leaning your way, and he wasn't sharing her arm rest.

(Smile) I know. (Smile)

I'm glad that's all that happened, because I feel like he is a very good friend, and us not talking about "our relationship" makes it possible for me to feel somehow at ease with him. I don't feel like I owe him anything, or should be a certain way with him, or look a certain way, or need to give him anything in return.

Do you really mean that?

I want to give him the same thing I get from him—caring, comfort.

Love?

I don't know what love is. Really. To say there is any love at this point seems too scary. Let's just keep it at friendship and caring right now. I think Tammy would feel better about that too.

Aren't they "just friends"?

There may be an unwritten rule that best friends can't date the other best friend's former boyfriend. However, that rule is broken a lot it seems, so maybe there's a rule but everyone knows that you don't have to follow it if the relationship you are developing is real. I don't know. Better to be friends right now. But I must say, his warm arm brought so much comfort, soothing, like I could have held onto him forever.

I wish you could feel my arms. They are always there for you too.

GA. You know me inside and out, and better than maybe I know myself. I feel your arms around me sometimes. It feels very comforting and I can sense that somehow, whatever happens to me, that I will be OK. You give me that. But Rick is flesh and blood. He's in this world, and that's where I am too, at least for now. And I hate to admit it but every cell in my body wakes up when he touches me. And that's confusing to me when I think of everything that is going on in my life, and what I should be thinking and doing, whatever that means. I think it's all good. I never thought I'd use that trite phrase, but I'm going to use it now when it comes to Rick. It's all good. Can we leave it at that?

We certainly can.

Don't get possessive with me! Now get over it! It's good to feel good. How's that for a profound thought? That's all for now.

Monday, September 10
Evening

Dad didn't come home 'til 8:00 p.m. He reeked with alcohol. He brought us cold tacos from Taco Bell and sodas with the ice already melted inside. He must have stopped at the bar on the way home and got caught up with conversations there.

Are you worried about him?

I made Luke macaroni and cheese for dinner around seven. He was, as you could guess, playing computer. I didn't even try to stop him. I just put the plate of macaroni and cheese on his desk and walked out.

Are you worried about your DAD?

I AM ignoring your question. I'm NOT worried about him. I think he is a loser for getting drunk and not even calling. I can't do everything anymore. I can't keep cleaning up for him and Luke, or get Luke to do his homework, or cover for Dad at dinner when he's late. So, I'm not worried about him. I'm trying to let go and cope. If he starts drinking again like he did after Mom died, it's like, how could he do this to me? That's the thing. It's always about him, when it needs to be about me. Sure his wife died, but she was Luke's and my mom. So he drinks and gets all distant and stupid and I just have to pick up where he left off? I thought he was getting better. Maybe this is only a one-time thing. We'll see. I don't want to think about it. I really don't. It's too much!

Rick walked me home today.

I know.

If you know everything then why do I even bother telling you? Like, I think it would be better for you to say like, "Oh really?" This is for my therapy. I need to write these things down and tell you, and you don't have to keep being a smart aleck and giggling and saying, "I know," and idiotic stuff like that. OK?

Wow. You are in a good mood—not!

SHUT UP! I'm not in a good mood. Or maybe I was 'til I started talking to YOU!

Whoa. I'm sorry. I won't say "I know" anymore, or giggle or say anything stupid when I have the least hint that you want to be serious. I promise.

It's OK. I'm sorry I'm in a bad mood. It's the Dad thing. I feel lost there, and like he brought me coffee this morning but it was black. He knows I put cream and sugar in it. He asks me how I am, but starts talking to Luke when I try to answer. Now if he starts getting drunk again I feel like giving up, but I don't know what that means. OK, OK, enough of that. Let me tell you about Rick!

Yes. So you were saying he walked you home.

Exactly. I think Tammy must have been sick today because she wasn't in class. Rick was waiting for me when I got out of history class and asked if I wanted to hang out. My instinctual reaction was to say, "No. Sorry." That's just what I do because I don't have too much energy to hang out. He came back with, "Can I walk you home?" He smiled like he'd thought out what he would say if I said no. I smiled back at him and said, "Sure." Then I explained that really it was just that I get so tired and had nothing to do with not wanting to hang out with him. We talked about everything it seems. We stopped on the steps of my porch and sat and kept talking 'til dinner.

What did you talk about?

Ha ha. Funny thing is we talked about school, politics, and current events. He likes current events, and you know I do too. We also talked about kids in our class, like who were the bullies and the nerds, and who would probably end up being drug addicts and prostitutes and who would end up being movie stars and stuff. Maybe those are the same people?????? Ha ha! It was all in fun.

He could see when I was getting tired and asked if I wanted to lean on his back, so we were back-to-back talking.
How was that?
SEXY! (If only you could hear how I said that. Sooo funny, like "Sexxxxxyyyyy!" in a *Price is Right* kind of voice.)
Sexy, huh?
I'm not going to go into details with you here. It was fun. It felt good to lean my back against his.
"Sexxxxxyyyyyy!"
It was. Like lightning running up and down our spines. How's that?
"Sexxxxxyyyyyy!"
Ha ha. I tell you not to make fun, and then you go ahead and do it anyway.
You started it.
Yeah. And I can tell that you are jealous of Rick.
Hahahahahaha. Get real! I don't get jealous.
Well, do you mind if I talk about this stuff with you? I mean, is it OK?
Nicole. I don't know what to say. My job is to be here for you. So, I will be here for you, for whatever you want to talk about or whatever you need. That's my job.
But is it hard for you to hear about Rick?
Girl, I'm your angel, not your lover-boy.
Yes, but I'm perceptive enough to know that you care about me, and I can tell you get a little jumpy when I talk about Rick. Please don't tell me this is my imagination.
I know this is going to sound like a cop-out, but I am going to plead the Fifth here and remain silent. Sometimes we have to do that, you know. Sometimes you need to deal

with certain things as if you were all by yourself, so you can make your own decisions and be your own person. As much as I may want to help, I can't interfere with that process. How I feel is truly irrelevant when it comes to helping you in your life. Like you said, it's about you. It's not about anyone else but you, as far as I'm concerned. So, tell me whatever you want. Ask what you need. I'll do my best. Yes, I care about you, but let's keep this about you. That way I can be the most help to you.

Can you help me with Dad? Can you watch over him? Can you put a worm in his beer so he stops to think before he drinks too many?

Yes. I can. I can needle him in ways he'll never dream came from me. It will look very natural, as if it were an accident.

Don't kill him or anything!

Oh no. I'm working from the inside. Maybe he needs to feel a little pressure though. Don't you worry about a thing. You have your fun with what's-his-name and I'll take care of business with your dad. And I'll put in a few requests for Luke too. Maybe we can ease him off the computer.

Oh, Angel! I should have asked you earlier for more! I'm very excited.

Me too. But remember, it will be subtle. That's how we work.

Tuesday, September 11
Evening

I'm watching the news. I like the news. I don't know why but I've always liked surfing news channels to see what's happening in the world. Isn't that sick?

I don't think that's bad. That's good. You care about what is happening in the world. We need more people to care about the world. That's what I think.

So, today's news had lots of stories about 9/11 and about terrorists still trying to attack and kill people. Why do people do things like that? It seems so evil to kill innocent people. That's really sick. That's one of those questions I need some clarity on before I leave this planet. Why does God let these people do these terrible things? You there?

Of course. I'm all ears.

I don't want you to answer why I have to be sick right now. I might be able to believe that this is just the way nature is and crazy bacterial stuff happens. But I don't understand evil. What is that all about?

What do you mean? Can you be a little more specific? I really do want to talk about it with you.

OK. So I want to tell you a story about how I found out about "bad people" like robbers and killers and people like that. I can't ever forget that time. One summer evening, as people were out and about, I turned on the TV and watched this woman sitting in front of a mirror combing her hair. I was very young and had not seen much of anything of an adult nature on television. As she sat there a dark figure climbed up a tree beside her room, snuck in her window, and crept up to her. I was mesmerized. Then he grabbed her. I remember he had a big knife. I screamed in absolute horror. It was the first time I had ever seen anything like that. I ran crying for Mom and Dad. I think I found them outside. I didn't know what to say. They kept asking me what was wrong, but I didn't know how to answer them. I didn't know what I had seen. But I knew it was bad.

Sorry that happened to you.

Well, that's only the beginning of the story. The next morning I was out back playing on the swing set. It must have been a Saturday because Dad was home. Both Dad and Mom were working on something near the house. I'm not sure what it was, but they were working steadily on it. Come to think of it, they were always working! Anyway, I was about fifty feet from Mom and Dad, but it seemed a lot further away as a kid. As I sat there swinging in the swing I heard this terribly loud buzzing, or rushing sound. Suddenly everything became dark over my head. It was a huge swarm of bees. They seemed to circle just above me. I screamed and ran for Mom and Dad. The bees didn't hurt me, but they scared the heck out of me. Once again I was crying in Mom's arms. Mom tried to comfort me but it was like the event the night before and this event were too much for me. Finally I stopped crying, and I remember distinctly that a very important question came to me. It was like the question of all questions, and the core of my being needed to know.

What was it?

I asked Mom, "Is evil real?" I remember her asking me more specifically what I meant. I asked her if there really are bad people who hurt other people like that person on TV. I remember her look of concern, and a brief moment of contemplation, like, "How am I going to answer this?" And then she just said, "I'm sorry to say, but yes. There are people like that."

Oooh.

Yeah. I get chills even now thinking of it. But it was the truth. I had asked for it. I believe if she had told me there was no such thing as evil or bad people I would have felt even worse, because I had seen it. I knew it was true. I just needed confirmation. Anyway. That memory has always been with me. It was my first existential disappointment. I made that up. Don't even know what "existential" means, but it sounds like it fits here. It was the beginning of the end of my innocence. I know everyone goes through it, and some people go through it in the worst ways, but I thought it was something unusual to actually remember that. What do you think?

I remember the day. I felt so bad about the TV show, but couldn't stop you from turning it on. I did shoo the bees away though. You couldn't see me but I did do that.

You're such a liar. Anyways. Here's the question. Is evil real? I know there are bad people in this world. Why?

OK. So, I'm just a guardian angel. I am not like those angels who come down and make big proclamations or utter revelations to people while they write them down on scrolls and things like that. I'm not God's right-hand counselor or anything, or Gabriel's backup vocalist. I've never even met Gabriel.

Stop stalling!

Listen. I'm going to play the therapist game with you and turn it around. I will help you, but you have to answer the question, really. What do you think? Is evil real?

What a cop-out! What a loser! Give me a break! Answer the question! OK. I'll start the conversation. Do I think evil is real? Yes. I always want to kick people who say it's not real, like, "Oh yeah? How about THIS?" They'd probably just smile at me and limp away.

So, what is evil?

Um. Evil is doing bad things to people. It's thinking and wishing for bad things too.

What is bad?

Bad is evil.

Not fair.

Let me explain. Bad is anything that is malicious or destructive, or hurtful. That kind of thing, I guess. What do you think? I'm having trouble here. So you MUST know more than me about the subject.

Sure. But don't hold my answer as God's word or anything. Don't shoot the messenger! Ha ha. That's an inside joke for us angels. The original Greek word for "angel" means "messenger." Never mind. OK, so I think that evil is the absence of good, or the absence of God. Now I don't want to wax too theological on you here so I'll try to keep this fairly simple and practical. The Creative Force in the universe—

You mean God?

Oh. Yeah, but I've found some people don't like the "G" word so I thought maybe you'd feel better if I—

Just say God.

OK, God, or whatever you want to call that—

Get on with it!

Sorry. God gave people the power to love and express that love to everyone, but God also gave people the freedom not to love and express that love. Why?

Because we need to be free?

Yes. Because love needs to be free. If we were puppets of some Creator, forced to love, it would all be a sham, not much fun for God either, who likes us, I am guessing, to return that love freely. So, when we let that love flow into us and through us in acts of love, then we are basically doing what we are here for. And it's fun too. When we turn that positive energy from the Creative Force and center of all things—

God!

Yeah, when we turn that positive energy, that love, toward ourselves and our own wants and needs, to the exclusion of others or even at the expense of others, then you might call that . . .

The "E" word.

Yeah. That "E" thing.

EVIL!

Why not? Some people don't want to use the word "evil," Nicole, because to them it conjures up images of satans and demons and "the devil made me do it" slogans and all that. Let me say that they are on to something. Evil is human-made. God didn't make evil, or anyone called Lucifer or Satan. These guys are human creations. Are they real? You don't want to get kicked in the shins by one of these fellows. Seriously, they are as real as I am. But both they and I are really no different than you. And that's all I can tell you or, as they say, I'd have to kill you.

No you wouldn't!

No. I wouldn't. It's just a saying. I thought you'd like that I'm up on all that hip street talk and everything.

That's not street talk. It's secret agent talk.

Oh. Whatever. Have any questions?

Um. Yeah. What did you say? LOL. So, what about these terrorists? They seem unbelievably misguided to say the least.

I think you're right. Anyone in their right mind can see that killing people is just wrong. It's an act of evil. At the same time, these men are so delusional that they believe, or at least some of them believe, that they are doing the will of God. That doesn't make it right, or any less evil. However, it is possible that these men may not have evil hearts. Just like the nineteen-year-old soldier who is called up from the reserves and finds himself aiming at and shooting one of these men we are talking about—is he evil? War is hell, as they say. But that doesn't mean the young soldier who does his duty is going there. So, what am I saying?

Evil begins in the heart. Is that what you are saying?

No, really. What am I saying, because I'm not sure I know? I'm getting lost. I think I can say with a clear conscience that I may actually be saying something angelic. You can't judge the heart of anyone, I mean, absolutely knowing for sure what they are like inside. To say someone is evil is to make a judgment reserved for that person in front of their God. Judge a person's acts. Put them in jail. You might even have to fight against someone to stop them from hurting you or others. Do what you must, but give people the benefit of the doubt. Give them room to change too. Judgment and hatred against someone never helps that person change for the better, and only makes things worse for the hater.

Alright GA. So, is evil real? Here's my answer: I believe it isn't the cartoon character rendition we see on the Christianity Channel. Oh, and not what is depicted on Al Jazeera either, apparently! It's not that simple. But we can turn our hearts very dark if we want to, and we can hurt people. So, yes, evil is real. Mom was right. Unfortunately, there are people like that. But is that it? Seems depressing, like the great Creative Force you talk about left a bunch of kids at playschool with an assortment of weapons of their choice, and now they all run around shooting each other. I know it doesn't work that way, but that freedom thing does leave the door open for the bad guys to do a lot of damage. It seems wrong to let people act out so much aggression and stuff. Doesn't it?

Here's a secret right from the angels in heaven. This may be hard to comprehend, but it is absolutely true. You've probably heard the phrase, "The good guys always win in the end." Well, they do. When it's all added up, the good guys never really lose. I know that's hard to see. But if you take the big picture, the long-term view, I mean the eternal view, it's true.

What do you mean?

Well, Nicole, I think it is important to point out that there is so much more love in the world than hate, and there is so much more goodness in people's hearts than what we might call evil, that basically, you can jump for joy right now. Go on!

No, really. I don't quite feel like it right now. You go on.

I know it's hard to see, but goodness and love are all around. Just the fact that the vast majority of people are willing to live in peace and cooperation with one another shows how strong that force for good is in the world.

Well, that's certainly a positive note!

It's true. And I believe that the Creative Force and center of all things—

God.

Yeah, that Creative Force of Love is so powerful that it lives and moves in all things, and that it is inherent in the order of all things. It's just so big and vast, this love and how it shows up in everything. That's what you are seeing when you look at life through those baby brother eyes you were telling me about. It's so strong and in and around everything! Even when destructive things happen, the way it has been set up and run by the Loving Force, all is turned so very gently to the best it can be, to the greatest good, to the way of Love Itself.

So, basically it's all good.

Yeah. In a way.

Mrs. Dobbs uses that phrase all the time in class. I hate it.

Yeah? But you said the same thing a few days ago.

I'm trying to be positive, but it's not always good, is it? Sometimes it's very bad. But . . . But what? I'm lost again.

But good can come out of anything if you let it, Nicole. It doesn't make bad things right. It doesn't give people an excuse to do harm either. It means open your heart, look for the good in all things and in others, and it is going to happen for you.

What is going to happen?

Like I said, if I told you any more I'd have to kill you.

Man. You are a twisted angel.

Wednesday, September 12
Evening

Aunt Melinda is the most evil despicable insane mega-lomaniac demon-bitch who ever walked the earth. I can't believe she came by today and gave Dad crap about me not going to the "right specialists" when she doesn't even know what specialists I am seeing right now! She just expects Dad to be wrong and launches in on him like a crazed dog with rabies, foaming at the mouth and biting his neck, maybe like a vampire or a freaking werewolf-bitch from hell. He slammed the door in her face and he should have. After what she did to him, to all of us. I don't want her around. I wish she was dead! She won't leave Dad alone! Damn it! You there?

Uh . . . Yep. So, don't hold back. Tell me how you're really feeling. (Smile)

Yeah. You can laugh because you don't have to deal with her. I've never met someone so sick and who hurt us so badly.

What happened? Sounds like a long history.

She wasn't always like this. Aunt Melinda is Mom's sister. She lives in a big house in a really posh neighborhood about an hour away. She married into money and has always acted like she could grant everyone's wish of those of us relatives in less fortunate circumstances. She has one child about my age. James. He's nice, and her husband is nice too. In fact she used to be really nice, but got really mean when Mom got sick and hasn't been nice since.

So she changed when your Mom died?

When Mom died she got this way and never got better. I think I'm ready to tell you about it. It's hard stuff. But I need to get it out.

Go for it.

It won't be nice.

I can take it.

I know. OK. I'm so angry at Aunt Melinda that it makes me sick in the stomach. She told Dad that he killed Mom.

Really? I thought your Mom died of cancer.

She did. Aunt Melinda is a control freak. Mom wanted to die at home. Dad had everything set up and things were really quiet 'til Aunt Melinda moved in. She basically stormed in and told us to get out of Mom's room, "Go make yourselves useful," because she was now taking over. No one wanted her to take over. There was nothing to take over.

So basically she shoved you out of your mom's room?

Well, it was a fight. I mean it must have really sucked for Mom. This was a day and a half before she died. Dad kept trying to get Aunt Melinda to calm down and kind of move her out of the room so he could be with Mom alone, I suppose. It got bad. I think Aunt Melinda believed she had the right to be with her sister, and that this had precedence over Dad's rights. I'm not sure what she thought. She is totally nuts. I mean she is a wacko!

So what happened?

Me, Dad, Luke, Aunt Ellen, and I forget, maybe someone else, were there with Mom. Mom was in and out of sleep. It was the drugs they gave her. They made her loopy but they kept the pain down, I think. So Mom was asleep, and Dad was holding her hand, and we were all really peaceful and I felt the angels around.

Yeah. I know.

So then in comes Aunt Melinda, who had been out shopping. She storms in right to Mom, starts shaking her and saying, "Catherine! Catherine! I got you your favorite drink! A chocolate shake!" Mom was not going to wake up right then, so Aunt Melinda started shouting louder and shaking her. I thought she was going to slap her. Finally my dad says, "Stop! She's been peaceful like this for some time. Don't disturb her." I was so glad to hear him say that. But I had to run from the room.

Why?

With Dad on the other side of the bed, Aunt Melinda almost threw herself over Mom's body at my dad, shouting. She was screaming. "What? Do you think she is going to heaven or something? You don't know anything! I'm a nurse! You're nothing. I'm a nurse!"

Wow!

She sounded just like the Wicked Witch of the West. I ran out of the room while she and Dad just went at it over Mom's dying body. Poor Mom. Hope she was too far gone to hear it. We had all fled Mom's room and were crying. Only Dad and Aunt Melinda stayed in there yelling at each other.

Then what happened?

Oh, it got worse. Dad called Aunt Melinda a few names. They weren't very creative. I think he said, "You atheist bitch!" Aunt Melinda left the room and it got really quiet for a few minutes. Then Aunt Melinda took Aunt Ellen aside and they were talking, and then she came storming around the corner and down the hall to Mom's room again. She said to Dad, "That's it! We're taking Catherine to the hospital!" It was crazy. Mom didn't want to go to the hospital. She had said she didn't want to die alone in that kind of place. She hated needles, tubes, and machines and things. I had thought that it would be good if she died at home with us there. I started crying all over again.

And what happened?

Dad got really mad and said all kinds of things about how Mom was going to die and the hospital couldn't do anything for her, and that she wanted to die at home, and that hospice people were coming in tomorrow. That's when Aunt Melinda said that he was killing her. Then he ran down the hall and left.

He left?

Yeah. I thought that was the end. Here we were at the mercy of this insane woman. I wanted to run out too, but I felt if I stayed quiet and did what she said, I'd probably be OK.

Did your dad come back?

He did. A little later. Here's what happened. Aunt Ellen and Aunt Melinda started talking more about it, and it seemed like Aunt Melinda was softening up a bit. I think she might have felt bad that Dad left. Anyway, don't tell.

Don't tell?

Yeah. Don't tell. I am so afraid of Aunt Melinda I don't want anyone to know what I am about to tell you.

Don't worry. Angels keep a lot of secrets. You're safe with me.

I believe you. While they were talking in the kitchen I snuck back into Mom's room. I knew if they were going to take Mom to the hospital I might never see her again. I went in and she was awake! I held her hand and sobbed and told her that Aunt Melinda wanted to take her away to the hospital. She looked really comfortable and sort of half here and half somewhere else, which surprised me. She was so peaceful when everyone else was so messed up. But she spoke. She said, "I don't want to go." I heard that and didn't even pause for a moment. I ran back down the hall and shouted, "Mom is awake!" They stopped talking and went in. I think I heard Aunt Ellen say something like, "Ask her." Aunt Melinda talked right into her face, like a drill sergeant, and said, "If we can get you better, will you go to the hospital?" Mom just looked at her and said, "I don't want to go to the hospital." Then she fell back asleep. ___

You did a good thing.

Yeah. I guess I did. Am I going to cry every time we talk?

Probably. What happened next? How did your dad get back home?

After Mom had said she didn't want to go and had fallen back to sleep, Aunt Melinda seemed like she lost her power. I think it was only about ten more minutes and she coldly grabbed up all her things, announced that there was nothing more she could do, and left. She came back in and said, "If she dies tonight, don't bother calling me. I need to get some sleep because I have to work tomorrow."

No! You're making that up!

I swear to God and hope to die.

I wouldn't do that if I were you.

Oh. Sorry. I promise it's all true. I remember every bit of it. So, then Aunt Ellen called Dad on his cell phone and told him that Melinda had left. He was just across the street standing in the field, cooling off, I suppose. He came right back in and apologized to every one of us individually and then went back in with Mom.

Did she die that night?

No. She just slept a lot, or was unconscious. I don't know. I just don't know. That's all for now, but I want to finish the story about Mom later. OK?

Are you going to be alright?

Yeah. I guess I needed to say that stuff to get it out. I felt like if I told on her—

Aunt Melinda?

Yeah. Like if I told you what she did, then maybe I could stop hating her so much.

Did it work?

No. I hate her more, after remembering it all.

Why do you hate her?

I hate her for disturbing Mom, and for what she did to Dad, and for being such a control freak and so . . . so . . . so . . .

Blind?

Yeah. I was going to say, "so completely seeing things only her way," or "only seeing her side of the picture," but "blind" is the right word.

Why do you think Aunt Melinda was like that? Try to imagine, and this might be hard, that I was her guardian angel too. What would I be thinking about her?

Ouch. That's hard. I think you'd be thinking, "Time to trade up." Or maybe, "Who the hell did I piss off upstairs?" LOL. OK. Let me try. OK, so you are her guardian angel. And you are thinking that you are working overtime with her. You are sad because she is so screwed up. You want her to be happy, and she is having a hard time being happy. It's easier for her to make others unhappy.

That's a good start. Let's see. She is a nurse?

Yep.

Nurses are trained to keep people alive. I bet she is such a good nurse that she can't not help but believe that this is her job. I mean, she's like a soldier fighting death. You even described her as a drill sergeant. She believes that death is the greatest enemy, and that all must be done to fight against it, at all costs.

Yeah. That's pretty screwed up, if someone you love is dying of a terminal disease. You have to let go sometime.

Exactly, Nicole, and this is where your Aunt Melinda is having a hard time. She probably spends lots of time saving people at the hospital. Now her sister, her own flesh-and-blood sister, is being attacked by the enemy. What can she do? She tries everything to fight against this enemy. All she tries seems to fail. She can save so many, but not one of the ones she loves the most. She feels helpless, alone, frightened.

And let's add angry, hateful, accusing, controlling, a goddess-like opinion of herself.

Sure. Those things are part of her too. I think she made mistakes. She was wrong to say those things to your dad. She miscalculated how sick your mom was, or at least was afraid to admit it. And the fact that she left, well, that could be used against her to say that she is one bad woman, leaving her sister to die like that. On the other hand, I think what it was really saying is that she was so hurt and felt so helpless that she had to leave. She may have even realized somewhere deep inside that she was out of control and hurting people and that your dad would come back if she left. Her leaving may have been a personal sacrifice.

Hmm. Maybe. But we don't really know what she was thinking, do we?

No. We don't. We don't know what is going on inside that poor woman. And you don't have to like her. But do you have to hate her?

No. I don't. Though I believe it is going to take some time to let go of that hate.

Can you forgive her? Forgiveness just means letting go. Can you let her go, set her free from your anger?

I don't really know. I close my eyes right now and feel all those feelings I have about the whole thing and I want to let it go, but something just says, "You better hold on to some of that anger because she deserves it!" I'm only telling you the truth.

Thank you. Well, forgiveness in this case might be something you have to do in layers, like peeling an onion.

But onions stink!

I know. I don't know why I used that analogy. I knew you wouldn't like it. OK, so forgiveness comes in stages. Is that better?

Better. Basically I hear you saying, "Try to let go of that anger for her, even if it only falls away a bit at a time."

Yep!

Can I add something to that? I mean you are the angel but I think I can see something that I want to say before you do.

Go for it!

The reason forgiving is important is because holding onto all the hate and anger hurts mostly ourselves. I see how all that stuff Aunt Melinda is holding onto is killing her. She looks like one day she is going to be walking out of the shopping center and then literally explode into little pieces of meat all over the parking lot.

Spontaneous human combustion.

Know about it?

Yeah, it's only reserved for the really bad ones. Boom!

Really?

Duh. LOL.

OK. So, if I can just let go of this anger toward Aunt Melinda, I'm going to feel a lot better. It's heavy. It burns! It smells. It sucks.

Are you ready to take the first step?

Depends on what it is.

Are you ready to commit to forgiving Aunt Melinda? I didn't say you had to completely forgive her all at once, but can you make a conscious decision to let the forgiveness begin?

Oh, make me puke! I look up into the air. I see the ceiling above me and I am now feeling inside my heart. I want to say that what she did was wrong, and that she needs some help, maybe several of you guys could go over there and rough her up a little.

(Smile) Hmmmm. I'm having a hard time with this. Breathe. Breathe while you can breathe, Nicole! I forgive everyone! I let them all go! I let her go. I let her be her. I am sorry that she is so sick. I release my hate. I forgive ....that bitch!

Funny. But I know you really did start. I can see into your heart. And I saw something else in there too. It kept coming to the surface but you kept swallowing it down. I saw it. You have to let it out.

I know. Dad! Now that I remember what he did that night I am so proud of him. He didn't run away. He just got some air. He was never going to leave Mom with her. He was there all the way. He held her hand until she went to the other side. I'm sorry Dad. I am sorry I have hated you. You did the best you could do with her. It's just that I want you to be there for me. I want you to be there for me.

That's all!!!!!!!!!!!!!!!!!!!!!!!!!!!!!!! I can't do any more!!!!!!!!!!!!

Puncture Wounds

Why did You create me?
I didn't ask for this.

The coldness of her hands,
And his heart.
You created me to kill me
Again and again.
"Stop stabbing me.
I'm already dead."

N. M. B.

Thurʂday, September 13
Afternoon

I read your poem. It's sad. Are you going to tell me about it?

I think it's pretty self-explanatory. I'm not in the best mood. I'm tired. I'm tired of writing. I'm just tired. Let's not talk about that poem. I'm not ready to do that.

Is there anything you want to talk about? You said there was more about your mom that you wanted to share.

This is not easy. I'll try. But I'm blank right now. I'm a dry spring! No more water. Too much gushed out at once yesterday and last night.

What was it like when she died?

I have to tell you. I spent some time alone with her before she died. She was in agony. She kept repeating after every gasping breath, "Kill me. Kill me. Kill me." It was like a poem or a chant.

Kill me.

Kill me.

Kill me.

Oh dear God!

Kill me.

Kill me.

Kill me.

Oh.

Kill me.

Kill me.

Kill me.

Kill me.

I sometimes say that in my head again and again, and somehow it brings me comfort.

Comfort?

I know. I don't get it. But it does. She was touching it right then, death, life . . . Maybe when I say it over and over again to myself I feel closer to her, to it. Maybe I'll do the same chant when I die. Um . . . She had a knack for the dramatic. I think some people would quietly bite their lips and just take the pain. Every little "kill me" helped her release it. But I have to tell you something special.

What is that?

When I touched her? When I patted her head, sometimes she'd stop her chant and quiet down. I felt really helpful when that happened, like my touch was giving her peace.

I have no doubt that it was. It was your love coming through. That's the most powerful spiritual energy there is. It's healing too.

I know. I could feel it. I could feel it move from my heart, down my arm and through my hand into her head. It just went right where it was needed and calmed her right down. She breathed differently too, when she felt it. She wasn't in such a panic for breath. It was like a kind of thirst inside her was being quenched. Like when you are really thirsty and breathing between long gulps of cool water. It's so good, you just love it, and can't get enough soon enough. That's what it felt like. She told me that it felt good and wanted me to stay all night with her. I did. I slept on the floor and got up and put my hand on her every time she started getting anxious. This was before Aunt Melinda came on the scene. Dad was still working when he could, so I got to be with her a lot. It was sad, but it was the best time of my life too.

How so?

It was her and me. She said she loved me so many times, I think she said one for every year I wouldn't have her.

And you?

Yeah. I said I loved her too. Most of the time we were quiet together, between the groans and the "kill me's". Feeding her, giving her water, ice. Holding her hand. Patting her head. She apologized a lot, for saying stuff like "kill me" and also for dying. That was hard.

Do you think she knew she was going to heaven?

I don't know, GA. Even in the end she was still being my mom. She wanted me to believe. I could tell by her comforting words to me. But in the end she looked more like she was getting ready to slip into the darkness only with hope there was something on the other side. She looked like she was trying to be brave.

She was brave, wasn't she?

She was.

I know this is hard but what were her last words to you? Do you remember?

Yes. It was the day after Aunt Melinda left. I got my report card that afternoon, and had gotten all A's. I was so excited I ran into her room. I realize now that I did the same thing Aunt Melinda had done. I spoke loudly and shook her arm and said, "Mom. Mom. I got all A's." She pulled herself awake, like out of some deep, dark place which held her down, and she looked at me with struggling eyes, like it was hard to stay awake, and she just said, "Goodbye." That was it. Then she went away. We all stayed with her that night as her breathing became quieter and more and more shallow. Then, like magic, we all came around her bed, and I patted her head, and she stopped breathing. It was early morning. . . . She died.

⁂　⁂　⁂

To be honest, I cried for a couple hours after writing that last part. I think it was good for me, but I still feel pretty sick. Maybe that's the chemicals. I can't write anymore about that. But I did want to say one more thing.

Yes. What do you want to say? I'm listening.

I had this pain in my heart for the longest time when Mom was dying. I told Dad I thought something was wrong with my heart. It hurt and felt heavy, and I even found it difficult to breathe sometimes. He didn't take it seriously, so I just lived with it. But the very moment Mom died, at that very moment, the pain in my heart went away. I never had it again.

A Poem about Mom's Passing

I took her hand.
It was cold, brittle
skeleton bone
bruised black skin.

Then a puff of pulse
blood, warmth,
A squeeze.
An "I love you."
A tear.
A gurgle.
A silence so loud.
Like steam escaping a broken wreck,
the spirit ascends.
She quietly lingers,
breathing between our bodies and lungs.
And somewhere between our rest and cries,
She slips away unnoticed.

N. M. B.

Thurʃday, September 13
Night

Dear Guardian Angel,

I've been thinking about Mom all day today. Talking about her death brought so many memories and feelings back to me. I haven't had any outward signs that she is with me. But I feel her inside of me, or inside I feel her. I mean, when I get in touch with my own insides I can feel her in me and all around me. It's hard to explain.

I understand, because it's a spiritual thing. Sometimes spiritual things are beyond words. But they are very real, more real because they exist in the heart and soul.

Remember that dream I told you about her waiting on the path for me?

Yep. Sure do.

I wrote a poem about it this afternoon in my poetry book. I'm going to share it with you. Thank you for helping me feel connected with Mom again.

Reunited

I'm feeling close to Mom again.
She's waiting on that path still.
She's not in any hurry
For me to burst out our front door
And skip across the street
To walk with her again.
She is in no hurry,
Because she sees me step out that door
And down that path
Every day.
On the way to school,
Or meandering by the lake,
Or getting picked up by Tammy,
And bringing ice cream home for Luke,
Or just walking out to see
If she's still there.
She's not in a hurry.
Because I do see her there.
I see her here!
I will cross that road someday.
When I've learned to look both ways,
As she would want.
But today is just another day.
And the sun quite literally

Has broken through the clouds
Behind me.
Time to go out and play,
To greet my mom
Some other day.

N. M. B.

Thank you GA. I wouldn't be able to do this without your support. You've helped me understand so much about life and maybe even more about death, just by listening to me talk about Mom. Death is such a strange thing. I'm still dreadfully afraid of dying, but if you're with me I know somehow I'll be alright. You will be there, right? Whatever happens? Wherever I go?

Of course. I will always be there.

Then I don't need to be so scared.

I love you, GA.

Nicole

Friday, September 14
Dark Night

Chemo. . . . All alone this time—no little old ladies. Sick, tired. Not going to dwell on it, no use in that. . . . Aunt Ellen took me because Dad had to go to work. Figures. She really is a clean person. I mean her house is really clean and her minivan is spotless. I was praying I wouldn't throw up in her car. When we got in to go to the Cancer Center she showed me two paper bags double lined with plastic and said, "Hey. Don't worry if you get sick in the car. Just use one of these. It's fine." That was a relief. She's so nice. I didn't get sick 'til I got home. Only threw up once. She stayed with me 'til Dad got home and was like my private nurse while I rested. I'm glad she's around to help out.

Yes. I can see a place for her in heaven when she's completed her time on earth. She has many angelic qualities already.

She does. Well, I'll vote for her if you have to vote people into heaven.

No, it's not an electoral system. People get to decide for themselves whether they want to go to heaven or not. Really it's what's inside that counts, and people who go to heaven have already learned to live in heaven before they get there.

How?

Just by learning to be good and loving people.

That sounds reasonable for people like Aunt Ellen, but I've been having a hard time being happy and loving and all that. It was hard to get to school this morning, knowing I had an appointment with "Dr. Drip" later on. I'm getting tired easily. The doctor gave me some pills to help with the nausea. He told me it was normal to get tired easily. Can't believe I have to do the chemo again in another week. He says I'm doing well with it! That's a surprise, knowing how sick and tired I feel right after it. If people feel worse I really feel sorry for them. I saw Tammy hanging all over Rick after the bell this afternoon. I don't want to believe it but I think she's trying to ensure that he and I don't get any closer. Rick has been going out of his way to talk to me and walked me home twice, no, three times this week. That should make me happy, but I'm too tired. It just gets me more depressed that I don't have the energy to care, it seems. Rick asked if I wanted to hang out and I said, "Not today. I have to go for treatment." He looked at me sadly and said, "OK." That killed me to say that. I'm not sure why but it did. Like I had to remind him that I wasn't normal. And his look, I kept thinking he wasn't really sad for himself, that I couldn't be with him, but like he felt sorry for me. So I started questioning whether maybe he's only hanging out with me because he feels sorry for me. Oh, jeez. It just got me depressed again. I'm down. It's so easy to fall into that pit over and over again.

What pit is that?

The pit where I don't move anymore, or think anymore. It's so easy to stop trying, living. I want to tell you so much more. I want to ask questions too. I need to get to the bottom of it all in case I do die.

The bottom of what?

Life! What's it mean? What's the purpose? That sort of thing. There are more things for us to explore together while I still have the strength to do so. If I die I'd like to understand life a little better, and if I live, well, I'll be all the wiser.

Well then, let's get started.

Hmm. Now that I think of it, it's not that easy. Right now it is very difficult to continue to just have a conversation. You know what I mean, do I have to go into it?

No. I understand.

Maybe this will pass. Knowing that eventually I'm going to have surgery to remove this thing, I feel like I'm waiting on the front porch for someone to pick me up and take me somewhere. So, you know, like I don't have time to get into a conversation. I keep thinking it's too late to have a conversation, because they might come at any minute. Actually, I don't THINK that. I feel that.

I get it.

So, what do I do?

If you want to talk to me you might just have to start that conversation. Even if the car comes, what prevents me from getting in the car with you? We can keep on talking.

I am feeling worse. See my arms? They are bruising up. I'm sick and the medicine is making me bloated. But I know you care for me. You will be there for me. I was thinking in the waiting room today how perfect you are for me. You just get it, and even if you joke around sometimes a little too much, I can tell that you really love me. You are my best friend. . . . Man that's pathetic.

In what way?

Well, I guess it's only pathetic if you are a figment of my imagination. Which I suppose you are, but you are so much more. I really believe that. I really feel that I can hear you deep inside of me, and I do believe in angels. I do believe you are there, and you talk to me.

So then what is so pathetic?

I don't know. There is the critic inside that tells me I'm a little messed up. No, it tells me I'm a lot messed up, and how pathetic it is for me to talk to a make-believe angel friend. What a pathetic lonely nerdy ugly stupid desperate little girl!

Hmmmm. How can I help? I want you to talk to me. I want you to get what you need.

How about a sign? A sign you are real.

What kind of sign could that be? Truthfully? The signs have been all around you all your life. Remember that time you were thinking about your mom and you put on that CD and wanted to listen to song number seven, and I just made number seven come on for you without you pushing a button?

Yeah, that was cool.

That was a sign.

Sure, or a messed-up CD player.

Remember when you had that dream that Mark was going to dump you, and you asked me to give you the dream two more times and you would know that this was from me. And you did have the dream two more times?

And he did dump me.

You were ready though, because of me.

Why did I need that? Was I so pathetic that I couldn't be like other girls who just deal with it? I am so weak and pathetic that I had to have some pre-warning to prepare for it?

Perhaps you are special. Perhaps it doesn't have to do with you being weak, but rather you have a gift. It could be that my reality is a gift for you, and always has been.

I like to think that.

Get serious. All your life you have had signs from me. All your life, girl!

Ha ha! Yes. Some strange things have happened to me. So what does it all mean?

It means that a lot of strange and wonderful things happen to people and they discount them as coincidences, or dumb luck, or some slip of the mind, which then turns into a convenient recall that allows them to believe in magic. As a matter of fact, it's easier to say that there is a truly magical world around you unseen, a world of knowing, connection, meaning, angels, and that sort of thing, than just a one-dimensional world of accidents and coincidences and meaninglessness. I'm real. I'm so real. You know that.

Yes, but you always leave room for doubt. I remember when Mom was diagnosed with cancer you were there. She thought it might be something serious, but we really didn't believe that. When she went to get the test, I remember getting up that morning and letting the dog out. I turned around to go into the kitchen and heard a scratch on the door. I turned back again and . . .

And the dog was back inside the house just wagging his tail at you.

Yes! I knew I had let him out. Some would say I had just gotten up and maybe slept-walked a bit and dreamt I let him out. But I did. And he was back inside.

But that's not the important thing, Nicole. What came to you after that?

When I saw that the dog was inside again, I knew it was you, and that you were telling me something, touching me in some way, telling me something I needed to know. THEN I remembered Mom was going for a test, and I knew that it was bad news.

I know.

I knew you were just touching me, telling me in such a playful way that you were there, and that I needed to be ready.

I know.

And Aunt Ellen came over and I told her I knew that it was going to be bad news about Mom because of that special sign. Aunt Ellen believes in that sort of thing, so it was easy to tell her. She knew too, I think. So when Mom told us, we already knew.

And you can say that it was all in your head, or you can say that it was me. I have been there all of your life, and have shown you signs all the time. But you can always disbelieve. You could look at that little occurrence with the dog as a lapse of memory, or a strange coincidence of some sort, but you saw it as a sign from above. It was you who discovered the magic in that. Most would shrug it off as a quirk and leave it at that. Nothing seen, nothing learned, nothing gained.

That's a good thought, that me being a weirdo is a gift.

Everyone is a weirdo in one way or another. We all have our strange moments. We have our peculiarities. That's what makes each of us unique. Believing in the magic, in a message behind every coincidence or oddity, makes life extremely interesting, doesn't it? Being open to signs from above is being open to direction and meaning. It's a good thing.

You do know how to make me feel good about myself. Thanks.

You're welcome. So, want a sign? Sure. Just watch. Just look. Turn on those baby brother eyes you talk about and look out at the world. You'll see so many signs you won't believe it. They are there all the time. You just need to see them.

It's funny how many times things like that have happened and how I can still doubt so much. But really, how important are those things anyway?

I know what you mean.

The way you have been the most real to me is not by things I've heard or seen or experienced out there. It's been how I've felt you in here. I've felt you in my heart, and heard you there so many times. You are the one who brings me calm and comfort, and you are the voice of reason in my head. You are that gentle whisper that says even if the worst thing happens that it will be OK, that I am never alone, and that there really is a reason for everything. You are so loving, gentle, so there for me.

I'm so glad to hear you say that. I mean it hits me right in the heart to hear that. I don't completely understand why things happen the way they do, but I feel blessed.

Yeah. It may not be that there is a reason for everything, like I don't believe God does stupid things to people to teach them some cosmic lesson. That's not how it works. But there is meaning behind everything, and everything does have some sort of magical way of having good things come out of it. At least I hope so. So, I don't know. There's something really cool about this world.

This whole world! Like heaven and earth.

Yeah, by getting to know you they seem so much like one world, like they fit together perfectly.

Like earth and sky, or soul and body.

Or even like lovers. . . .

Whoa. Speaking of signs, have you not heard the phone ringing?

Yeah. I looked at the caller ID and decided not to get it.

Who is it?

Ha ha. It's Aunt Melinda. At least I'm fairly sure it is.

What do you mean? Doesn't caller ID tell you who is calling?

It does unless you block it, which Aunt Melinda does, because, I suppose, she feels she's too important to just let her name go out there to anyone. In fact, it's really funny. When she's calling and you look at the phone, instead of her name it says, "Unavailable." LOL. Think about that one. I have never seen any caller ID say that before. It doesn't say "Unknown" or "Unknown Caller" or just "Incoming Call" or anything like that. Somehow the phone company found out about her inner personality and came up with a new name—UNAVAILABLE.

I don't quite understand.

Well, it's probably better that way. I was talking about her insides, and not in a nice way. I suppose "Unavailable" is better than, "Horse's Ass Calling" or "Here's Megalomaniac Mel."

You're being mean. But I understand now why you aren't answering the phone.

I *am* being mean, but she scares me. She really does. It will stop ringing at some point, won't it?

Want a sign?

Sure. . . . How did you know?

I heard your dad come in and pick it up downstairs.

Oh. Too bad for him.

Maybe . . . (Smile) . . . Maybe not.

Now I'm not sure I'm following you.

You wanted some help with good old Dad. Here comes Aunt Melinda to the rescue!

No! Did you get her to call?

I didn't get her to call, but I did whisper a few concerns in her ear. You're right. She's a control freak. Now let's just see what happens.

I wish I could get excited about this, but I'm beat. I should get some sleep.

I agree. Goodnight.

'Nite.

Saturday, September 15
Night

Not much time to write today. I saw Rick this afternoon. I took him down to my favorite place on the lake. It felt right. I told him this was my special place, and about the fishermen. Then the guy with the pipe actually came by in his boat, puffing away. We both laughed and waved to him. We only stayed for a while. It was hard to get down there. Tiring. We stayed 'til the sun was turning the water colors, just so I could show Rick. He loved it. I think he really understood. He said, "Nicole, you are such an artist." I thought that was a great compliment. I'm not sure what he meant, maybe that I can see things a lot of people don't see, like I have the eye of an artist. Not sure . . . but it felt good.

When we started home he could see that I was having trouble, and truthfully I was also going through one of those dizzy spells. He took my hand and that helped a lot.

Then what happened?

Nothing.

Really?

Don't you know?

No, I don't.

Then he had to go somewhere with his dad so he said goodbye.

Oh. OK.

Then he kissed me.

Like did he kiss you on the cheek like he was saying, "I really care for you, friend"? Or what?

"Or what" is more like it.

Hmmm. Congratulations? Isn't this rushing things? How's Tammy doing?

Oh, man. Can you give me a break? I feel good today. It was one of the best days of my life. I am planning to talk to Tammy this week. She'll be fine. She's over him, I know it.

I'm glad for you. I really am.

Well, you keep an eye on him, on all of us. Keep us out of harm's way. Can you do that?

I'll give it my best. Right now I'm still working on your dad.

I'm cleaning up more beer bottles today than I was a week ago. You better try harder. And don't forget about Luke.

He's on my list. Do you want to talk about something? Any spiritual questions?

Not tonight, Angel. I need to rest.

Sunday, September 16
Night

I didn't have to call Tammy.

What happened? I know she came over but you told me not to say, "I know." So what happened? Did she come over?

Yeah. She called and then she came over. She wanted to talk.

About what?

Sigh. You know what.

Maybe.

Yeah. About Rick. She was like, "You betrayed me."

Really?

Yeah. Like, "I've been your friend and helped you even when you're down, like with this cancer and everything, and I invited you to come and be with me and Rick, and asked you to hang out with us and go to the movies and walk around at the mall, and then I talked on the phone with you for long hours when you realized just how sick you were getting, and I tried to comfort you, and I listened to you." (That part about listening was bull.) "And you and I are supposed to be best friends and you purposely went after Rick and stole his affection, which isn't fair because he has a big heart and obviously felt sorry for you and you took advantage of that by coming on to him and even when you knew that I still liked him and wanted him back you took him to the woods and made out with him."

She said that? Is it true?

No. You know what happened. I told you. It was just a little kiss. It was a really *good* kiss but just a little one.

Well, "Hell hath no fury like a woman scorned."

Bible?

Yeah. I think so.

You are not kidding. I felt bad like maybe I didn't understand that she and he still were working out their separation thing, and I could have stayed away in honor of our friendship, but I was so needy. It felt so good to be with him, and feel his touch. And he is a nice guy as she says. So I felt sorry for her like maybe it was wishful thinking on my part that they were totally over and that even when she was hanging all over him again I thought that was to show how powerful she is as a vampire seductress rather than some clinging Snow White damsel in distress. I felt sorry for her for about two seconds, that is. Then when she hit me with that line about him just feeling sorry for me and me taking advantage of that, well, I could have kicked her in the you-know-whats, if she had any.

Interesting. So, what did happen?

I cried and told her the truth.

That sounds like the perfect thing to do. And did she forgive you?

No. She said she could tell I was faking it and that if I wanted to be her friend I should be honest with her, which really surprised me because I was honest. Then she said as she was leaving that she didn't want Rick to drive a wedge between us and that I had her full permission to do whatever I wanted with him because I was dying and she would overlook it because of my condition.

Who made her Goddess of the Universe?

My thoughts exactly. She said that she would still be my friend because it would be wrong for her to leave her best friend in this time of need, but that it would be a distant friendship for a while so that she could heal from this travesty.

Did she use the word "travesty"?

Ha ha. I don't know why I'm laughing but she did. Before she could leave I said, "I have never taken anything from anyone. You just have to face it that he wanted to be with me. That's your problem. You deal with it. And I'm glad you'll still be my friend, even if it's from a distance. I'm sorry if I hurt you. I really am."

And?

The door slammed as I got to the "hurt you" part. But I know she heard me.

How are you doing with all this?

I'm numb. I keep thinking I should cry but I'm numb. I feel like an Oreo cookie. I'm hard on the outside and all mushy on the inside. And it makes me sick, like in waves of sickness when I think too much about it. I can feel that right now. Woooooooh. Here comes the sick. Sitting here I think the anger at her for being so uncharitable toward me keeps me from being completely sad about my best friend walking out on me like that.

What about your part?

I knew you were going to ask me that. I don't know. I truly don't know what my part was in this. I sincerely thought she was over him, for the most part. Why is life so complicated????? So now I have Rick but no Tammy. As much as I care about Rick I don't really know him like I know Tammy. Tammy has always been there, even if I usually have to go play in her world and ignore mine. It's still fun. She has a really great world she's created for herself. Argggggghhhh. Is that how you spell it? Like AAAAAAAAAAARRRRRRGGGGGGGGGGGGGHHH-HHHHHHHH! Dad's got his beer. Luke's got his computer games. What do I have?

Loverboy?

I am going to kill you!

That would be a first, I believe. Look, I may be your angel, but I'm getting as conflicted as you when it comes to this soap opera with Rickie Boy. Part of me says you're lucky because I know Rick has a good heart. But part of me says you are really rushing things and maybe you should slow down, or even consider not being involved with some boyfriend at this critical time in your life. I mean, you have me. You don't need some runny-nosed, hormone-driven teen idol wannabe putting his hands all over you comforting you. If you stopped this right now you might be able to get Tammy back. She's important to you, isn't she? Slow down. Give life a chance to unfold.

Do I have time? Do I have any time? Do you see me? Do I look like I have all the time in the world? I can't wait to get this operation over with so I can go on with my life! It seems like eternity waiting, and just getting sicker from this chemo.

I hear you. I do. I'm sorry. It's just that I do care so much. Hey. I noticed you are wearing your scarf all the time. How is that?

I don't want to talk about it.

OK, I respect that. But can you see that this might not be the end of the world right now? Give Tammy a few days, that's all. You'll be around in a few days, I promise, and even longer than that.

I want to see Rick. I want to feel myself in his arms. Do you get that? I know you think I'm going too fast but I need so much to be loved, touched, held. I find myself dreaming about just being in the warmth of his embrace. Do you know what I mean? Can you relate to that?

Yeah. I can relate to that.

I'm so glad to hear that, because it makes me feel like you do understand. And I need you to understand and be there for me.

Oh. I totally understand. And please. I'm always here. Look, as your angel guardian if you are feeling crazy about him, why don't you give him a call right now? Just talk. Talking is good. Really! Just call him.

It's too late. I'll see him tomorrow at the prison. I mean . . . school.

Monday, September 17
5:45 p.m.

Dear GA,

My head hurts. Actually, my hair hurts! It feels like someone has been pulling on it.

They say it's going to come out.

I know that. Some of it is already coming out with the brush. But it feels like, I know, it feels like when you brush your hair against the grain, pulling it back? How that hurts? Strange. . . . Just saw Rick. I invited him in. Dad doesn't like it when I do that but Luke was home so I think it's OK. Rick opened the fridge and asked, "Can I have a beer?" I was like, "No way!" Then he showed me that the fridge was packed with like a case or two of Molson's Golden. "At least he has good taste," is what Rick said. I had told him about Dad's drinking. Rick and I talked about Tammy, and he told me that she really was making a bigger deal out of it than she should, and that they were done, and that she had said that they were only going to be friends and that he could do whatever he wanted. He said that she knew that he liked me. So he was surprised when he told her that he did like me that she reacted like that.

How did she find out about the kiss or the alleged "make out"?

Rick's a nice guy. He took her at her word that she was over him and that they were moving on. So after he told her that he and I were more than friends she asked, "Did you make out with her?" He said that we kissed. Then she exploded into a whirlwind and disappeared into the clouds.

Really?

I think he meant figuratively. You may be able to do that but I haven't met a mortal who is that talented yet. It means she had a cow.

A cow.

Don't play dumb with me. You told me the other day that you had to "plead the Fifth" and if you know what that means then you know what it means to have a cow, and all those other dumb sayings you pretend not to know. Right?

Hey. Don't have an effing cow over it, OK? Sometimes I do and sometimes I don't. So exuuuuuuuuzzzzzzzzze meeeeeeee! Then what happened?

When?

After you talked.

Oh nothing.

Right.

Nothing I want to share with you at this time. It's between Rick and me.

Yeah. But you really shouldn't do that in front of Luke.

It wasn't in front of him. He was on the computer. Anyway. We just kissed, that's all. You probably know that already, watching every panting moment.

It's not nice to mock your guardian angel. I'm worried about you. Slow it down.

Mind your own business. I'm done for today. 'Bye.

Wait—
No. 'Bye.

Tuesday, September 18
Evening

Why do I feel like I'm hurting Tammy if Rick and I are seen together at school? I waited in the classroom until Tammy was out of sight, and I could see through the window that Rick was outside waiting for me on the path out front by the road. It seems stupid but I do feel guilty and sneaky. There's no reason to be that way. I try not to rub it in. I hope she can get over it. Don't say anything GA. I know what you think.

Friday, September 21
Night

Dear Guardian Angel,

I am sorry I haven't talked to you in days. I've been preoccupied with other things. I think you understand. Like I've been seeing a lot of Rick and cleaning up after Dad and worrying about Luke, so I haven't had time to do my homework, and no time at all to write to you. But I feel so sick now. I think I better write something. I need to remember that this journal helps me a lot. I need to make time for it.

I'm glad you're back. I missed talking to you. So, what's been happening?

So much. As you can see . . . I'm continuing not to do so well. Let me take off my scarf and show you.

I already know.

It fell out overnight. Yes, I'm speaking figuratively, but it did fall out really quickly once it got going. It surprised me. Look at my arms where they put in the drugs. It's still better than putting a tube in my chest.

Do they do that?

Yeah. So, I don't want that, but I need to wear long sleeves to cover up these poked and bruised arms. And look at my face. Notice? I didn't think my eyebrows would fall out, but look. They're gone!

You are beautiful, Nicole. You are really so beautiful, even without hair.

I look like crap. . . . Like vanilla crap on a sugar cone!

You look like . . . you're sick.

Thanks. Thanks for not lying to me. I suppose the ups and downs are normal. I mean I *am* a teenager. I'm supposed to be emotionally unbalanced and all over the place, aren't I? One hour I am way up, hanging with Rick, or talking with you about life and happy things, or giving Luke trouble about computer games, and then the very next minute I get sick, sad, tired, and scared all at the same time. Is that normal?

It is very normal. You've been through so much and have continued to be strong and very positive. I'm proud of you. You are not a quitter.

Thanks, Coach. But you don't have to give me a pep talk. How can I quit? What would that look like? There is no place to go to get away from this. I have no choice except to face it. When it hurts I can't run off somewhere where there is no more pain. I've sort of tried that with Rick. It doesn't work. I can't turn my numbness into feeling again. I can't look in the mirror and pretend I'm not changing. I could break the mirror!

I've heard some say it's bad luck to break a mirror, but that's probably not true.

Bad luck? My mom dying when I'm ten and me getting cancer when I'm sixteen could be called bad luck, don't you think?

Do you think so?

I can go to that place where it's all bad luck. It's a dark, deserted place. It's a place beyond sadness, beyond anger. Dad has been hitting the bottle hard and I think Luke is checking out too. Like he hardly says hi when I poke my head in his door. He comes home and sits in front of his computer. He even skips dinner most of the time now. I don't really blame him. When Dad's home for dinner he's already half looped. I thought you were going to help with that? I'm wondering about Rick and me too.

What do you mean?

It's moved quickly. We didn't talk at all this week. It's like he just wants to get physical right away. I mean that's OK. Really, I get so much from him in so many ways. He makes me feel cared for. I need that. Wow, do I need that! But I was hoping we'd get to be deeper and deeper friends at the same time, and explore life together. I do like to talk.

I noticed.

Ha ha. But our relationship isn't very deep, not like I thought it would be. He like talks for a few minutes and then gets way affectionate way too quickly. I wish he talked to me the way you do. I think he has the potential but it seems like it's going the other way, like into superficialdom. Is that a word? I suppose some of this is my fault. I mean, it's not like I stop him. . . . Oh well.

"Oh well"?

And I still wonder how Tammy and I are ever going to get back together. I really thought she would call me or say something after a few days. She said she would, and she knows I need her. I'm not sure what to do about that. So, what's left? Add to that the sense of impending doom this cancer brings to me and it all gets very bleak. Though people are still around I feel like they're not really here. When I think about the sickness I see it inside like death is sneaking up on me in the darkness. It's like all the creatures of the forest have fled in the night and I'm the only tiny animal left behind, screaming in the darkness, just before it's eaten by the wildcat. It's a scream of horror. Imagine looking up and seeing this cat hovering over you with those glowing green eyes opening its mouth to devour you. I'm a little screaming rodent about to have its head bitten off!

Nicole, you are so very dramatic. No wonder you got A's in drama.

Thank you. I don't even have to try very hard to be dramatic.

I know. It's very real. That's what makes you so special. I'm sorry you feel abandoned. I'm here for you emotionally, spiritually, and any other way you need me. I haven't forgotten about working on your dad either. I need to be careful not to mess with people's free choices but I've been doing some subtle things and I think they're working. I think things might heat up for him quite quickly. In fact, can you—

Stop. Let's not get into a conversation where you're try-ing to make me feel better. I need to be here today. I need to scream while I can, like a little animal before I'm eaten.

Yes. But can you hear that?

I hear the leaves crackle under the wildcat's paws as she approaches me.

She's here.

Yes, ready to pounce.

No. I mean listen downstairs. SHE is here. They're yelling.

Someone's yelling?

Surprise, surprise! Look who just showed up. Look out the window. It's your Aunt Melinda's Mercedes!

Crap! She came over.

That's your dad taking her on. Open the door a crack and listen.

I'm afraid. I'd rather hide behind the bed, in case she comes up here.

OK. Quickly open the door a crack and hide behind the bed, and I'll stand here and relay to you what I hear. Can you do that?

Fine. (I'm hiding now. I'm afraid.)

They're talking about you. Your Aunt Melinda is asking about your health. She's concerned for you. Wow. Your dad isn't buying her placid approach. Wham! He's calling her names already.

What's he calling her?

That's not important. You're right. He's not very creative in his name-calling. She's one tough cookie. Is that what you say?

One tough bitch might work better.

Yes. She's tough. She's not taking the bait. She's calm. Ooooh. She's cold, calculating, smooth. She's a warrior if I ever saw one. She's sticking it right into his chest.

Alright. Enough commentary! What's she saying?

Do you really want to hear?

Yes! Yes!

"You are not going to kill your daughter like you killed Catherine. In the name of God I won't let you do that. Nicole needs more help than you can give her. You are not paying enough attention. She is slipping away while you're drinking and out doing who knows what? It's not work obviously, because this place looks like a refugee camp. If you don't straighten up and give her the help she needs I will have Child Protective Services in here and take her away, and Luke too."

I hear Dad. What's he saying? What's he saying?

Are you sure you want to hear?

Yes!

"Get out of my house, you insane woman. Catherine died like she wanted to die, at home, peaceful, with her family." Ohhhhh. Your aunt interjects. "You killed her." He says, um, "She wanted to be at home. Not tortured with needles and tubes and insensitive bitches like you." Oh boy! Oh boy, oh boy.

Now what?

I can't tell. She's talking in a hush. Sounds like she's threatening him again. Oh my. No!!!

What?

She's coming up here! Hide!

Close the door!

I can't. I'm hiding too.

Close it!

Fine! It's closed.

Did you lock the door?

Shhhh. She's knocking.

I know. I can hear her. Did you lock the door?

Yes. Shhhh. Listen. What are they saying?

I can't tell. Dad's saying something. I can't hear what he's saying.

I can't either. Listen. They're going back down the stairs.

Maybe he told her I wasn't here, or that I was sick and asleep?

Just wait and be quiet.

I think I'm going to be sick. Not a good time.

Hold on a second. Count to ten or something.

One. How do you know counting will work? Two.

I saw it in some movie.

You're such a liar. Three, four, five. What's happening?

Keep counting.

Six, seven, eight. This is ridiculous.

Look, Nicole! She's leaving. See? There goes her car.

Phew! Whoa!

That was utterly frightening!!!!

Tell me about it!

So, do you still feel sick?

No. It worked. But you made that up. There was no movie.

I know. But I had to do something. Look, maybe you should go downstairs and see how your dad's doing.

No. I'm too afraid.

He could tell you what happened.

I can't. I just can't. This is too big for me. It's not about me, really. They need to work that out.

That's true. But what if . . .

What if she tries to take me away?

Well, I was wondering . . .

I won't go. Dad's a good father. This place isn't that dirty. I'll start cleaning more, fix up what he can't get to. I'll clean up the bottles. And there won't be any evidence that anything is wrong. Nothing is wrong here. Isn't that true, Angel? Dad isn't doing anything wrong, is he? I *am* angry with him. That's what makes what Aunt Melinda says so scary. I think he is checked out emotionally most of the time. This place does get messy. He hasn't been there for me the way I wanted him to. His drinking just makes him more distant. But to be taken away from him? Wow!

Would you want that?

Never.

Then there is a good chance it will never happen, if you don't want it to happen.

I hope you're right. But I don't know what to do with the anger. And I also feel guilty for putting him through all this. And I am afraid that Aunt Melinda will destroy our family and hurt Dad and Luke even more. And I love Dad at the same time. I'm confused! How can I feel all of these feelings at once? This is insane! I feel like I'm going to explode.

Things will work themselves out. They really will. Can you take some deep breaths and try to relax? Remember that you can only take care of so much. The rest, well, you just have to trust. It will all work out.

Easy for you to say, Angel! But I do believe you. I can't solve any of it today. It's late. The wicked witch is gone, the castle secure, the door locked, and I'm here with my angel. Time to get some sleep.

A beautiful idea, and sensible too. I'll be with you here all night. You can rest safe.

Thank you, Guardian Angel. I don't know how I could do this without you. Goodnight.

Goodnight, Princess.

No. Just call me Nicole.

Pardon me. I thought with you talking about the castle being secure and everything that it would be fitting. Why don't you just relax and let me be nice to you?

Actually, I find that quite condescending and something my dad would call me in his idiotic, drunken, and clueless fatherly attempt to parent me.

Sorry.

It's OK. "Princess Nicole" says turn out the light and be quiet.

Yes, Your Highness. I will be quiet, but it's your turn to turn out the light.

Jerk!

'Night.

A Dark Poem

As a new day ends,
The killer gives birth,
In her tub of perfumed oils,
And dragon scale pealing pain.
She wins again.

Hatching another lie,
To herself, and to Herself.
A new day ends,
Inside the nighttime
Of her moonless sky.
As she cries out for the light
Of the fire within.
But receives no comfort
In the baby's cry.
It is, after all,
Just another lie.

This poem is dedicated to my favorite evil aunt—Melinda.

N. M. B.

Sometime in the Middle of the Night

Can't sleep. I'm wishing Mom were here to keep me sane, quiet, safe. She was the only person who never judged me. She was my nurturer, champion, partner, coach, greatest fan. I remember coming home from school and talking for hours about my day. She would listen intently all that time, and give me such praise. She was the warm nest where I could always return. When I couldn't find anyone to play with, she would drop everything and play with me. See this scary rag doll on my shelf? We had a game where we would hide this thing in each other's room, or drawer, or I'd hide it in her car. It was so ugly we would try to hide it in each other's stuff. I guess she won, because I still have it. And you know, I could ask her anything. She couldn't answer all my questions, but looking into her quiet eyes I could see that she knew there was an answer, even if she didn't know what it was. I can smell her now. As she passes by, I smell the flower of her spirit, the breath of her soul, the serenity of her way of being. I miss her touch, those soft arms, that warm cuddling embrace. . . . I'm missing you, Mom.

Saturday, September 22
11:00 a.m.

I told Luke I'd give him forty dollars if he didn't play computer this weekend and went out and played with some friends at least today or tomorrow.

Forty dollars? Isn't that a lot of money?

He's a hard bargainer. I know he'd do well at business if he can learn to do something besides computer. So I said I'd give him twenty bucks and he said, "How about forty?" And I knew this was my only opportunity make him do it, so I said, "OK. Forty bucks. I'll pay you Sunday night."

Great.

Yeah. And then he said, "How about forty for today and eighty for today and tomorrow?"

You didn't agree to that, right?

No. I said if he stayed out 'til dinner both days I'd give him fifty.

So now it's fifty?

Yeah. And I had to pay him half of it up front. But I only have twenty on me so he said I could pay all the rest tomorrow if he could finish up this one part of his game before he went out. I said that was fine.

And?

He left five minutes ago.

You talked with him at 9:30! That was almost two hours ago.

Look, he's gone. OK? I did it.

You did, didn't you? Good job.

Thanks. Yeah. Now I've got to clean up today in case Aunt Melinda comes over with Child Protective Services.

Do you think she'd really do that?

I've learned, GA, anything is possible. I don't necessarily think she'd do that, but stuff happens. I mean look at this house. Stuff has definitely been happening in here. It's a dump. Aunt Melinda must have been impressed with the stale beer smell throughout the downstairs.

Nicole. How are you going to keep cleaning up when you can hardly walk to school without getting tired? You need to take care of yourself.

What choice do I have?

You have choices.

Like what?

Like not covering for your dad. Like letting him take care of his own mess he's making of his house and his life.

But it's my life too! That's the problem. Oh dear God! I'm tired already, just thinking about it.

Isn't there another way?

Like what?

I'm not going to give you all the answers. Think about it. What's the problem here? Are you the problem?

No.

Is Aunt Melinda really the problem?

Part of it.

She's not the problem. At least she's not the cause of your problem here. She's seeing something she doesn't like and she's dealing with it the only way Aunt Melinda knows. She's trying to solve the problem.

And what is the problem?

You tell me.

No.

Yes.

No. It's complicated, really complicated. . . . I've got to get cleaning.

Please. Don't.

I'm going to clean up today, while I still can. I promise I'll think about this more tomorrow, or some other time.

Oh Nicole!

Goodbye for now.

Sunday, September 23
Noon

Dear Guardian Angel,

This morning was almost interesting. Dad almost did something fun with me, but . . .

But what?

But it didn't happen. He was going to take me to church today. It wasn't as if I was thrilled out of my mind to go to church, especially in my condition. But the idea that Dad wanted to take me somewhere really appealed to me. We're pretty much CTE types.

What's that?

Christmas, Thanksgiving, Easter—CTE. That's when we show up at church.

Yeah. A lot of people do that. I don't blame them with some of the garbage that's dished out by a lot of preachers on Sundays.

All the same, I was looking forward to getting dressed up and wearing a really beautiful scarf around my head and jewelry of Mom's to match.

What happened?

He didn't wake up in time. I tried to get him up but he wouldn't get up. He said he was sick and couldn't go.

Drinking?

Probably.

I see that you're already dressed up, ready to go. You look gorgeous.

Thank you.

Did you get all ready to go and then find out he couldn't take you?

No. I decided to get dressed up anyway, just for fun. It feels good. See, the purple scarf with the white moons and stars on it? It matches this amethyst necklace of Mom's.

I like the black dress.

Yeah the dress matches my eyes. You know, those dark circles? Ha ha. I'm glad it still fits, but my face is so puffy. I think we should have church here, just you and me. Let me turn on some music.

Classical music sucks.

Oh?

It does. This is so hyper. Why does anyone like classical music? It's manic. They say rock music is manic. It's not half as manic as some classical music. People just like it because it's old. Some of it sounds like the people who wrote it needed an enema. Really stuffy! I'm turning it off! Do you like classical music?

Some. The music in heaven is far superior to anything on earth though.

Really?

Yes. This is because musicians are able to play exactly what they feel, and the harmonies are, well, out of this world.

Ha ha.

The way people connect in heaven is so complete and complementary that the harmonies are spine-tinglingly beautiful. Imagine voices connecting on all levels, singing from the depths of their souls. It's not stuffy. Listen to this. I mean to the harmony.

> *Amazing grace, how sweet the sound,*
> *That saved a wretch like me.*
> *I once was lost but now am found,*
> *Was blind, but now I see.*

Can you hear the voices, octaves above and below the melody? I'll sing it again:

> *I once was lost, but now am found,*
> *Was blind but now I see.*

I can faintly hear it. It sounds like it's coming out of the clouds, far away, hundreds of voices.

Thousands, singing in such perfect harmony. Sing it with me and listen.

Alright.

> *'Twas grace that taught my heart to fear.*
> *And grace, my fears relieved.*
> *How precious did that grace appear*
> *The hour I first believed.*

I love that last part where half the heavens changed their note on the word "believed."

And the retard at the end!

Yeah. And the retard.

You didn't know I knew what a retard was, did you? It comes in when you slow down and milk it at the end. This is fun.

You have quite a voice.

You too. Thank you. Just singing that song was like the best church service I ever attended. Too bad this page can't record what just happened. No one will ever know.

Sometimes that's the beauty of it, that no one knows but you and me. It's our secret. Like the tree that falls in the forest when no one is around, and people wonder if it makes any noise.

Does it?

The whole point is that it's a secret of the forest. No one knows but the trees and those who live there. The squirrel knows. Believe me!

The secrets of the trees! I like that. We should sing again sometime.

Any time.

Are there lots of harps up there?

Not as many as people think. We don't sit around on clouds playing harps. There is way too much to do, especially for those who are assigned to watch over people on earth. That's a full-time job, as you know.

What do you mainly do when you watch over people? Do you just watch, and occasionally jump in when they get in trouble?

Sometimes we do that, but that's the exception rather than the rule. We mostly work on their minds and souls.

How?

Not by any coercion, or really any observable means. We help people feel better, and give them options. For instance, when someone is really down about something, we whisper some hopeful comments to them. They hear them as if the comments are their own thoughts, which, in a way, they are.

I think I get it.

Sometimes we try to help them feel better by breathing on them.

Really? That sounds gross.

Angel breath is nice. It's really not a literal blowing of air on them, but rather sending them some positive feelings as gentle as a breath of fresh air flowing to them. It's hard to describe.

Apparently so. Will you breathe on me? Just blow a little comfort this way?

That does sound gross now, doesn't it?

Hey!

I said it's like breath. It's more of a special blessing or wishing well to a person, which they can accept or not. Have you ever looked at someone and just wished them the best or maybe sent them a big, silent, "I love you"?

Maybe. . . .

Well that's it. That's what we do. You should try it. Just try blessing someone in your mind, like just whisper in your mind to them, "God bless you." Or wish them the best. Give them a big silent, "I love you!" It will make a difference.

We can direct our positive vibes? That's so hip! That's so hippie, I mean.

Wishing well to people is not just for hippies, it's for everyone. Just think what the world would be like if everyone consciously expressed love to each other, if only in a concentrated thought, even once a day! It would change everything. People forget about each other and stop caring. One special time devoted to wishing others well, even once a day, would change that.

If they did it once, they'd probably want to do it more. I can see how it would help make everyone's day a little brighter.

Who are you going to wish well to today?

To you?

I knew you were going to say that. That's wonderful! I'm honored. I really am. But how about sending some love to someone else?

Too late.

Oh . . . Nice! Thank you. That was a good one! Woo hoo! That made my day! Yowzah! Okey dokey! That's a lot of lovin', girl! Now do me a favor. Share that love with someone on earth. Choose someone who needs it more than I do! Come on!

Um, I'm thinking. Rick is too obvious. He gets too much already.

Tell me about it.

I already sent some forgiveness Aunt Melinda's way. That probably got squished crossing the road! There's Tammy. Where is she??? I'm not ready to go there. I'm waiting for her to make the first move. Does the dog count? And there's Luke.

And?

I hate it when you can read my mind. When I looked at Dad lying there this morning I felt so much anger but also so much sadness. When I think of how life kind of went sideways or more like right down the tubes for him as well as me—I mean he lost his wife!!!!!—I feel sorry for him. I'm beginning to understand he went through a lot. I couldn't help but notice as I was trying to wake him up that he had a little bit of the baby Luke look on his face as he was snoring away. I don't know. . . . I feel angry at him and also feel sorry for him at the same time. I'm conflicted.

Why don't you send him some love and then start a new page and let's talk.

I suppose I could do that.

You are growing!

It's grow or die, or in my case, grow *and* die! I know, I know, *maybe* die. Jeez. I'm sick of that. OK, here goes. Dad, I wish you the best.

How did that feel?

Empty. Totally empty.

It was, wasn't it? Let's talk. Turn the page.

A Turn of the Page

I hate him. I hate him. I hate him.

Thank you for sharing.

I HATE HIM! I HATE HIM SO MUCH I COULD SCREAM!

Go ahead!

AAAAAAAAAAAAAAAAAAAAHHHHHHHHHHHHHH-HHHHHHHHHHHHHH!

Thanks for sharing again. More?

AAAAAAAAAAAAAAAAAAAAHHHHHHHHHHHHH-HHHHHHHHHHHHHH!

That selfish bastard! He doesn't care about anyone but himself! He is so stupid, and self-centered and lazy and mean. I HATE HIM!

Yes, but how are you feeling?

Don't mess with me! I'M ANGRY!!!!!!!!!!!!!!!!!!!!!!!!!!!!!!!!!!

OK. More?

There is always more. It never runs out. I hate him so much.

I thought you said you were beginning to understand what he went through?

I hate to think about that. I do understand more what he went through, but that doesn't make me hate him less.

Why not?

I'm not sure. . . .

What have you seen recently that has helped you understand him?

When we talked about Mom dying and how he acted I really see now how much he loved her. He really did. She was such a support to him. As personalities go, she had the bigger personality.

What's that mean?

She took up the empty space. He relied on her. She helped him come out of himself, come out of his quiet introverted place. She had such a big impact on all of us that when she left the void couldn't be filled.

Is that part of why you are mad at him, because he couldn't fill the void?

I don't want to admit that. But I do understand how that may be possible. When she died, he tried, but not very hard.

He didn't know how to cook or clean or do the laundry or anything. Mom liked to do that stuff so he never did any of it. And he tried to talk to me but it never got very deep or sincere. If I got hurt he'd basically pat me on the head and say, "There, there." I mean what's that?????

He couldn't replace your mom. You know that, don't you?

Once I just said, "Dad. Shut up and just hold me!" That was soooo embarrassing because that was in front of my friends when I got hit in the back by a baseball. He squeezed me for about two seconds and actually put his hands right on the sore part and it hurt even more. But he was like that with everything, even when he was sober. He's an idiot. Can't you see that?

Aren't you being a little hard on him?

Shut up! I just wanted him to love me, but he didn't have time.

Is it possible that no one could fill that void your mom left? Who could? She was your mother. Dads just aren't built the same way. I know this may be hard to accept, but it sounds like you were expecting your dad to fill in, and when he couldn't, you got mad.

I hate you.

No you don't.

OK, I don't. I think it's true that I wanted Dad to be everything. I understand how he couldn't be. But I still think he fell short. He didn't try. He's lazy. He won't give me what I want. He only goes halfway.

What do you want?

I just want him to pay attention, and maybe not treat me like I'm a nuisance. He gets frustrated with me as soon as I say anything, and gives me some pat answer. He's asleep!

What is it that you want?

You already asked me that!

I know. I think what you've wanted is love.

Yeah. You got a problem with that? Isn't that what we've been talking about? Love is that wonderful force of life! Love is what angels are all about! Love makes the world go round! Blow some love-kisses to the people who need it the most! OMG, you are so incredibly naïve! You have no idea what I've been through!

Maybe I do.

If you did you wouldn't have such a sappy view of life. I just want to die sometimes. I just want to die!

You may get your wish.

Good. I hope so.

And why is that?

Because life sucks!

Be more specific.

Life sucks! How much more specific can I get? It sucks. Cut me a break!

Life sucks because your father couldn't love you the way your mother loved you?

You are cruel.

He's far from perfect. You wanted him to be able to take up where she left off. You wanted him to take up the space of a mother's love which is beyond measure, unconditional, nurturing.

I miss her!

I know. Do you see how your dad couldn't do that? I know you wanted more. You expected more. You needed more. Even if he was Superman he couldn't be everything for you. He isn't a god, you know.

Believe me, I know that.

He's not some god who is capable of meeting your every need but refuses to grant you all you need and deserve. He couldn't do that. He was hurting too much. He's a frail human being like you and me. And he was wounded when she died, just like you. It's not surprising he didn't have the energy to keep up with all that his little girl wanted. He was grieving, exhausted, alone, and I guess trying the best he could.

I doubt that. He could have done better.

I know you doubt that. The little girl inside was left alone. When her mother left her she looked up to the only person left whom she knew loved her, and would provide for her. She needed him more than ever. She wanted assurance that everything was going to be OK, that she was still loved, that she would always be loved.

Rip my heart out, why don't you!

She wanted that and more. She wanted her mother! He could be her supporter. He could be her provider. He could be her protector, even clumsily try to comfort her sometimes. He could be her father. But he could never be her mother, no matter how he tried. He could never be her mother. And that's what the little girl needed the most.

I miss her so much.

I know.

I don't think I can ever fill up that empty place I've been wanting Dad to fill all this time. Way down that little girl is still so mad.

That little girl may always feel that way, because she is a little girl, and will always believe that her dad can do anything if he truly wanted to. But there's also a big girl who knows that he is only human, and can find a space to let him be human.

I still say he's a horse's ass.

Well, you are acting like a stubborn mule!

Alright. What you're saying is extremely painful to accept. You know that, GA! I'm only sixteen. What do you expect? I'm working on it! But I want you to admit to me right here, as my guardian angel, who cares so dearly for me, that he could have done better! Admit it!

Oh, Nicole. He has major issues.

Then admit that sometimes he wasn't very good. Sometimes he blew me off. Sometimes he didn't have the patience when he might have. Sometimes he didn't listen and he went right to judgment. Sometimes he forgot me. A lot of times he forgot me. He may have been doing his best but sometimes that sucked! Admit it!

I admit it. Yes. Sometimes his best wasn't very good.

Thank you. Thank you. Thank you. And he is getting worse! He blew me off today. He promised he'd take me out this morning and he blew me off. So, can I be mad about that?

Oh, you naïve child! Is that what you called me? A naïve angel? LOL. Touché! You can be as mad as you want to be for as long as you want. But do me this favor. If you are going to be mad at him, can you tell him? Can you talk to him about how much his behavior is affecting you? You said, "He is getting worse." I'd say, "IT is getting worse."

You mean his drinking?

It's beyond drinking. I mean his alcoholism.

Damn it! He's got a problem and now I have to take care of it.

No. You have to take care of yourself. And the way to do that is to let him know first how much he means to you and how much you want to have a relationship with him, and then how his drinking is affecting you and your relationship. I think it's the only way he'll be able to grab back on to life and be able to be there for you.

Do you think . . . do you think he's getting worse because of me?

Nicole, it's not your fault. I think your mom getting sick and dying started him on this path of trying to ease the pain by putting down a few beers at night. And this habit has been catching up with him. Now, you said his drinking slowed down at one point, but ever since you were diagnosed with cancer he's been drinking more and more. Imagine, and I know this is hard and I repeat, it's not your fault, but imagine the pain of watching his little girl fade away into sickness. He's feeling your pain, your sorrow, your sickness. He's afraid. He's so afraid he's going to lose you that he can't cope with it. The drinking is his asinine way of dealing with all of it. He's medicating himself with the wrong medication. That's all.

That's all? That's enough. Asinine! That is definitely the right word to describe him.

His behavior.

Yeah. But do you think he can stop drinking? And if he does, do you think he will start being there for me? That's scary. What if I ask him and he doesn't listen to me, or if he quits drinking and he's still an uncaring, asinine . . . ass?

That's a chance you'll have to take.

Yeah. After six years I'll just change everything! I'll walk in there and wake him up with a bucket of ice water and tell him my heart. Then I'll walk out and . . . what? I don't think I can do this. I'll think about it. Is that OK? I will consider what you're saying. That's all I can do right now.

That's good enough for today. Thank you for being so open with me.

Thank you for being so hard on me.

Any time.

I wish I could resolve it all right now. I wish I could change it all with the snap of a finger or a wave of a wand, or yell or something. I picture that little girl you were talking about as stuck way down a dark hole.

Let me pull you out of that pit. Let me take you in my arms and lift you in flight.

I wish you could. I really wish you could. If only I had time. I have so much growing to do and so little time. I can't do a lifetime's worth of work in a few weeks. I can't. No one can.

Let me lift you out.

I wish you could.

Monday, September 24
Back from the Doctor's

Dear GA,

We waited for an hour to get into the specialist's office and he spent five minutes with me. Why do they check your blood pressure and look at your tongue when they know very well that the reason you are there is because you have a brain tumor? And then they check your lungs and listen to your heart. That all took about four of the five minutes.

Then he asks me the same questions, and some of them don't make any sense at all like, how's your eating, and are you sleeping OK? He talks to my dad like I'm not there, about what they want to do. They are going to do some more exploratory stuff soon, he said, but he wanted me to increase the steroids.

Steroids? You haven't said a word about these.

Yeah. I forgot to mention them. That's what's puffing up my face. Dexamethasone is what the bottle says. Isn't that what those wrestlers take and it ends up making them way too bulky and some turn into killers?

I don't think he'd give them to you if that happened.

I will be big and stwong. These things make you beeeeeeg and strawwwwwwwwng like Awnald Schwarzenegger.

What do they do for you?

They stop the swelling, and then they do something else. Oh, they can help with feeling sick too. But they can also make you gain weight and look like a He-Man. So, that is not fun. Let's see. Now that I've lost my hair, if I gain a hundred pounds and my face keeps puffing up like this, I can become a WWF wrestler!

Good. Good. That's so positive! What's WWF?

Oh, you are such an ignorant angel. Never mind. I was being sarcastic. But that does lead me to a question. Actually, I've wanted to talk about this for a while, especially when I'm in a good mood.

It's good to see you in a good mood. What do you want to talk about?

Speaking of hot bodies . . . of which I have not anymore. I want to talk about boys.

Boys? Oh, is that why you are in such a good mood?

Yeah. And I want to talk about love. I want to know all about love.

Are we going to be talking about Rick? Don't you have a girlfriend you can talk to about this stuff?

You know I don't. . . . I never thought we'd end up not being friends. Even when she got mad at me I didn't think it would last this long. I can't talk to her. Not now! Not about Rick!!! I have to talk to *you*. Could we talk about love and I just won't mention any names? He *is* my boyfriend! I've been thinking, if I end up dying, I will probably miss out on a lot, and I think that's unfair.

You mean missing out on love?

Yes. And all that comes with it.

What if you don't die?

Oh. Well. It can't hurt to know a few more things about love, can it?

Most people learn the hard way, I suppose.

That might be true, but I don't have time for all of life's lessons to just come to me. Give me something to hold onto and think about right now. Please. I remember there was one story from the Bible we learned in Sunday school about this woman who was going to die, and she went with her friends into the mountains and celebrated her virginity or something before she died. Maybe she mourned her virginity? I can't remember. But that's how I feel. I don't want to end up mourning my virginity. Really!

So, do you want to talk or do you want me to give you permission to get . . . ?

Shut up! YOU are an evil angel. That's not what I'm talking about! I want to know about love. How do you know when you're in love? Isn't it good to express love if you're in it? Just tell me something, anything about love.

OK. I'm going to give it to you straight, but in a roundabout sort of way.

Great!

Love is a lot of things. There are all kinds of ways love is expressed. Think about it. There's romantic love, passionate love, love between a mother and daughter, or parent and child, love between brothers and sisters and friends, and you can even love your dog, or love a good chocolate sundae! Love, in terms of say, what you might be interested in now, is pretty much nature's way of getting you to do your part to keep the human species populating the planet.

Get out! It's more than that!

Wait. I'm starting from the beginning here. Bottom line, it's easy to feel these hormonal blasts going off in your system and fall in love in seconds with people you find yourself physically attracted to. This kind of falling in love is like smelling chocolate baking somewhere. You just have to find it, and when you do, you must have it.

That's a good example. I love chocolate! So life is like a box of chocolates after all?

I'm not sure I understand.

You are so pathetic. You totally know what I'm talking about. But love IS more than a sexual attraction, isn't it?

Absolutely. Falling in love is a very special part of life. When you fall in love you feel as if you could live and grow with that person forever, and that no one has ever felt as good as you do when you are with the one you love.

Yes. That's so true. . . . What's wrong with that? Sounds good!

There's nothing wrong with that, because that's where you start. If you didn't feel like that, you would never get involved with someone. If it was all work and no play, or all stark reality and no fantasy, you'd run the other way.

That's pretty pessimistic! You must have been burned in a few love-relationships over the centuries, huh? Were you once on earth? Did you fall in love?

This isn't about my personal life. But I suppose you won't listen to me if you think I'm some kind of prissy angel who never experienced what it's like to be in the world and in love. People have so many silly ideas about angels. Like, where did they get the idea angels are sexless beings? Look that one up in your Bible. The word "angel" just means "messenger" not "neutered toad"! Yes. I've been in love! I've lived in the world and felt all the hormonal rush of youth and the passion of lovers and yeah, OK, I've been hurt by love too.

Wow. It sounds like you have a story to tell. Can you tell me? I really want to know.

Honestly? That would be breaking the rules. As your guardian angel I'm supposed to keep the focus on you and your life.

But I want to know!

I suppose I could tell you some sappy story about myself. Like I could tell you I was in love once. And I could tell you she was a princess and she and I were going to get married and let's see, then she dumped me for some Robin Hood type and all that. Or maybe it was me who was the Robin Hood type and she dumped me for the guy with all the land and loads of cash. Does it really matter? The point is, I loved. In fact, I was one of those idealist poet types who fell in love more times than I can count.

No!

Yeah! Truth is I never settled on anyone while I was on earth. Nothing seemed to work out. But once you get up here it becomes a lot clearer what this whole love thing is about, like what real love is, and what's possible, and I know this might sound crazy but it's not too late for love once you become an angel. Poets know it. Lovers know it. Love lasts forever.

Totally.

Yeah. And people don't get that and they misunderstand what angels are and what they can be, like people who die go to heaven and people in heaven are called angels. So like people are angels and angels are people and love, well, love is love!

Can angels love people?

Yes! Of course!

Can people love angels?

Yes! What separates you and me right now is just the door between two worlds. We're all the same. Just think of me as someone who has a head start on you because I happened to get here a little sooner than you did, and I've learned a lot since I've been here, and my job is to quietly share that with you and lead you here. But let me assure you that love goes on forever. That's what makes heaven heaven. Can I get back to my original point now?

Wow! After hearing that, I'm not sure what your original point was. Sure. Go on with your original point. (Smile)

I was talking about different kinds of love. Where was I? So it all starts out with a spark and then it turns into a flame and all that romantic hormonal stuff. But then real love has an opportunity to grow out of that, in a whole new way. In fact, if you want true love, the kind that lasts forever, you must let it grow.

How? What do you mean?

Real love is something that grows between people. It is cared for, nurtured, supported, fought for, and even prayed for. Real love isn't something you just fall into. It's something you grow into together. And you keep growing in it and it keeps growing in you.

Most of my friends are very pessimistic about love. They like to have sex but don't want to be hurt by caring too much. That's not what I'm interested in. I've already been through that phase from "guys are gods" to "guys should all be castrated and wear shock collars." I do think some people make more out of sex than it should be. I mean that's all people talk about, whether it's "don't do it" or "this product will help you do it better" or "if you are going to do it, then use these" or "doing it just might kill you." I think love and sex go better together. That's why I'm asking you about it.

Love and sex do go better together. That's very wise of you.

It's easy to be wise when you have nothing else to be. But what about when you have a choice? If I am going to die I want to know love. I want to experience it from the very depths of my inner soul to every sensation of my body. Remember, I'm very dramatic. I want to feel it *all*! I want to experience love inside and outside. I think I'd appreciate life much more if I knew all about love and all the various features of love!

Life is what you make of it, Nicole. That's true with love too. The important thing to remember, and this is with any sort of thing you may call love, is it's an incredible force for good. Use it that way. Use it responsibly, let it grow, nurture it, share it. You see, love is not about you, it's about someone else. It's about wanting someone else to be happy and fulfilled, and of course you want that back in return, but it's really about how you can share yourself and your life with another for their happiness, as well as your own. But they come first. That's what makes it LOVE with a capital "L".

"I'm not sure why you're saying this. If I'm in love I would assume I don't have to worry about all those things. Love is good, really good, just like you say. So, I think expressing that love in all the different ways you can, would only be beautiful.

OK. Let's talk about Rick.

I didn't think you wanted to talk about him.

I decided we might as well get to the point. Here's the question, Nicole. Are you in love with Rick? I mean have you looked inside and asked yourself if this is about loving him or about using him to feel what love might be like? Do you love him?

I do love him. . . . FINE. I don't love him like *that*. How come you know me so well? It's not fair! I love him, just not with a capital L. But it's still love with a little l.

OK. There's a significant difference between love with a little l and love with a capital L. But I'm just telling you how I see it. You don't have to listen to me.

You've never liked Rick.

I like Rick. He's a really nice guy. If you love Rick, well, maybe you should wait 'til you get better and not be so heavily involved with him, if you know what I mean.

So what if I die?

If you die? You won't die. Do you believe me? Love never dies. Think about that one. Love can never die.

Well what does that mean? Like I can love after I die? Do angels make love?

That's a personal question.

Not really, I didn't ask it about you. Can I ask you a question along those lines? I mean a personal question about love?

I'm not very comfortable with that. But I guess so.

Do you love?

Of course, angels are like the epitome of love. They are the love-beings of the universe.

I know that. But can you love, like, you know?

Like, I don't know. What?

Love with a capital L! Can you still fall in love?

Sigh. Can you write that? Sigh. Thanks. I think you've got me there, because I just explained that this falling in love is nature's way of procreating the human race, but I suppose it's more than that. Can I fall in love? I can. I can because even if I'm called an angel, I'm still human. And human means more than just being frail, like you might say, "I'm only human!" I can't use that. I mean angels are supposed to be beyond that. I can't even say, when I make a mistake, "I'm only an angel. What did you expect?" All of this can turn into a real complex for the perfectionist-type angel.

You're stalling. You really get intellectual when pressed about some personal issue.

Hey. I'm only an angel!

Hardy har har! So, you CAN fall in love?

I can.

Then you really do know what I'm talking about.

I do. It's human. To be human is more than just being a creature of the earth. To be human means to love. We are children of the Great Loving Creative Force.

You mean God.

Yeah. We're created in the likeness of God, and that likeness is pure love. We are human because God is HUMAN. We love because God is LOVE. It's all about love. Like John says, "All you need is love."

John Lennon said that. But I'm sure it's in the Bible too.

Yeah well, you know, it's true. That's why everybody says it. So, yes, I can love. I can love because I'm human, just like you.

Do you love?

I do. More than you could possibly imagine right now.

How much? In what way? Can you tell me?

Nicole! I'm already in trouble breaking the rules talking about me rather than about you. That's all I can say right now or I might get reassigned to someone else if I keep saying things about myself.

Can you tell me?

(Smile)

Are you going to ignore me?

It's for your own good. And mine.

Oh, please!

(Smile)

Wednesday, September 26
Evening

It seems like I've been with Rick every waking hour this week. Today he asked if he could come in and I said, "Not today." That was because I had so much homework, and I'm tired of the intensity of our relationship to tell you the truth. But he said, "Please?" So I let him in and didn't get anything done! The only place he doesn't go with me is to the hospital. I wish I'd see less of him and more of my family.

Really? Do you mean that?

I don't see Dad and Luke at all it seems. We haven't had dinner together—I mean Luke, Dad, and I—since last week. Either Dad is late or Luke is too busy on his game. Aunt Ellen has been taking me for my new treatments which are scheduled every day!!! Can you believe that? I am missing a lot of school and I'm falling behind and there's too much pressure!!!!!

You haven't told me about the new treatment.

I've been in denial about it.

Radiation.

Yeah. It's not as bad as it sounds, but there's something about the word "radiation" that scares me. They shoot a beam at my head to burn the cancer cells and shrink the tumor. What if they miss and hit my brain?

I'm sure they know what they're doing. I've never heard of that happening, so you don't have to worry about that. But what's it like? Is it like the chemo?

Besides itching on the back of my head, and feeling tired, it's actually not that bad of an experience. It all depends on where they aim that ray gun.

Is there really a ray gun?

Ha ha. Technically I suppose there is, but it doesn't look like a gun. It's just another big machine to lie in while it makes funny noises and stuff. It is really funny in a not-so-funny way that you have to go down into the basement of the hospital to get it, because that's where all the radioactive stuff is and they don't want regular people exposed to it. You can get cancer from radiation, which is ironic. With all of this stuff, like chemo, radiation, even the steroids, it's like so primitive!

What do you mean?

They have fancy machines doing all the work but it's still like the old days when they would drill a hole in your head and cut out a piece of brain to see if your headaches would go away, or when you had a bullet wound on your wrist they'd cut off your arm. I think someday, actually, I hope someday people can look back at this time and how they treated cancer and say, "Isn't it great we've learned how to cure cancer without having to cut, poison, and burn people to fight it?"

I never thought of it like that.

Well, I think when you go through it then you really see how bad it is, but since you're so sick and afraid to die you let them do it all the same. Now I'm just caught up in the machine, and I'm hoping when the machine is done with all its cutting, poking, prodding, poisoning, burning, and humiliating, that then I GET BETTER!

You will.

Really?

You've got to be positive.

Oh. I thought you knew something, like God handed down a reprieve. Oh yeah, it doesn't work that way. So, what do I do? Be positive? That's hard. I feel so powerless, like I have no control over this cancer or the cure. I'm a puppet, a meat puppet.

Maybe there isn't much you can do about the cancer or all the tests. How about what you can stop doing? Like . . . What's one thing not to do? Is there something you can stop doing?

The only thing I can think of is not being so afraid. I can stop going into a panic about it all. I think . . . I can stop trying so hard. I can try to let go of the fear I suppose, at least a little at a time.

And?

And . . . um . . . enjoy the day?

Brilliant!

How about cope with the day?

OK!

How about make it through the day?

Nicole. Let's keep it positive.

Fine. I'm going to try to focus on what is happening right now, and just experience it, not control it, try to make it more than it is, or cling on to life, or push it away for that matter. But just, maybe just observe it. Yeah, even enjoy it if I can. And when it's not that enjoyable, remember that this won't last forever.

Grandma used to say, "Remember, this too shall pass."

Didn't everybody's grandmother say that? It's trite but it works. Also, let's recite all the other clichés which seem to have some value as well. One day at a time! Just for today! Um . . .

Let go and let the Great Creative Force of the Universe take over.

I think there's a different version of that saying for non-PC angels, like "Let go and let God?"

Isn't that what I said?
Anyway, speaking of time . . . Gotta go. Homework!
'Bye.

Friday, September 28
4:30 p.m.

Dear GA,

I got the morning in at school today, but I'm not sure how long I can keep up, missing school here and there and still doing everything I'm supposed to do, like the homework and stuff. They have it worked out so that certain girls keep me informed. Lianne gives me the homework and Skye fills me in on what I've missed in class. That's an extra assignment for them. I hope they're OK with that. But it's not the same as being there, and I do care about grades. Maybe I shouldn't, but I do! I've never had a grade below a B+ except in PE. I'd rather quit than get bad grades. I've got to seriously think about how I'm going to do this from here on out. Oh God! Why is it so complicated?

You need to slow down. Just tell your dad and . . .

And he'll have another six-pack for dinner! Crap!

What is stopping you from talking to him? . . . Why won't you answer me? Nicole!

I'm going into a self-induced coma. Do you mind??? I want to go blank inside, stop thinking about it. It's too big. Didn't you say something about letting go? I'm trying. I'm feeling like I have to uncomplicate my life at this point, and not make it more complicated. Is "uncomplicate" a word?

Doubt it.

You know what I mean. The point is, I have to start now.
. . . BRB

※   ※   ※

Sick again. . . . So sorry.
I'm always sick on Fridays. Chemo day. You know that. It's
true though, when I get worked up I usually end up puking.
I've got to go. I have plans. See you later.
'Bye.

Sometime in the Middle of the Night

Hi.
Hi. What time is it?
I'm afraid to look. I just want to tell you one thing. Then
I think I could sleep.
Rick?
Yeah.
That's what I thought.
It's not what you think. Or do you know already?
*No. I took the evening off. I got some reading done, sat
around a bit, caught up on some sleep. . . . Oh no. You look
upset. Maybe I should have been there!*
Some things are better done in private. I had to be on my
own for this.
What happened?
He asked me if we could go further, and I said "no." Don't
reply with, "What do you mean?" Thanks. At least he asked!
I thought that was good of him, and he didn't ask again.
In one way I'm hearing you whisper to me, "There's time.
There's time for all the good things. Just be patient." I'm also

hearing you say, "You have to let go." This is a time of letting go, of working things out, and letting things settle, isn't it? That's what I need to do. He'll be OK. . . . I'm so relieved. OK, part of me is really pissed. But love lasts forever, right GA? I'm counting on love with a capital K. I mean L, but something wants to say K. Ha ha, it must be the tumor. Love with a capital K! Yeah. I'm losing it. What's new? Don't answer me. I'm actually feeling very peaceful inside. Peace. Soothing peace.

OK. I know you're all worked up and can't turn off the thinking.

You're right.

So, I just want you to trust me. Do what I say.

OK.

Prop up the pillows behind you and just let yourself lean back onto the pillows and relax.

OK.

Take a few deep breaths. And let your mind start getting peaceful. Now I want you to imagine you are leaning back into my arms. And feel my warmth around you. It's real. No need to think about anything. Just relax. You're safe here.

OK. I'll do that. I'm going to stop writing now.

Saturday, September 29
Noon

Dear Guardian Angel,

I'm surprised how good I feel on so little sleep. I'm here in the den gazing out the open window after a quiet walk. The weather has been so warm for this time of year, like summer.

I'm glad because I can still get out, though it's overcast and rained a little here and there. I'm still feeling very peaceful inside. Not too sick either. How are you today?

I'm fine.

That must be a drag, always being fine. Are you really always fine?

Um. Well, I can have good days and not-so-good days. But I don't really have a bad day. I used to, but I don't anymore. I'm growing.

That's cool. If you didn't have a not-so-good day then you wouldn't appreciate the good days. And you are growing? That's really cool, because people often think about angels as being rather . . .

Static?

No, I was going to say boring, but static works.

Thanks. We are not static or boring. It's fun being an angel.

Is heaven fun?

It's a blast.

People keep growing there? Forever?

Yep. One day at a time, as they say. It gets better and better and better.

Wow! That could make you crazy thinking about how long FOREVER is.

Think about forever as today. Every day in FOREVER is today.

That's so deep.

I know. I'm a deep person.

It's so weird to think of you as a person, but I guess what you've been telling me is that angels are people too.

Exactly! That's exactly what I've been trying to get through to you. You and I are not that different.

I'm feeling that more and more every time we talk. So, even if I'm not always great physically, I do feel good inside when we spend time talking together. I'm in the mood for a conversation.

I'm always ready to talk with you. What do you want to talk about? I'm all ears.

I'm getting so deeply connected to nature again. One good thing about all this is I've come to see how important parts of my life are for me, like going outside, and being near water. It's too cold to wade in the water right now, but I love even being near it. Even after having such a hard time falling asleep I found myself waking up early this morning and went outside.

Early?

Nine a.m. is early for a Saturday, isn't it? I got up and took my new scenic route to the lake and then walked north 'til I hit the stream. After the rains it's got a really full flow going, not the usual trickle it often ends up being in the heat of August. I didn't play in the stream. I sat under a tree and just watched it and listened. Hmmm. Sigh. Breathe. OK.

What?

Now I'm sad. Not sure why. As soon as I heard the stream all these memories came flooding in. I hope I don't die. I haven't spent enough time down there by the water.

I hear you.

I know what I will miss. I will miss that sound, hearing the sound of the stream flowing along toward the lake. That trickle of water. Today it's more than a trickle, it's so soothing. I will miss the color green. I like all the other colors but I'm going to miss that one, that green of the forest in the middle of the summer, and that wet wood scent of the forest, and that warmth when the sun is shining down on my head and my face. I'll miss those things. I will also miss the sound of the wind. Maybe it's trite to talk about that. A lot of poets have talked about the sound of the wind in the trees, haven't they? But that doesn't mean I don't have the right to do so. I'm dying. I can be as trite as I want.

Yes you can!

Thank you very much! Trees! The trees seem alive to me. When the wind flows through the branches and leaves, each tree has its own sound, a whisper, and they talk to each other. When I sit down by the lake, right where the stream flows into the lake, and hear the water and the trees, I already feel like I'm in heaven. But it's a still day today.

Yes. It is.

When I think about the really sweet times, today I am reminded of playing in the stream. Luke and I would stand in the stream for hours, making little dams and waterways, and waterfalls, and tiny lagoons, and islands, and peninsulas and docks, and swimming areas for the little imaginary people who lived there. I loved to make fairy houses with two stories, and a garage, patio, furnished rooms made out of bark and sticks and leaves. Tammy even made tiny pieces of furniture to go inside the houses, like tiny beds, and dressers, and a table and chairs. We really thought the fairies inhabited them. Mom occasionally put a few pieces of candy inside the houses with a thank you note from the fairies. She was fun. . . .

※   ※   ※

You've been silent for a while now. What's that about?
I went blank.
That was a long "blank." What are you thinking about?
There is something about remembering things that makes me so sad. I know. You don't have to remind me that I might not die. I get that. So, I don't think it's only that I am sad that I may not be able to do those things again. The truth is, I haven't made a fairy house since before Mom died. I've played in that stream possibly only once this year. I can't remember. But there's something else about it that is just sad. I think it's that when I take myself back to those times, I feel the wonder of life and the security or trust I had in the world. I see that this is now gone. I think it's something that I must have grown out of. I know Mom dying and this tumor have altered my life in a cataclysmic way. I can imagine some psychiatrist right now saying, "Of course her sense of safety and security has been damaged by events." I'm guessing that's what a psychiatrist would say? But I think it's also just sad to treasure these memories as things gone by, never to return, at least not in the same way.
When is the last time you really played in the stream?
It's been a while. Talking about it makes me want to do it.
I'm thinking you need to go play in the stream today.
I'm thinking I have homework.
I'm thinking soon it will be too cold to play in the stream. When Luke gets home you should go with him.
Yeah. Isn't it great Luke's out with his friends? He's either glued to the computer or wandering off who knows where, but I'm glad for him. . . . Fine. If he comes home in time I'll ask him to play. But I think he's gone for the day.
How much did you pay him?

Only twenty.

For the weekend?

No, just for today. So let's keep talking. I think the times I felt most alive were when I was quiet. Those times in the stream, or watching the trees or feeling the sun were peaceful times when I forgot about everything else and lost myself in the sounds, or in searching for the perfect rock to plug the hole in the dam I was making, or really trying hard to make that little fairy home nice for little people I really thought existed. There also seemed to be so few times when I felt such peace. It seems there is so much pain in this existence. Many times I tried to have a good time when I was older because I was trying to escape the pain. I realize you can't do that. Trying to escape pain by trying to have a good time does help alleviate it for a while. I'm not saying having a good time is bad. But what amounts to a truly good and meaningful time has so much more to do with not try-ing, forgetting, letting go of working so hard to be happy, and just being. Just *being*! That's the place where I found the happiest times. But there seems to be so few of them, when I look at my short life.

I don't know what to say.

I know. I can sense that. Maybe Rick would go with me to the stream. That would be fun. I should call him.

Hang on. We're having a good talk right now. Anyway, I'd like to respond to you by affirming your experience that the best times are when you're not trying. I also think the best times are when you lose yourself caring for someone else, or in loving others, and doing things for them. True?

Yes. And guess what?

Here's Luke!

Sorry, you were just on to something. I don't know what he's doing back so early, but when he walks in I'm going to ask him if he wants to go to the stream.

Sounds good to me.

I'm not sure what he's doing out there. He hasn't come in yet.

OK.

Here he comes.

OK.

I'll ask. Hold on. . . .

※   ※   ※

He said he was pooped. He gave me back the twenty bucks and said he needed to do homework. That really doesn't sound like him. Hmmm.

Interesting. Does that mean he may go later?

I'll ask. . . .

※   ※   ※

Yes. He might. I'll check in with you later. I'll get some homework done before we go. 'Bye.

'Bye.

Saturday, September 29
Late Afternoon

It's been raining ever since you came up with the idea I should go to the stream with Luke.

That's too bad.

I walked down there by myself for just a few moments. The walk took me ten minutes. I'm a slow walker these days.

I stayed for less than five, and then walked back. I just wanted to hear the stream again. I wanted to experience it with my eyes and ears wide open, even if I did get a little wet.

Notice anything?

Yes! When you stand by the stream and focus on one place right in front of you, and listen very intently, you can hear the stream not only in stereo, but in three places. I could hear the trickling water directly in front of me, and then a different sound of trickling water just upstream and a third sound of trickling water just downstream, all at the same time. I never would have noticed that if I hadn't been consciously thinking to myself, "What is so cool about listening to streams?" It's something I wanted to know before I died.

There is some Bible passage about the voice of many waters. I wish I knew the Bible better. Maybe it was Shakespeare.

Don't you guys have to know the Bible?

The Bible is important, but there are many people from many religions in heaven. That's something people find out when they get here.

Are they surprised when they get into heaven?

No. They are surprised when others get into heaven. Heaven is a big place. A lot more people get to heaven than you might think.

I'm going to look up that "many waters" passage. I'm guessing it's in the Bible. BRB . . .

※   ※   ※

I can't find it!

What?

I can't find a Bible! Dad's on the Internet, and I can't find a Bible! I know we had one.

Ask your dad.

Maybe. BRB. . . .

❊   ❊   ❊

This is no joke! I just asked Dad if we had a Bible and he says, "It's right here on the table!"

What's so surprising about that?

He must have been reading it. It was right on the dining room table. I didn't know he had it in him!

See? Open your eyes and you find out all sorts of things!

Don't know what it means. It probably means he met some floozy fundamentalist Christian chick at work. Anyways. I've got it and I'm going to look up the verse. Hmmm. The concordance at the back of the Bible has like four references to "water." Duh. I can think of more than that off the top of my head. Let's look up "many." Nope. This is going to take some time.

When you're done flipping through the pages, ask your dad.

He won't know.

He might.

❊   ❊   ❊

You are ON today, my angel friend. He says it's in the book of Revelation, or maybe Isaiah. That narrows it down to two books. Hang on. Hey! If you're an angel can't you find out where it is and tell me?

It doesn't work that way.

How convenient! HEY! Found it! It's right there in the first chapter of the book of Revelation! He sees this guy in the middle of these lamp stands, and he's all flaming and everything, and it says, "His voice was like the sound of many waters." God, I suppose.

No doubt.

I wonder what that means. The voice of many waters is a comforting sound. The waters I've heard are very comforting. It sounds Native American! They talk about the Great Spirit who lives and moves in all things. That sounds similar, doesn't it?

I'd say they are probably talking about the same thing. The voice of many waters is the voice of the Great Spirit.

And any other name you might have for God. Isn't that right? I mean whether you call God the Great Spirit or Jesus, or Allah, or Jehovah, or even your favorite politically correct term, what was that? Was it the Great Creative Force of the Universe? It's all the same God, just different names. It must be.

It occurs to me that the voice of many waters may mean that God, or the Great Creative Force and all that, speaks through many religions, as many waters from many different streams.

Cool!

It's one God, many voices, through all the different ways people see God and express God.

But some are better than others, aren't they, GA? They have to be.

How's that?

Some say God is love, like you do all the time. Some say God is angry and vengeful. Some say God wants them to fly airplanes into buildings. Some say God wants a certain race to rule over all. Some say all who don't believe in a certain God are going to hell. I mean they can't all be right.

True. So very true! Some waters are clearer than others, I suppose. Some waters soothe the soul, and some, well, some rush like a torrent and destroy everything in the way. Want to know a secret? Don't tell anyone I told you this, because they would never believe an angel said this.

I promise. What?

Every religion has its imperfections.

So, are they all wrong?

No. All the really solid religions are very far from wrong. They are very right. Any religion that teaches people to love one another, or to obey certain laws that help people respect and honor each other, is giving the world a gift. But all religions only know so much. They are all trying to describe the same thing—life. Some do a better job at that than others. Some open the heart, bring people together, bring spirit and meaning to people's lives. Some shut people down. But no religion is perfect. They only point the way to perfection. They are not perfection. People get in trouble when they think they have all the answers.

I know why.

Why?

Because when they think they have all the answers they stop looking.

Exactly. They stop looking and they stop seeing the value in others who do not see things their way. So religions are like maps pointing out the terrain and showing us, to the best ability of the author of the map, the way.

The way to God.

Yeah. The way to the top of the mountain.

Some people would argue it's better to not belong to a religion because of what religion has done to the world.

It's not religion that has hurt the world. It's the people who have used religion in all the wrong ways, or the way people have taken religion and made it something it wasn't supposed to be. The problem with any good thing is that people tend to organize it and end up ruining it.

So the various religions aren't really flawed. People are.

I'd actually say both. I think all religions are designed by God with imperfections built right into them. They are, I suppose, perfectly imperfect.

What do you mean?

They have imperfections so that people don't take them too literally. They are imperfect because they can only speak to imperfect human beings. It's like a frog trying to talk to a tadpole about what's beyond the mud hole. The tadpole will never understand the frog completely. The frog needs to speak in tadpole language, and within the framework of the tadpole's experience, so that the tadpole can understand. But what the frog can say to the tadpole is limited. The tadpole has never even been out of the water. How can any explanation of the bigger picture be anything but fuzzy in order for the tadpole to begin to understand?

Therefore, many waters? For us tadpoles?

Hey! That works. Why not? But when people throw out religion just because it's been abused or misunderstood, they are like tadpoles throwing away the frog's explanation in preference to believing that all there is to life is this little mud hole.

Don't throw the baby out with the bathwater?

Well, that's right. That's ingenious. Did you come up with that?

Give me a break!
What do you mean?
'Bye.

Two Worlds into One

If I am the tadpole
You must be the frog.
Someday I will leave this mud hole,
And hop away from this bog.

You know that, don't you?
And you prepare me the way,
For the night I leave this darkening pond,
And take in the first breath of day.

Kiss the frog, Nicole!
Kiss the frog!

N. M. B.

Sunday, September 30
11:30 a.m.

Hi Angel. I don't know if I'm really pissed at this point or just really upset. I haven't heard from Rick all weekend! I e-mailed him last night and I can see that he opened it, because if you're both on AOL you can see that kind of thing. He might be busy, but that's never stopped him from coming over before. He could at least respond to my e-mail. Do you think he's mad at me?

I don't know and . . .

You don't care, right?

Didn't say that. And since you're finishing my sentences I'm not going to tell you what I was going to say.

Whatever! Be like that. I'm gonna just chill here. I'm sitting here on a sunny Sunday morning with a huge cup of coffee, extra cream and sugar so I can taste it even with these screwed-up chemo taste buds. Dad's still sleeping it off, Luke's asleep. I'm listening to this CD of Norah Jones. I don't even know who she is. It's one of Dad's CDs but it's good, mellow. It's perfect for this morning's conversation with my angel.

Good. I'm glad to hear that. Yes, this music is very nice. Her voice is calming. This is the kind of thing I like to listen to as I'm floating down a meandering river in the celestial mountain region.

Do you really do things like that? How about today you tell me something about your life so I can get my mind off of mine? Would you do that for me? Do you river raft or something? Is that what you're saying? Tell me about it. Are there mountains in heaven, and trees and rivers and all that? I'd never really thought of angels having fun like that. Do you have a raft or canoe?

No. I go inner tubing. A bunch of us get together fairly often when on break, and spend all day floating together through the most beautiful scenery, and in the purest water. It even tastes better than the purest drinking water available on earth. It's got a sweetness to it. I know that could sound gross, but it's not. It is so fresh and pure and living that it has a hint of sweetness. It's very cool.

That sounds amazing.

It is. Sometimes we float under magnificent trees folding together above us, with life of every kind living in the branches above. Sometimes these can appear like jungles with all the animals you have on earth, and it's like a safari. Other times it turns to a warm fall day as we pass majestic mountains jutting up from the riverbed arrayed in fall colors, red, orange, yellow, purple, blue.

Purple, blue?

Yeah, actually, and thousands of other colors too that you don't have on earth. Fall here is amazing. Actually, everything here is amazing.

How do you listen to music as you're floating down the river? Headphones? Don't tell me you have iPods.

In heaven, music just shows up when you want it. Music and feelings are very close to each other. So when you are experiencing this feeling of rest, relaxation, and reflection, well, on comes somebody like Norah Jones, or one of a thousand beautiful pieces of music from folks here. Sometimes, the atmosphere breaks into a symphony when passing a majestic mountain or golden city. Now this is hard to explain. Don't think you get overwhelmed by it or anything. It really works with how you're feeling inside. I think it probably comes from the inside, like there is some receiver inside of us that picks the music and then plays it.

Can others hear your music? Or does all your different music clash at times?

No. That's the beauty of heaven. This is kind of deep, but since we are all pretty much enjoying the same thing, or feeling the same way about what we are experiencing, we basically hear the same music. Now no one feels exactly the same, so the music that person is hearing may vary slightly, and what we hear is his or her variation of the theme, so to speak. So, say, the eight of us may hear a wonderful symphony, where one of us is contributing more strings, while the other may bring in the kettle drums and another one the brass section.

Like an orchestra.

Yes.

Do you ever listen to rock music?

Hell yeah.

Ha ha ha.

Sorry. Had to do it. Yes. When we play games together, or fly across the oceans at light speed, or work hard together on some project here on earth, man we rock!

You're kidding!

No. Not everyone appreciates rock music so not everyone has that experience. But my friends and I have a blast. Heaven is a fun place. Sometime, whenever you get here, I'll take you down the river.

Would you?

Of course. I've been thinking about that a lot lately.

You have?

Yes. I don't know when you may come over here, but yes, there will be a day when I can show you all of this. I haven't told you the half of it. I know you love nature. You will be amazed at what you see here. You'll think you died and went to heaven!

Ha ha.

Sorry.

I can't wait. I want to do that. I want to go. Will you really do that with me?

I will.

You make me very happy, GA.

You make me very happy, Nicole.

I do? You know, you sound pretty cool for an angel. So you hang out with people and run off for the weekend in your SUVs and party on the river?

We don't need motor vehicles, unless we want to do something where they play some special role. Like car racing or just hanging out in an old Chevy and talking.

Yeah?

People like to do things like that. They like having similar circumstances to what they had when on the earth, so some like to park on a ridge, gaze over the valley with oldies playing off the old radio, and just talk with their girlfriends.

They have girlfriends?

Yes. I've been trying to tell you that. People fall in love here, of course. Love is love. What would heaven be like without it?

They have girlfriends?

Yes. And people here are nice to each other and respect each other, and really grow to know each other so much more quickly and deeply than on earth.

They have girlfriends!

And boyfriends. And they may even get married and live happily ever after too. How's that?

I'm kind of blown away by that. I don't know what to say. I'm sort of embarrassed. Do you think if I die young I'll find someone in heaven?

I'll bet my wings on it.

Do you have a girlfriend?

Uh. Nope. Not really.

What's that mean? "Not really?"

Well, I'm feeling like I don't need a girlfriend right now. I'm happy with the way things are going for me. Things are looking up these days. Not the same pressure I used to feel about it.

The whole dating thing is too much pressure. Like how do you know you met the right person, and what if it's the wrong person and all that?

People are so transparent here in heaven that you can see right into their hearts and know what kind of person everyone is inside. You can see right away if this person is the kind of person you want to be with or not. In the long run, you'll find the one you really want to be with, and you know he is perfect for you and you for him. It doesn't mean there won't be work ahead for both of you. That's unavoidable. But you'll want to be together forever.

Like a soulmate?

Yes. That's exactly right—a soulmate.

Um, so what if your soulmate likes swimming in the ocean better than floating down a river? How does that work?

Personally, I like the ocean and the mountains, and jungles and the desert. It's all here. So, just like on earth, people do different things together, share time. If two people are really different then they won't be together. It works the same way on earth. You need to have things in common to get along, but variety of tastes spices things up I guess—no pun intended.

What I'd give to be able to taste again! Heaven sounds so cool. Do you have a house at the beach or doesn't it work like that?

Yeah. Got a house everywhere. That's just sort of how it works. I love the one we start out at by the river. It looks fairly modest from the road leading into the woods, but when you walk in the front door it opens up to a cathedral ceiling with windows facing the winding river in the valley below. It's all made of wood and beams, with a stone fireplace in the middle, three stories of bedrooms, lofts, an open kitchen stocked with everything you'd ever want to eat, a big-screen TV, satellite radio, and shelves with all sorts of adventure books and drawers full of games.

TV? Satellite radio?

And then in the living room one very nice, well-worn blue couch faces the fireplace and a smaller version of the same couch faces the windows overlooking the mountains and valley below. Two rocking chairs, some gorgeous lamps, old Persian rugs. They just look old. It's all very clean.

Big-screen TV?

I wanted it. We don't watch it much, but it's fun to have it there. After a hard day of floating down the river it's a wonderful thing to be able to cuddle up in blankets on the couch and watch some five-star movie with a happy ending.

Why do you need satellite radio?

I was kidding about that. Remember, the music just comes on when it's wanted. So, yeah, that is pretty much satellite radio. You can get it anywhere, anytime, and the channels are limitless. And the best thing is—no commercials!

Sometimes I think you are pulling my leg!

What do you mean? I'd never pull your leg, except that time at the top of the stairs, but that was more of a push. Heehee. Really sorry about that though.

No. I mean sometimes I think you are just playing with me, telling me things I want to hear. It sounds so beautiful and really like a lot of fun.

It's true, Nicole. I am telling you what you want to hear. And it's also true that everything I'm telling you is real. I promise. It's not like we just jet set around and play all the time though. We work a lot. The work is fun, like being someone's guardian angel is a lot of fun. It's the joy of my life, especially when I can really make a difference in some way. But it's a job, and there are responsibilities, chores, challenges, and all those things that make life real. So, life is pretty balanced here. But I have to admit that it's a blast. That's one of the reasons why they call it heaven, I suppose.

OK. So I am expecting that whenever I get to the other side, you'll take me tubing on the river.

I most certainly will. But it sounds like you might like the ocean better.

I like both. Just like you.

I thought that was the case.

Are there mosquitoes in those jungles? How about crocodiles or snakes?

No bugs. All the animals are nice too.

One more question. This is kind of embarrassing but . . .

Shhhh. Don't ask. Some things are better kept secret, because then they can be a wonderful surprise. Life's like that. You can't know everything. That way the future unfolds like a new gift before you every day.

Um. I was going to ask if there are bathrooms in heaven.

No you weren't. But yes, there are bathrooms in heaven, and plumbers too.

Plumbers? Sounds too much like earth, too real.

Plumbers are people too! They need a job when they get to heaven, right? Heaven is very real. That's what I've been trying to tell you. It's more real than anything you've ever experienced in your life.

What does that mean? The clogged toilets are REALLY clogged? Great! Luke will love it. Can't wait!!! OK gotta go check my e-mail. Thanks for entertaining me with that story. It is fun to think about. I hope heaven is like that. It would be fun.

Sunday, September 30
Evening

Just a Poem

The leaves are contemplating their colors,
But the warmth has kept them green.
The mist rises off the lake as the cool rain falls.
This is my favorite time of year.
I'm glad to see it again.
I am paying special attention this time.
I am playing with animals near the stream.
I am smelling the golden grass,
And listening even more attentively to the trees.
"We are akin to all that is."
I heard that somewhere.
I am akin to all that is,
And all that ever was,
And will be.

N. M. B.

I wish we could send e-mails to heaven. It would be even better if we could attach files like pictures and short videos.

That's a great idea. I'll take that back to home base and submit the idea for review.

Nice thought. I am sure they would have come up with something like that already if it were legal. But I suppose that would break the rules of how the whole heaven and earth relationship works.

Perhaps. What would you do if you could send e-mails to heaven?

I'd be taking pictures of all of us and sending them to Mom. Sometimes when I see something really awesome I say inside myself, "Mom. You should see this!"

Monday, October 1
Afternoon

The phone has been ringing all afternoon, and it's you-know-who.

It's you-know-whom, I believe.

You know what I mean.

You're obviously not going to answer it. So, why bother thinking about it?

Do you ever get unwanted calls in heaven?

Never. No sales calls, no surveys, no disgruntled employees, no old girlfriends who can't let go, no mother-in-law prying into your affairs, no IRS calling, no Fraternal Order of Police to ask for money, not PTA, school committees, or irate neighbors.

Does the phone ever ring?

Come to think of it, it doesn't ring. Angels know instantly when someone is going to call and they pick up the receiver before it has a chance to ring.

What if it's someone you don't want to hear from?

That doesn't happen. It's always someone you want to hear from. That's one of the perks of heaven.

Cool! And I guess Aunt Melinda must have gotten the message I don't want to talk to her, because the phone stopped ringing.

I noticed. How was your appointment today?

What a joke!

What do you mean?

My regular doctor . . . he's OK. I've been seeing him since I was small, and he's funny. Even when I was diagnosed with cancer, he kept me laughing with the most disgusting jokes. But I saw the surgeon today. You always hear that some of those guys think they are gods. He was pretty cocky.

Oh?

Well, he didn't really ask me anything about how I felt. He just talked to Dad and acted like I was a machine he had to fix, or a farm animal getting in line for castration. Do they do that?

Frankly, I'd rather not think about that.

It sounds appropriate for what I'm trying to say, like I'm just another sheep in line for shearing.

Now THAT I understand. But what did the doctor say?

Not good. The tumor isn't responding to any of this stuff they're doing. He wants to do another biopsy and after that they are going to set up surgery to take it out, probably in a few weeks.

Why another biopsy if they are going to take it out?

I don't know. The first one wasn't a big deal. They put me out so fast I don't even remember it. It was kind of a "no-brainer." LOL. See? I can even make stupid jokes like you. But I do have to go into the hospital for the biopsy, even though he said that it was a routine thing. So, I guess that's the answer, it's routine. They are going to increase the chemo though. He said . . . God, it makes me dizzy.

Are you OK?

Yes. Sorry. It makes me dizzy to talk about this stuff. The ultimate goal for all this treatment is surgery to remove the tumor, but what the surgeon is saying is that it's so big it's pushing against something bad, and if they shrink it then they can cut it out . . . dizzy, sick . . . dizzy . . . man I hate talking about this . . . If they can cut it out. No, I mean if it shrinks they'll have an easier time cutting it out. Soooo. They're going to fire all their guns on this thing and see what happens. My head hurts even more already just think-ing about it. Anyway, I bet heart surgeons are nice because they fix people's hearts. I think brain surgeons are too up in their heads to feel any empathy.

Very funny.

Thanks. His name is Garry Waltzel. I think I want to make him a present for fixing me when this is all over.

Really? That'd be really nice, Nicole.

Yeah. It's going to be a plaque, with his face on it. And it's going to have a quote etched into the shiny metal under his photo. It will read, "Let go and let Garry."

Oh, great!

I am really getting tired of all of this. I want to get it over with. I've had it with these treatments already. I'm worn out. I feel like I've been on a diet of Liquid Drano sometimes.

There's the phone again.

Ughhhhhhhh. I've gotta get out of here.

Good plan. Call up a friend and get outside while there's still light in the day.

What friend? I have no friends.

Maybe you should call Tammy and try to straighten things out.

Not a chance. I do miss her. She has to make the first move, though. She was the one who said she needed distance. I'm starting to wonder what kind of friend she really was. If she was my best friend, how could she just leave me like this?

What about Rick?

He didn't even try to find me today.

Tuesday, October 2
Evening

[A sketch of several gravestones appears on this page. G.R.S.]

Angel, I needed to talk to somebody today. I needed a friend. Nobody. I even asked Emily and she said she was busy and then asked Skye and she was busy, and I think people are avoiding me because I'm sick. The old friends are gone. I give up on Tammy. I don't know what happened to Rick. He waved to me today when I was in class. That's it. I looked for him after school. Nowhere.

Well at least Rick waved. That's something.

If he was with Tammy I'm going to kill both of them!

Do you think?

I'm paranoid I suppose. I think anything's possible, especially anything bad. It seems to work that way.

That's pessimistic.

I know. I did end up having a good time this afternoon, even if I was by myself. I needed to talk to someone, so I thought if no one would talk to me—and you don't count because I wanted to talk about girl things—

Thank you.

I decided maybe I'd go to see Mom's grave and talk to her. I hadn't been down to the cemetery in so long because I know she's not really there in the grave. But something drew me there, like I had to connect with her in this world, on earth. At least that's what I thought when I started down there. The graveyard is probably a good half-mile, maybe more like three-quarters of a mile from the house. You go by the lake and it's sort of on the other side, so it's further than it looks. It's getting a little funky to walk distances anymore, but I made it there all by myself.

You might not want to do that anymore alone.

I know! I feel so weak now that I'm home, like sick-weak. But let me tell the story. When you get there the graveyard is in the woods, really natural looking because people like to preserve the natural setting there. Mom's grave is on the lower side of the hill, near the edge of the woods by the creek. You can hear the creek if you listen hard.

Yep.

Alright! Is this interesting you?

Very much.

Then what's this "yep" stuff?

I've been there. That's all.

Well, at least act interested, OK?

Nicole, I am extremely interested. I think it's touching you went to see your mom's grave today. I want to hear about what happened. Did you have a good talk with her?

I didn't! Don't make me cry now. I couldn't face her for some reason.

What happened?

On the way there I got so tired I was really wondering why I thought I could make it down there, and then as I came to the edge of the graveyard I felt empty inside. I'm such a wacko with my feelings nowadays!

No you aren't.

Well, I am, but thanks for being supportive. So what happened is I walked down the stone path toward the bottom of the hill where her grave is. When I came through a small grove of trees and saw her stone at a distance I just froze.

Really?

Yeah. I couldn't go near it. I'm sad about that. I just couldn't and I have no clue why I couldn't. I stood there a distance away and did nothing.

Maybe because you know she's not really there.

Yeah. She isn't there, right? I mean she's in heaven.

Yes. She's in heaven.

But she would have talked to me if I had gone to her grave and asked her to talk to me, don't you think?

Sure.

Then I hope she wasn't waiting for me!

Nah. She probably knew you weren't really going to go there anyway.

Hmmm. I'm thinking maybe she was with me anyway, because I didn't feel alone. Was that you with me? Or do you think it was her?

Probably her. That's my bet.

Well, someone . . . So, while I was there I thought I'd look around and maybe do some exploring, look at some other graves.

Oh. OK.

Yeah. It was good. Wandering around I noticed there was a section of older graves in a place by itself, not so far from the creek. It was obvious that these graves were the first to be placed here. They all faced the water, and were well worn and old. Some of them were from the 1800s, like 1860 and up to 1900. Then they must have expanded the cemetery.

Cemeteries are interesting, aren't they? They carry a lot of history. Think of the love and memories that are focused there for the people who are buried there. It's why they say cemeteries are holy ground. They are so full of honor and memories, and sadness, but also hope, and beauty.

Yes, I know what you mean. I was looking at the different gravestones, and some have epitaphs and quotes, and sometimes the dates themselves tell you something, like those who died young. I wondered what the stories were behind the etching on the stones. I'd make up a story about them. Like a lot of people died in February of 1869 and nothing anywhere says why, but I thought maybe some sickness or plague came through.

Plague?

I mean like the flu or something. It's a small cemetery. Eight people died that month. It doesn't sound like a lot of people but I think it was. Some were old, but there were two children and one woman in her twenties. A grave of a boy sat alone by itself.

There is probably a history book somewhere where you can look that up.

I know. I'm too lazy. I don't really care that much. But there was that one grave all by itself that I found myself drawn to. It was a little grave with a smaller stone than the others. What was written on it made me want to cry. It said:

Little Barry Stevens

Ten Days Old

"Rest for the Little Sleeper"

A child ten days of age.

Yes. I wonder why he died. It sounds like he slept a lot. It sounds like he never woke up. So sad for the family. There was a date there too, in the 1800s but I don't remember exactly when. It wasn't with the others.

Yes. "Rest for the Little Sleeper." They must have loved him very much.

I know. It really hits me deep and I'm not sure why. I think it might have to do with the sweetness of babies and all the hope for their future. I'm having a hard time with words. I wonder about why that baby didn't get to be all he could have been. At the same time I know that his parents must have cradled him and held him for those ten days and given him so much love.

You told me about looking into your brother's eyes when he was a baby and seeing so much. Are you sad that little Barry Stevens' parents may not have been able to experience that same thing with their "little sleeper"?

You'd think that would be the case, but I am thinking that the gift this little baby gave his parents wasn't necessarily in his eyes, but in his restful sleep. The epitaph must have meant that. They must have hoped so much that he would wake up, and then maybe they realized that he wasn't going to, and then they just loved him, until he went to sleep for good.

❉   ❉   ❉

You've been silent for a while now.
Yeah.
What are you thinking?
I'm thinking about Luke. He is a quiet boy. He's so quiet. It's funny. He'll go and do things with me, when I ask. But he never asks me to do things. He plays video games most of his free time now, except when I pay him to go out and play.
Has he ever had friends?
He used to have more. Boys used to call him. Sometimes someone would call and invite him over. Sometimes he'd get invited to play some nerdy game with a few other nerds.
Would he go?
Yes. And then he'd come home and go into his room and play games by himself. . . . Nobody calls him anymore. I think he has friends on the Internet, but that's different than in person.
But you've gotten him outside several times. I've seen it. It's cost you a fortune.
True. But maybe it's a good investment, because I know he's not out there playing by himself. I hope. . . . No, I've seen him with kids. I don't know. I just worry about him.
You care about him a lot, don't you?
Yes. Sometimes I forget about him. That's so wrong, but I get overwhelmed and don't pay much attention to him. I

feel bad about that. I used to talk to him more, when he was younger. I'd tell him stories when it was our bedtime. I'd make up these elaborate stories about his stuffed animals, Teddy, Linus, Freddy, Cutie, and Modie.

He had all those animals?

Some of them were mine. I'd tell stories of the five of them going on adventures together. They would fly on magic carpets, visit the ant people underground, fight Gendor the half-man half-ant king, find elves and magic potions, have to answer riddles from ogres under bridges, rescue fair maidens and have all sorts of adventures.

Sounds like you were a good big sister, and you have a good children's book to write someday.

Most of it was based on other stories I'd read or seen on television, so I don't know. But it was fun because the one stuffed animal, Cutie, who I think was a bear, was a very naughty bear. He would get in trouble a lot, or say sassy things to the evil Gendor, and throw inappropriate things from the flying carpet.

Like what?

Never mind! I was just a kid trying to get a laugh. And boy, would Luke laugh. I remember talking to him and he would smile and have that sparkly look in his eyes as if he was there with these animals. When I cracked a joke about Cutie he'd giggle and kind of spasm in bed for a moment, like a shiver of joy or something. They were the good old days.

Hey. You're only sixteen. The good old days can't be that far back.

Well, the stories came to an end when he turned ten.

Why? Did he just grow up and lose interest?

Probably. But in reality I ran out of stories. I started singing to him instead. That was fun. I made up songs. Some were serious, and some were funny. I can't remember any of them now except one that was about Cutie that went:

Oooooh bapah!

Oooooh bapah!

Oooooh bapah bapah bah boooh!

That was the chorus, and then there was some storyline between the choruses, but it's gone now. I think the memory eaters in my brain got that memory. . . . As he became older we did less together. When we were young we slept in the same room. When I moved into my own room, it just stopped.

Would he fall asleep when you told him the stories?

Ha! Yes! He would laugh a lot, and sometimes I'd talk for a half-hour or more. But he'd usually stay awake until I said I was done, and then fall asleep immediately.

Rest for the little sleeper?

Yeah. You got me. That's what makes me sad. He was always so sweet. And I feel sad that he's so alone now. I never talked to him about Mom dying. I hope Dad did but I don't know. He became more and more quiet and I think sadder inside. Why am I such an ASS? I should be doing so much for him!

It's not too late.

It feels like it is. Not only did he lose Mom, but now if I die I feel like he won't have anyone. I know I just said I should be doing more for him, and that's the truth. But him losing two family members is going to do him in. This isn't making me feel very good.

I know.

When I think of sad things like this, I really get in touch with how bad I feel, I mean physically. It's funny, well, funny in a sad kind of way, that when I'm in good spirits I almost forget I'm sick, except if I look in the mirror, and then scream in horror. Ha ha. Even when I puke or get headaches or dizzy, or forget things, I can sometimes accept it as the norm when I feel good about life. But when I get sad, I feel like I'm going to die. I feel every pulsating pain, the nausea brewing deep within, the numbness and weakness. My nose even feels funny! Ha ha. It does. It feels like someone is tickling it! What else? My leg hurts. What a walk! That's enough for now.

That's a lot.

The thing is, when I think of Luke being left alone that sadness starts in my throat, and then it's like a trapdoor opens and it falls into this cavern in my body and spreads out like a dark poisonous cloud. Anyway, here I am talking about ME again. I don't want everything to always be about me. It's about him. This time it's about him.

I know how sad you are for him. But that will not do any good, just to be sad and feel sick and do nothing. Are you sure you can't do something about it? You're not dead, you know. Really. You are still very much alive.

Oh, I am so twisted up! I feel like I want to do something for him. I feel like I could break through my own inertia and self-absorption and then try very hard to push through his walls and connect with him. It's all possible. But then I get this image of him waking up with that big smile and twinkling eyes, like he's hearing the stories about his little stuffed animals all over again, and then . . . and then . . .

Then you die.

Yeah. Then I die on him, right after he opens up to me and believes again. I can't do that to him. I love him so much. I love him more than anything in the world. I am sad about this. There is nothing I can do.

Nicole. You can do nothing, and he will stay isolated as he is now, and maybe even some of the sadness of you dying (if you die) will be deflected by the walls he's put up. But if you do break through and show him how much you love him, it doesn't mean life will become worse for him in the long run. It may look like he will open up only to be hurt more, and there is some truth to this. But mostly, he will gain so much. He will have his sister again, and know about her love, and never lose that, ever! I know we were just talking about all the love and honor and spirit you can feel at cemeteries. Those stones are reminders of all the good in the world, and the good those folks brought to the world. But they are inanimate objects, those stones. Think how much more those memories of your love, your courage, the strength of your character, and all you did for him and meant to him will be cherished by your brother, forever etched into his heart!

So, what you're saying is that if I get him to take off his armor and then I die, it won't be like I opened him up and took a sword and stuck it through his heart?

No. It may feel like that. But life is about loving people, and risking, and getting hurt, and healing, and growing, and feeling joy, and everything life has to offer. If you love him and show him that love, it will remain with him, help him, and even sustain him when you are gone. You have a chance to make a difference to him. And remember, life is forever. You can take him for that river ride too, when he gets here many years from now. And wouldn't it be better for him and for you that when you see each other again there is great joy and laughter, rather than the colorless shadows of memories gone by, and no real connection forged between you?

That sounds scary. OK. Got it!

Do you really understand? I didn't mean to scare you. You really have a wonderful opportunity in front of you. You have time. Even if you only had today, you have time.

I'm thinking. Feeling. I'm staring into space. I don't know where to start. But I have to start. I will. There is too much to do. I can't do it all. I can only do a little at a time. I need and want to take time for him, and I need to take risks and reach out to him. It doesn't have to be intense either. But it can be real.

Rest for the Little Sleeper

Little Barry Stevens
Ten Days Old
Rest for the Little Sleeper
Your life story now told.
As you open your eyes
And see heaven's springs
Enjoying the life
That all heaven brings,
Remember your mother
Who held you so tight,
And your father with tears
Who buried you that night.
One day you will meet,

And they will look into your eyes.
The joy they will feel
Will fill the skies.
Then together
You'll go out and play,
And race and run around,
And act like children all day.
When the energy has waned
And your love grown deeper,
May you all find your peace:
Rest for the Little Sleeper.

N. M. B.

Wednesday, October 3
Afternoon

Hi.

Hi.

Read this e-mail:

"Hi Nicole. I'm sorry I haven't been able to see you since Friday. I've been doing a lot of thinking. It isn't fair to start a serious conversation over e-mail because there's too much room for communication to get all messed up and not be able to hear each other. I really do care about you. That's part of the problem. I know you may not have much time to see me, but I am wondering if we can get together tomorrow to talk. If that doesn't work out, maybe there is a time this weekend if you feel up to it. I'm really sorry I haven't been in touch. Just know it's been painful for me too. TTYL. Rick."

First question . . . What's "TTYL"?

"Talk to you later."

*Oh. I thought maybe it stood for "Truly testing your love,"
or "Totally trashing your life" or "Trying to . . ."*

Stop.

OK. So, what's your take on this?

I was going to ask you that exact question. I've been reading it several times over and what I see here is a big kiss-off.
That part about, "I've been doing a lot of thinking" is like the
opening for every "Dear Jane" letter.

And John too.

Exactly. If it were followed with, like, "I've been doing
a lot of thinking and I'm sorry for what I've done," then it
might be positive. But when the "I'm sorry" comes before
the "I've been thinking," then you know it's not good for the
recipient.

Interesting. I concur with your analysis. Continue.

So then he says, "It isn't fair to do what I'm about to do
over e-mail." OK. He doesn't exactly say that but that's what
I'm reading between the lines. And then he talks about there
being a "problem." You still with me on my analysis?

*Yes. However, he does want to talk in person, and I think
that gives you some hope. Most men, and believe me, this
comes from guardian angel experience, most men would use
e-mail to end it.*

Cowards!

*That's one way to put it. Now teenage boys? I think you
would agree with me that they can be even more callous.*

Agreed. Bastards!

*But he wants to talk. And he says, "There's too much
room for communication to get all messed up and not be*

able to hear each other." That's good, because it sounds like he wants a two-way conversation and to hear your side, and maybe there is some sort of compromise.

Do you think this is just about our physical relationship? Like he wants to make some deal so he can get more because I said no? OMG!

No. No. No. Well . . . maybe . . . Hmmm.

Can't be. He's not like that.

He might be.

Do you really think that? Do you think that's all he wanted from me?

No. I don't. He even says he cares about you, and you know that's true. I think just like you've been feeling . . . what was that word you used? . . . . "conflicted," I think he's conflicted.

He is nice. He really is. It has to be something deep and I'm sure, like you say, it's about the relationship and how we can do better. But notice he doesn't say, "I love you" at the end, or even signing it, "Love, Rick." It's just "TTYL." Damn it! I'm going down. It's over.

Wednesday, October 3
Nighttime

I e-mailed Rick. Told him maybe we could meet this weekend. Ha ha.

Yes. Very funny, since you're dying to meet with him and you have time tomorrow, and probably could even fit him in after treatments Friday if you really wanted to.

I know. I have to wait. It has to do with my dignity. If he has to wait a few days he'll think I'm doing fine without him, and not some needy little love-refugee just waiting with outstretched arms for him to feed me some of his love and attention.

Love-refugee—you have a way with words. I have to remember that one.

So, that's it.

No it isn't.

What do you mean?

There's more. I can see it in your eyes.

Do you still look in my eyes? I'm feeling so ugly nowadays. Um. Don't answer me. Um. Yeah.

Nicole! It's not like me to get upset with you, but you're not telling me everything that's going on. You know that things are out of control, so why won't you talk to me about it? Forget Rick, just for a few moments, and talk to me.

. . . I can't.

Why not?

I'm so sick of crying. . . . I can't because if I do I won't have anything to hold on to. If I admit the whole world is in chaos, then there is no place for me to find comfort, peace, somewhere to lay my shiny bald head and just rest.

But—

I know. It's not there anyway, but I can pretend.

Stop pretending! Talk to me. Let's take this thing on together. Let's make a plan. You can get through this. It can get better.

I'm going to have to give you the short version if you want me to go to school tomorrow. I don't want to go to school anyway.

Well, go ahead.

How do I talk about this when it just happened? He's in the living room lying on the couch in basically a drunken coma. How do I begin? OK. So . . . Sorry. So . . .

I'll start. You found hard liquor hidden in his drawer. I believe it was Smirnoff's vodka, Jack Daniels, and some sort of liqueur. That was a few weeks ago. Then you started checking the trash and he had new empties in there regularly. So, you know and I know that he's way past a few beers at night.

Nice intro to tonight. I still don't know where to begin.

He came home drunk. How about there?

No. I'll start before that. He didn't come home at supper. He's done that enough times that it could mean either he was busy at work and forgot to call, like usual, or it could mean he stopped at the bar again. In this case, it meant the latter. By 7:00 p.m. I heated up macaroni and cheese and gave that to Luke. I asked Luke if Dad had called. He shrugged his shoulders. That's the problem with Luke. Sometimes you don't even know if he's saying "yes," "no," or "I don't know," or "I don't care." Probably all of them at once. So Dad didn't come home 'til 9:30 or 9:45. I heard the car pull up with a screech, and I could hear his footsteps as he ran to the door. Bang! The door flew open. Wham! He slammed it shut, and stumbled into the living room. Even Luke came running out it was so loud. Oh God! Oh God! Oh God!

What?

He was crying.

Your dad was crying?

Yes. He was crying and bloody!! He was bleeding from his head!!! Crying . . . Crying . . . Crying . . . Bloody . . .

I'm here. I'm holding you. It's good to cry. Let it out. I'm crying too. I'm with you.

I shouted, "Dad! Dad! Why are you bleeding? What happened?" Luke stood there with wide eyes, silent, in shock.

"Dad! What happened?"

He kind of went, "Mumble, mumble, sniffle, whimper, mumble, cry." I couldn't understand anything of what he was trying to say. He was so drunk I couldn't understand his words!

"Get a wet towel Luke!"

"Are thhhey thhhhere?" Dad mumbled.

"Who? What Dad?" I looked out the window. I couldn't see anyone. "Is who where? Dad! What happened?"

Luke came back with the towel and we put it on Dad's head. He was on the floor sitting up against the couch, so it was easy to reach his head. That's where he fell to when he came in, like he was hiding. I wiped off his head and he yelled, "Ouch. Jeez." That was the clearest thing he said all night. There were some little pieces of glass in his head.

"Watch him!" I yelled at Luke. I don't know why I yelled but I did. And Luke just looked at me like, "Yes sir!" or "Yes ma'am!" I went and got a serving bowl and filled it with water and got more towels. The first thought I had was we needed to get him to the shower to get the glass out, but like I realized he wasn't going anywhere! So I brought the water to him. I put a dry towel around his neck and soaked another towel and squeezed it over his head to get the blood and glass off his head. I told Luke to hold a towel over his eyes . . . tears . . . tears . . . He just let me do it, like he was a little dog getting a bath. He didn't put up a fight at all. He let us wash his head, and it wobbled a bit because he couldn't even sit up without wobbling I suppose. The more water we poured on him the more relieved I became. He had several cuts but only a few pieces of glass, sharp little nuggets of glass. It took a while for the bleeding to stop. I kept asking him questions while I dabbed his head. Luke put the towel into the bowl after we watered Dad down and then stood there and listened.

"What happened? What happened?" I kept asking Dad but he would only mumble a little. I was relieved when he stopped crying. That was as hard as seeing all the blood. The most I could get out of him was that he was in an accident. He said he hit a car.

"Did you hurt someone, Dad? Did you hit someone?"

"Pah cah. No. Pah cah," he mumbled.

"A parked car? Did you hit a parked car?"

"Uhh. Yeahuh." That's right. He said, "Yeahuh."

I need to stop for a minute. Get my breath. You know how I say I feel sicker when I talk about bad things? Remember that GA?

Yes I do.

Well, right now I feel like the meat is going to fall off my body. That's how sick I feel. It feels like my face has instantly rotted and is separating from my painfully pulsating skull, and my stomach is going to come up with the vomit, like the vomit will be in its own barf bag.

Do you want to finish the story later?

No. Let's get it over with. So it took forever to get out of him what happened, and there was a point where Luke and I started laughing because he said he hit one parked car and then he said he hit two parked cars, and then he said he hit three parked cars, and the way he said it was so funny we laughed. Isn't that crazy? And then he said something about losing "them" on the golf course. I'm like, "What?" He drove through the golf course. It sounded like he drove right through the fairways and greens and stuff. We laughed but then realized someone was chasing him. Then it got serious again.

"Who was chasing you, Dad?"

"Poleehuh . . . The poleeh."

"The police? Is that what you said, Dad?"

"Uhuh . . . I lost 'em." Luke and I just looked at each other. He apparently outran the police. Luke went over and looked out the window. I followed him over and looked out front myself. Nobody there.

"Do they know who you are, Dad? Did they get your license? How close were you?"

"Nah. . . . I dunno. I lossss em."

By then the bleeding had basically stopped. I wrapped a dry towel around his head the same way I wrap a scarf around mine. Dad dragged himself up onto the couch, laid down and fell asleep. Luke and I grabbed a flashlight and went out to look at the car. The front left corner of his car was bashed in and the headlight was broken. But the most shocking thing was that the windshield was smashed into one of those spider webs on the driver's side. His head had hit it hard enough to break the window. We looked inside and the bag was blown too. He must have blown the bag on the first hit, and then hit the window on his second or third. I hate to say it, but I looked carefully at the front bumper and underneath the car for signs he had run someone over. Uck! I didn't see any signs of that, thank God! Dad had pulled the car up to the top of the driveway and since there's a hedge on the right side of the driveway as you're facing the street, the damage on the car was hidden from the road. If there were any police looking for him I didn't see any go by. I think he really did get away before they got his license or they'd be here now. Don't you think?

That's probably true.

When we went back in Dad was out cold on the couch and Luke went in his room. I cleaned up all the towels and stuff, and put them in the wash, and then came in and sat here in a daze for a while until I got out the book and started writing to you. So, here we are, back to the present moment.

And how do you feel?

Surprisingly a lot better now that I've gotten through the whole story.

I'm proud of you for sharing that hard time with me. You're a very caring young woman. And brave too. So what will happen now? What's next? What will you do?

Go to bed?

You can't just leave it there! Can you? What will you do?

It's after 1:00 a.m. It took all my energy just to tell you the whole story. Dad's going to have to deal with his own crap when he wakes up.

He probably won't remember what happened.

That might actually scare him, when he feels the cuts on top of his head and sees the car in the driveway. He'll wonder, "What did I do?" And maybe he'll do something about it.

And if he doesn't?

I will.

That's what I want to hear.

I will talk to him no matter what. It already might be too late. If the police find out about this he could go to jail, and then I really won't have anyone to care for me.

I'm sure Aunt Ellen would take you in immediately.

Probably. But I want to be with my dad . . . what's left of him. Can you hold me while I sleep tonight?

Yes.

I need that.

Thursday, October 4
9:20 a.m.

Good morning.

Good morning.

What a terrible night!

You mean with your dad?

Well that too, but the sleep was horrible. Are you sure you were holding me?

All night.

It must be a combination of everything! I remember many dreams, but at the same time I was awake enough to feel like I hadn't slept at all. Do you know what I mean?

I think so.

So as you can see I skipped school, and from the sound of snoring coming from downstairs it seems Dad has skipped work as well. I hope Luke got off. I should check. Remind me to check, will you?

Sure.

Um. I felt this low buzzing vibration going on in my body all night long. Maybe the word buzz is the wrong word, but I can't think of another one. It's a slight feeling of needing to puke and like some weird electric, radiating, low-level pain all over my body? Oh damn it. I just can't explain it. But I have to.

If you describe it then it won't be as powerful, right?

Exactly. It feels like someone took my body and rubbed it with alcohol or some really strong-smelling oil, like have you ever smelled that tea tree oil?

No.

I feel like someone was torturing me so they started giving me an Indian burn with this oil all over my body by rubbing their hands on me as fast and as hard as they can, and doing it for like an hour, so the skin is red and inflamed. It's raw, and is there a word for like "hypersensitive"?

I don't know. I'm still stuck back at "Indian burn."

Yeah. My dad says when he was a kid he and his friends would rub each other's arms real hard and it would turn red like the skin of an Indian, and so it was called an "Indian burn."

Got it. So, back to your hypersensitive skin. It sounds dreadful, like you should be in the hospital getting some sort of medication for this. Painkiller?

I'm making it sound worse than it is in trying to get to the heart of it. If you take that raw feeling and then see it as having turned from burning into a smolder, like the fire is gone, add a little rubbing alcohol to the mix, that might do it. It doesn't make for a very good night's sleep. Then add to that my hands go numb! My whole arm goes numb! But the worst thing, GA, is when I wake up.

Oh. I thought that might be a good thing.

I wake up and this feeling all over my body seems to turn yellow.

Yellow?

Yeah. Yellow. It's a sickly yellow glow all over my body. It doesn't feel good. It makes me feel sick. But listen. This is important. This morning I realized that it's fear. Like my whole body wakes up with fear, every cell in my body. That's what it is! I'm not even thinking anything when I wake up, but it's like my body has been thinking all night, and worrying, and it wakes up terrified. And in the middle of this, or in the center of my body there is a smoldering, nauseating feeling. Sometimes I have to throw up first thing in the morning. It's so weird, this whole feeling. It's awful.

I'm sorry this is happening to you.

And here's the truth, GA. This fear makes me want to die so I can stop feeling it. It's ironic that the fear of death makes me want to die. But I don't even know if that's what the fear is about. The fear I wake up with is so visceral (I have no idea what that means but I think it's the right word), so deeply connected to every cell in my body, in my bones, running through my veins, radiating off my skin, and so concentrated in my heart and stomach that I have to throw up, that I think this fear is a fear of everything! It's so scary I just want to die. I just want to die!

It sounds like you can relate to your mom and her repeating, "Kill me," so many times.

Yeah. I thought of that. I think I understand more what she was feeling, and she died gasping for breath, so it was a terrible way to go. Seriously, I only feel this way for a few moments in the morning. Once I get up, or after I throw up, it goes away. That's the strangest thing about it. All this fear seems more connected to my body than my mind. My body worries when I sleep, but then when I wake up and take over, it calms down.

✻ ✻ ✻

You've been silent for a while. What's going on?

Well. I just got up, and when I sit here and get quiet I can still feel it. I'm sorry. I want to push the off switch and cut the power. Turn off the machine. Don't even ask, "What's the machine?" Life. Like the machine is obviously broken. Hear it? Someone turn it off before it really breaks apart and hurts somebody.

What are you talking about?

I don't know. I'm just free-associating, like there's this machine buzzing and clanking, and it sounds like it's going to blow up. So someone needs to run over and shut it off. OK. . . . OK.

So. Where do you go from here?

Coffee. Yeah. Let's get off of this bed and leave this awful state behind. God. It sucks to be me. But I know as soon as I leave this bed and go get that cup of coffee and check to make sure Luke got off that this whole nauseating feeling will dissolve away. I'll brew Dad a cup too. He's bound to wake up soon.

Thursday, October 4
11:30 a.m.

Luke did get up and go to school. Dad left too. I heard Dad get up at 10:15, and I decided to stay up here because I didn't want to be there when he started realizing he went off the deep end last night. He took a shower and got out the door in fifteen minutes. And then, ha ha, he came right back in.

Why are you laughing?

I don't know. I can imagine him walking out to the car in his computer geek clothes with his briefcase in hand like any other day, and then seeing the car and going, "Holy cow!" That's what he'd say too, in his hung-over, nerd-like way. He must have come back in and sat down to think because things were very quiet after he came in. I was somewhat afraid he would come up and see if we were here, but he didn't. He never thinks of others. He went out the door again about a half-hour ago. The car is still there so I'm not sure how he got to work. Maybe he took a cab or a bus or something. I'm going to jump in the bath and relax. Doesn't that sound nice?

Sure does. Don't forget the citrus soap.

I bought some really fragrant bubble bath. It smells like strawberries. I can't wait to try it out. Talk to you later. . . .

Friday, October 5
Evening

Hi.

That was a long bath, like more than a day long.

Sorry I didn't come back to write more. Yeah. I'm sick. Dad came home from work sober last night. Hurrah! What a break! I knew he'd learn. He never asked about what happened, but he looks at us like he's expecting us to say something.

Are you still going to?

Not if he quits. No need. I don't want to embarrass him.

Where is he tonight?

It's early. I'm not going to worry about it. Isn't that what you're always telling me? Don't worry?

True.

Rick and I have been e-mailing back and forth. I told him I was sick. I missed school today too, because my usual treatment was at 11:00 a.m. and I didn't feel like going to school beforehand. Afterward I just felt too bad to go. So I stayed home.

I'm glad you're taking care of yourself. What did Rick have to say?

He just said he hoped I felt better soon and we set up a time tomorrow to meet. He's going to come and sit on my porch because I don't have the energy to do much else. I'll probably feel better tomorrow than I do today. That's the usual. But I'd rather meet on the porch because if it goes badly I can just come right inside and don't have to slog all the way home from somewhere crying.

Got it!

I'll be back. I'm going to write more later. I promise.

Friday, October 5
Bedtime

I'm back.

Welcome back.

Thanks. Dad came home and went to bed.

And?

I have no idea. I stayed in here, doing homework and a lot of thinking.

That sounds useful.

Yeah. You know, I'm missing Mom like crazy right now.

I know.

I realized as I was sitting here, actually praying, that even when I pray . . . this may sound weird but sometimes I pray to God and yet I see her. I know she's not God but she helps me connect to God. Does that make sense?

It does.

That's funny. Now I'm doubting. Like, are there really people in heaven? To think heaven might just be a dream, or a hope, shared by a lot of scared people who are trying to understand what the heck they are doing here—that's intriguing.

In what way?

I suppose it's easier for me to believe than not believe. Death looks so final, but I have this deep sense within me that I will live forever. I just know it. It's not that I wish it to be true. I just know. But I do wonder why I know.

Because it's true?

Perhaps. I also look around at all the beauty of this world and know that it isn't all some cosmic accident. There is too much meaning in it, too much purpose behind every tree, cloud, and trickling stream. In some ways I've seen God in everything. I've felt God's spirit in me, around me. I've experienced heaven in Mom's arms, in Luke's face, at the water's edge, and I suppose I've experienced hell too sometimes.

What about me? Have I helped you believe?

Of course, GA. I have felt you, heard you, touched you. Truly. Not just in my imagination, but in that deep inner world, which is real. In some ways, like you say, more real.

And I don't even know what "more real" means except I know it's true.

You are on a roll, girl!

I know. But then I remember Mom passing, and even though there was so much beauty in the room, and peace, and so much of a sense of God and angels, there was something else. The horror of death, the terror of watching her body breaking and her life slipping away is also there. At one moment she's there, and then she's gone. That body on the bed isn't her. It's an empty shell, like a spacesuit no longer in use.

Isn't that evidence that her spirit has gone somewhere else?

I suppose it could be seen that way. At the same time, all that I knew, loved, experienced of Mom vanished with that last breath. "Goodbye." And then she was gone.

Gone from this world.

Yeah. And now she lives in the magic world of hopes and dreams come true. I hope! I hope that's true. I do miss her. I do want to see her again. I could see when she died that it wasn't all bad, and empty, and sad. There was something beautiful about it. I felt heaven around her. I did. I didn't ask to feel that. It was there. It was real. So, I am hoping to see her again.

You will. One day, and hopefully after you've lived a long and productive life in this world, you will pass over as all do. There you'll see your mother smiling with open arms. You'll run to her and embrace and cry sweet tears of joy.

That's such a nice thought. I suppose the other alternative is that I die and like that's the end of the show. The music ends, the curtain closes. "Dibiddy, dibiddy, dibiddy, the-the-

the that's all folks." Then when the lights go out it all disappears into darkness, into nothing. And I don't even know I'm dead, because I no longer exist. There is no me to be afraid. There is no me to cry anymore, or to long for love and comfort. There is no me to rattle the cage, or scream out in rage. There is no more me to be poked and bruised and feel the pain, and no more me to feel sorry for myself. There will be no more me, period.

How does that sound?

Honestly?

Of course.

It sounds untrue.

What do you mean?

It's not a bad way to go, to be nothing, but my inner heart says there is no such thing as nothing. You can't be something and then be nothing. Isn't that true?

Energy changes forms but never dies. Basic physics.

Like you know anything about that, but yes, it's even scientific. I don't care if I'm nothing when I die. But I know that I can't just disappear, and I know that Mom didn't just disappear. If I can love her even now, she's alive. I know it.

That's very good. I see you're in deep reflection. What's that about?

I want to go see her grave again before I have that operation.

Why?

I don't know. I need to talk to her there, before I get any sicker, before I have the operation, before there is any chance I may die. Even if I believe her spirit is in heaven, I want to go there, just one more time.

I must be psychic. Not a week goes by since we talked about him and he's in trouble!

What happened?

Luke got caught shoplifting.

Really?

Yeah. At the hardware store.

At the hardware store? What? Did he steal a screwdriver?

No. He took some electronic equipment. That's so him!

What do you mean?

Most kids steal candy. He's stealing something useful. He wanted to play computer games on the TV in the living room, so he stole some stuff to be able to do that.

Why did he steal it? Couldn't he have bought it or asked your dad to buy it for him?

Yeah. That's what scares me. He wasn't thinking. It must be because of everything that's going on. It's a call for help. I know it.

How did it happen? Do you know the story?

He was with a bad kid. It's really a shame. Finally somebody pays attention to him and makes friends and it happens to be the most disturbed kid in the neighborhood.

What's his name?

Danny. Danny's parents never punish him. They're like, "Please Danny, stop hanging your sister by her hair. She probably doesn't like it. Oh Danny, don't kill the little bunnies. They're so cute. Danny, please don't shoot the gun out the window." Danny is a brat. His parents whine about his behavior but let him get away with everything! They never punish him! Someday he's going to kill someone.

Sounds like he needs some help.

Yeah. Definitely. So I didn't even know that Luke knew Danny any more than being classmates. I would never have paid Luke to go out and play if I knew he was playing with Danny! I would have told Dad that he had to stop it. Luke says that Danny stole a lot from several stores, and that Luke was with him and felt bad about what Danny was doing. Danny dared him to steal something until he finally gave in. He said he went to the hardware store and stole some electronic components because that's the only thing that appealed to him. He got caught before he got out the door. They called here just before Rick was going to come over, and I had to tell Dad, and then we had to get Luke at the police station. Dad was so nervous about going in there. I suppose we know why. But they didn't say anything to him except that Luke would be getting some information in the mail about what would happen next.

Are they going to press charges?

It sounds like it. I hope he's OK. It's all been so much pressure on him just like on me. He's probably been under even more pressure with me and Dad checking out in our different ways. He looked terrible when we picked him up, wild-eyed, defiant, stone-cold quiet. I'm so worried for him!

You can worry, and even better than that you may want to do something about it.

I already thought of that. I'm going to talk to him. I don't care if he doesn't want to talk or swears at me, or tries to throw me out of his room. I need to make the effort. I'm so afraid.

Afraid of what?

That he'll become a criminal.

Listen, this may be nothing more than a phase. I think it's very sweet that you're worried and ready to help him out. This is a real opportunity to make a difference. But I'm sure he's going to be OK. Didn't you ever steal anything?

Oh yeah. I never got caught though. I only did it once but I still feel very guilty about it. My friend got caught. She would switch the tags on the clothes, so she could get a better deal. Someone finally caught on. I felt sorry for her though, because she was poor. She's in a much different place today.

So, maybe Luke will be OK too. But yes, talk to him.

I will.

What's happening with Rick?

I put our meeting off. I need to be here with Luke and Dad and figure out what more needs to be done. I'll see him tomorrow.

Sunday, October 7
Morning

Dad drank last night.

I'm sorry about that.

He fell asleep on the couch. I think he peed himself. He's sleeping in a puddle . . . maybe it's beer? I'm seeing Rick this afternoon.

Finally.

I just have one request.

What's that?

It's Sunday. I can't sing anymore, but I want to hear you sing another verse of "Amazing Grace" for me, just the one I'll write here. I want to listen and soak in the words. I need to feel them. Will you do that?

I will, with all my friends joining me.

OK. I'll write them down and then listen. That's all for now.

I'm ready.

> *Through many dangers, toils, and snares*
> *I have already come . . .*
> *'Tis grace that brought me safe thus far . . .*
> *And grace will lead me home.*

Sunday, October 7
Night

He dumped me.

Monday, October 8

Mirror, mirror on the wall
Who's the fairest of them all?
Snow White's skin has turned to gray,
Bruised cheeks and heart
She slips away.

Will they come to see her
With her hair now turned to dust?
Will even a tear fall from his eyes,
And cleanse her lips of rust?

O Queen of beauty, fear you not,
Snow White's body has begun to rot.
Even if she were to revive,
She will only ever be half alive.
And the beauty that once gave you chase
Has fallen from its place of grace.
A monster, she will roam the night,
As those that loved her flee with fright.

O mirror, mirror on the wall,
Who then is fairest of them all?
You, O Queen, have won the day,
For Little Snow White has passed away.

N. M. B.

Tuesday, October 9
Still Night

Gonna talk about it?

Fugly! That's all I have to say.

What's that mean?

I'm not sure, but I know if you combine the f-word with "ugly" you get "fugly" and that's how it went. OK?

Badly huh?

Badly for me. And it's always about ME. Don't you know that by now? Fugly!

Well, it is YOUR life we've been talking about here. Don't feel bad about it.

He said he needs to pull away because he realized that it would be wrong to get real physical and all emotionally connected when I'm so sick and fugly.

He didn't say that.

Not the fugly part, but that's probably what he was thinking. He didn't want to quote, "hurt me," and he thought we should quote, "just be friends."

I've heard that before.

I bet you have.

Yeah.

So, I agreed with him because what else was I going to do?????

Hold it! Didn't you truly agree with him anyway? Weren't you thinking the same thing before this happened?

Yes. But he dumped ME! Not fair! I should have said something first. That would have been better.

Better for you.

Yes, but . . .

I know. It's all about YOU anyway. So, how do YOU feel about it?

What a stupid question! I never want to see him again! I don't want to see anybody! I'm tired of all this drama! In fact, I'm sick of everyone! Everything! People are so stupid! When something hard comes up they just pull away, like no one wants to deal with their own crap. It's easier to walk away. I've noticed that with all my friends, not just Rick! They even look at me differently.

Who?

Everyone. I can see it in their eyes. They can be talking about anything. They smile and talk faster than usual, and try to be so upbeat, but I can see in their eyes they are thinking I am going to die. And that's weird!

Maybe they just care about you.

They look at me with that look. It's a long gaze, or they do it when they think I'm not looking. It's the kind of gaze that says, "Look hard, because this is going to be one of the last pictures you'll have of her."

Is that what they're saying?

I suppose it's sweet when people who know me look at me like that. But when people who don't know me that well start looking at me like that, it feels like I'm being violated, like I'm on display. Look at the freak! But don't let her catch you looking! They're like secret paparazzi who snap their memory shots while I turn the other way. And then there are those who just stare. They gaze right into my face and roll the hidden camera. "Let's get some tape for the news at eleven."

They don't all do that!

I swear all my close friends have backed away. Tammy, Rick, Em, Skye, Lauren, should I go on? Lianne, Steve, Kathy . . . More?

Stop. You know you're just feeling sorry for yourself. You know Rick just said he wanted to cool the physical stuff and be there as a friend. It sounded like he sincerely wanted to support you and like he cares.

You were there! Weren't you?

I couldn't miss this one. I'm sorry. I just had to be there, to help!

And did you help me?

I thought it went extremely well, so there was no need to intervene.

Why, Angel? Why is everyone pulling away?

Are they, Nicole? Are they really? Or are you also pulling away? I believe Rick is a nice guy underneath, and he woke up and realized that after you turned him down. And that's why he backed away from that physical relationship with you.

He more than backed away. He left.

True. But it's hard to be mature and do everything in the mature way when you're not yet mature yourself. Rick is just a big kid. But I think he's growing up and someday you can definitely be friends again, maybe even more than friends.

Too late.

What do you mean?

I already told him I found somebody else, somebody who loves me and cares for me and shows me respect!

What? Wow. That was a fabrication.

Really? How do you know?

Maybe you're doing something I haven't seen.

Maybe I am. But maybe you're just an idiot.

OK, I'm going to tell it to you straight out, Nicole. Stop feeling so sorry for yourself. Do you see your part in this stuck place at all? Do you see that you're choosing to look at the bad in everything? I know things ARE bad but you can make them worse!

Oh, Angel! I can feel myself pulling away from everyone. It felt like I had two choices with Rick, either cling all over him or push him away. I did make the first move to end it. I feel like the same thing is true with Tammy. I feel like I took the first step in ruining our relationship by dating Rick. Now part of me wants to fall before Her Majesty and beg forgiveness. But I can't do that. You know that. So I'm stuck here all by myself. Do you understand how that feels? Does anyone? Sometimes I feel like no one could possibly even begin to understand how I feel. Even the people who have decided to be especially nice to me, like all of the teachers now, saying special hellos with smiles and a warm pat on the back, or a sideways one-armed hug in the hall. They can reach out to me, even touch me, but I can't feel it. I mean I feel it but it doesn't get in. I look at them and say to them in my mind, "You can't help me. You don't even have the capability of imagining the kind of pain I'm in. You live in this perfect little protected life and in this world of complacency you look down at me, and throw me a mercy kiss." I can hate them sometimes. I hate them all!

Nicole!

What?

It's one thing to be upset about Rick, or about the trouble you've had with other friends. But when you start picking on the good people who are truly trying to help you, that's going too far. You're feeling so sorry for yourself you can't even see how sincere these folks are being and how much they care. You're the one with cancer. Not them. Live with it.

You don't sound like my guardian angel. You sound mean.

I'm trying to wake you up. They're good people who are trying their hardest to care for you. You're right. They can't know exactly how you feel. But they do care.

My intention is not to be a jerk about this, Angel. I'm describing this place I'm in which is so low, and so cut off from everyone, that I feel like friends and people who are attempting to be nice to me are just not getting it. Is that so bad? They don't get it! It feels lonely when they don't get it, and it does piss me off! It's frightening, the lack of love there seems to be in this world. I feel that way. I just do. I don't mean to say it's right, or I'm better than anyone else, or that they should easily act differently. I think they can't. They can't go to my depths, can't know the pain, can't feel the kind of fear I feel. They're not staring into the face of death! I am!

I hear you. I do. I hope I wasn't too hard on you. I just don't think feeling sorry for yourself and being judgmental about others is going to help at all.

Perhaps you're right. It's easy to be a prissy angel. Put yourself in my shoes. Jerk!

I'm only trying to help.

Go away.

Not before you answer one question.

What's that?

How's your family?

The same.

Is that all you have to say? How's Luke?

Right now he seems really nutty, like he's agitated and pissed off.

He probably is. Life hasn't been that kind to him lately. Are you going to talk with him?

I want to but I'm waiting for him to calm down a little. I don't want to push him over the edge. Like maybe he's fed up with all this and he might run away if people push him.

Is that why you've chosen not to talk to your dad too? Afraid he might run away?

He already ran away a long time ago, didn't he? I'm not afraid. I'm looking for the right time. Why don't you do me a favor and fix things. Wave your magic wand and make everyone a little more sensible and responsible and a bit more considerate and then my work would be a lot easier.

I'm an angel, not your fairy godmother. Did you call me a prissy angel?

I need a miracle here. I need someone to step in and grab Luke and tell him he's only got one chance to make it in this life and he better make the right choices. And then someone needs to take Dad by the ear and yank him to a few AA meetings and while he's gone throw out all his bottles and put an attack dog in front of the refrigerator so he can't stock it with any more beer. Then I need someone to just mention to Rick that his ex-girlfriend might very well die and he needs to at least realize that and be more than nice, and then tell Tammy to get over herself and come be my friend! Can you do that?

Can YOU do that?

No! Why do I have to do all the work around here? I'm not going to beg people to love me, or to do what I want because I'm dying!

How about begging them to do what they need to do for themselves?

You expect too much of me. If I could manage to put all my problems aside and let go of all my concerns including my pain and fear and disappointment and all that, and then talk to these other people to help them with their problems . . . to do that I'd have to be . . .

An angel?

Yeah.

Maybe that's the plan.

Not my plan. It's too much work.

Tuesday, October 9
Later

By the way, I'm having an operation next Monday, October 15. I suppose you knew that.

I did.

Yeah. They need a sample of my brain. They're going to drill a hole in my head and stick a straw in there and suck out a piece of the tumor.

Yummy!

Ha ha! That's what I was thinking.

Are you scared?

No. It's supposed to be routine. But the other operation will be soon, possibly as early as the first week in November. Dr. Waltzel said they'd decide next week. That's the big one when they do open my skull and cut out the tumor. I'm scared about that one.

I'll be there.

I know.

Wednesday, October 10

She came by again. Started a fire and left.

Your aunt? She lit the house on fire?

Figuratively. Not literally. It means she started more trouble. Yeah. This time the whole crew was here—Aunt Melinda, Aunt Ellen, and Dad. Luke and I were upstairs just out of sight, listening to the whole thing. It was the same old bull. Aunt Melinda told Dad that Luke getting in trouble was proof that he wasn't a good father. She said Luke was turning into a juvenile delinquent.

Hard words. Did you get mentioned in this bout?

Yeah. "As for your daughter, for all I know she could be dead in her room. You wouldn't know either. When's the last time you saw her?" What a bitch! He saw me this morning.

Did your dad take that from her?

He had no choice. Aunt Ellen chimed in before he could start cursing at her, I suppose. She is always the peacemaker, but I didn't find her words very comforting. Here she was trying to find some middle ground or solution, which I felt gave way too much credence to what Aunt Melinda was saying. I know she was trying to help, but she could have been stronger.

What did she say?

She said stuff like, "I can keep an eye on Luke. If things get really bad he can always move in with me." She also said, "Nicole is a very independent girl," which I liked hearing. "She speaks her mind. If she wasn't able to care for herself she wouldn't just lie down and die. She's a fighter. She'd be all over Brent." That's my dad. I think she's right. I would make him take care of me, if I needed more care.

Really? We can talk about that later. What happened next?

I was surprised that Dad just let it go at that. I guess he figured after Aunt Ellen's move it was now Aunt Melinda's move. He stayed silent. Then Aunt Melinda said, "Oh, God. I'm just trying to help. I promised Catherine I'd help, and for the love of God, I will not let her down." All this talk of God really surprised me because Dad had called her an "atheist bitch" when Mom died, so I assumed she didn't believe in God. Anyway, it sounded like under that evil black plastic

Darth Vader suit of hers there might be just a tiny piece of humanity left. Once again, Dad kept silent. Probably the smartest thing he ever did. When they were leaving, outside I could see Aunt Melinda break down in tears. I mean she was wailing. She and Aunt Ellen hugged for a while and talked, and then she got in her Mercedes and drove off.

Wow. So Aunt Ellen saved the day.

She did, I suppose. And Dad helped by keeping his big mouth shut. Dad asked Aunt Ellen what happened outside in the front yard. She told him that Aunt Melinda broke down and cried and said, "I told her I would do anything to save her, and I couldn't save her. I was powerless to help my sister and she died. I don't want to go through that again. I can't."

That's sad.

Yeah. Aunt Ellen got really choked up and Dad just sat there all silent.

Thursday, October 11
Evening

I'm spending more time in my room because I don't even want to see what Dad is doing down there. Look at my prison! It's all so nice but empty and useless!!!!!

Purple covers and pink sheets, teddy bears, children's books, the old comforter, all seem so pointless nowadays. I look at my brush and comb, which now lie on the dresser unused, and my bottle of shampoo and conditioner don't run low anymore. These things have become insignificant to me now. Or worse, everything irritates me. Why did Dad paint my room pink?

'Cause you're his little girl?

Because he thinks all little girls should have pink rooms and purple sheets, and look pretty all the time, and say the right thing, and only talk when they're spoken to, and stay out of his way when he's drunk, and pretend everything is OK, and I'm having a hot flash.

Maybe you should calm down.

Maybe you should . . . whatever! It's all pointless. What a joke! What a bad joke! I understand Mom much better now. She had it right:

Kill me.

Kill me.

Kill me.

Kill me.

Kill me.

Just kill me now!

When it comes to the end I would hope to be able to look at life with gratitude and see everything. I want to be able to say all that needs to be said to everyone I care about, whoever is left. I want to make a speech that all will remember, and maybe even publish, about life and death and hope! Then I want to say a prayer and go.

Sounds beautiful.

Yeah. The problem is, it isn't going to happen that way at all. I can tell right now that it's going to be hell. I mean HELL!

Why?

Because it's already like hell. Where is the love? Where are my helpers, those who will care for me? Right now I already feel so sick I can't get up anymore. I mean emotionally I can't seem to get up. I want to appreciate everything around me but the sickness from the treatments, and the dizziness, and the neck pain and the stomach problems, and that feeling of dying inside get in the way. I'm not trying to make a joke of it. Dying is shutting me down even now. What will it be like when I'm really dying? I'll be like a dog struck by a car, lying beside the road, panting a few last breaths, dazed, mouth dry and full of gravel, glazed eyes. Then . . . dead.

Sad.

No. Mad. Mad while I can still be mad. This sucks. While I can still scream or at least have enough energy on this page to scream in letters, I will. I hate it! It's not fair. Everything feels horrible. This shouldn't be happening! Why is this happening? Why is this happening? Why is this happening? If there is a God, why are you like this? Why do you let this happen? Why are you so mean? Weak? Far away? Why am I dying? Why doesn't anyone care? Why are you doing this to me? Why don't you grow up, GOD? Kill someone your own size! You bully!

God isn't killing anyone.

I know. When I said it I felt bad. But I'm still pissed. I'm getting tired. I get so tired now. I can't go to school. Being around people isn't helping me. I don't have the energy. I don't have the energy to do this. These are my last days.'

You are so dramatic. You may not die. You may get better. Chances are you're going to recover. You know that, don't you?

GA, I feel myself dying. Even if it's the chemo/radiation/drugs that are making me feel this way, it still feels like death. I am sick as hell. And I just know that in a few weeks I'm not going to be feeling any better. Here goes therapy:

Kill me.
Kill me.
Kill me.
I want to die.
Kill me.
Kill me.
Kill me.
I just want to end this!
Kill me.
Kill me.
Kill me.
I just want this to end!
This will end. This will all end.

Friday, October 12
5:30 p.m.

Sitting out the chemo high. Wooohooo! JK. Taking it easy after treatment. The usual consequences of this wonderful miracle of science. So, guess who said hello at lunch break?

Rick?

Nope. Yes, but not who I'm thinking about. Guess again.

Tammy?

Yep. At first I almost burst into tears, like, "What? What did you say? Did you say 'hi' to me?"

You didn't say that, did you?

I thought it, and almost started crying. She asked, "How are you?" And that could be viewed as a remarkable act of kindness because she usually just starts right in talking about herself. But she said it with a certain look on her face that seemed a little fake. I want to use the word "disingenuous" but I'm not sure what that means.

Insincere?

Not exactly. But like she knew something about me that I didn't know, or I didn't know she knew.

You may be looking too hard.

Not really. Right then Rick walked by both of us and said hi and he kept walking like he was passing by two ghosts. Tammy reached out for him but he got away and she said, "Rick, I'll e-mail you about that question you had the other day." Then she smiled at me and gave a little chuckle. I thought it was an evil chuckle like a, "Muhahah!" but that might be my imagination.

Knowing you and your penchant toward the dramatic, it's a distinct possibility.

Considering the way in which Rick practically ran by the both of us I think it's safe to say they're not an item or anything. If they were, that would really make me mad. Hey! Do you think that's why she's talking to me, because she got him back?

Do you really care?

Yes!!!!

OK. Why do you care?

Because it would be really wrong of her!

Just like it was when you dated Rick? It's a free world, Nicole!

I think I'm going to explode right now! You don't get it! You don't get how unfair that would be! You just don't get relationships! I'm mad at you!

Me?

Yes. You and everyone else. Deal with it!

You can be mad at me all you want. But why don't you give Tammy a break? She's reaching out to you. You want and need her friendship. If you have questions you can talk with her. Call her. E-mail her. Ask her to come over.

Get serious! You really are naïve and know nothing about how relationships work and you're not being sensitive to my needs or feelings about this at all! I'm not talking to you anymore today! Goodbye.

Friday, October 12
Night

OK. I'm back. It's late but I do want to talk. I'm still angry as hell.

At who? At me?

It's "whom," "at whom"! I'm angry about everything. I'm so angry deep inside about how screwed up this all is. I feel a lot of hate. There's a list of people I could probably point to as being those I hate the most, but the hate is more of a general thing that seems to just be flowing out of me right now, like a flamethrower. I know that's hard to imagine. It's more like, if someone gets in the way, they'll be exposed to my hate, and get burned by it. Right now I hate everyone and everything. I hate that people are so superficial. I hate that no one really seems to care about anybody, or not that much. I hate that people are so selfish. I hate that we all live these miserable lives and then we die. I hate that it's set up that way. I hate that I feel sick all the time. I hate it. I hate it. I hate it!

What's IT?

I already told you. IT is everything! I feel like I got ripped off. I feel like I was lied to about what life is supposed to be like. Someone misled me, promised me so many things, but then screwed me. I can go on and on with this, you know.

I'm worried about you. You're holding everything so tight and fanning those angry flames inside.

Oh, please! Don't give me some lame angel-lesson tonight. I don't need to hear about how I could do better, or come to some wonderful observation about how beautiful the world is and how grateful I should be and all that bull. I mean I'm not trying to hurt your feelings, GA. It's more like I want to feel bad right now. Do you get that?

I hear you. I don't know if I get it, but I hear you.

There's something soothing about feeling sorry for myself. I have to admit it. All this hate doesn't feel good though. It kind of ruins the self-pity thing. I don't really hate anyone for any legitimate reason, now that I think about it. Underneath that hate there's a really scared and upset little girl who's just looking for help. I don't even think she's looking for love at this point, which is so cliché, I suppose. But she is looking for understanding. Doesn't anybody get it? Can't anyone understand what I'm going through?

I don't think they can to the degree you want them to because they aren't you. Only you can understand what you're going through. They can try. And they can love you, which truthfully is more important anyway.

The thought that no one can understand exactly what I am going through is a very lonely thought, GA. Something about it scares the hell out of me. But it's true! I think when people realize just how alone they are they start reaching for God, don't you think?

I think that's true. Isn't that a good thing?

It probably is for a lot of people. How can it not be? Because I think if God is real, then God does get it, and does understand us like no one else. And if God isn't real, well, it gives people someone they can pretend is there to understand them.

That's pathetic! You believe in God! I know you do!

I do. I really do. The problem is I'm also beginning to feel like God is the one who lied to me about life and promised me so much but then screwed me over. "And God said, 'Here Nicole. This creation is all for you. Here is your beautiful family, your loving mother and father, and your sweet brother, and your friends. Here are all your hopes and dreams for yourself, and the world! This is my gift to you, Nicole.'" That's what God said. "And then God said, 'You shall not have your mother. You shall watch her die in pain and agony. And your father shall fall away, and your brother become silent. And you shall fear all things, Nicole. And this will not be the end of woes for you, because you too shall be stricken with sickness, and your body will ache, and your hair will fall out, and your face will turn from beautiful to ugly, and you shall lose all those you love, and you shall not receive any of my gifts, which I now take away from you.'"

What? Are you pretending to quote the Bible? Do you think God is really that mean?

I don't really know! You tell me! I mean you really piss me off.

Me?

Yes, you! Some kind of angel you are. You can't even help me.

Oh. . . .

Oh, now I've gone and hurt your feelings too. God I'm such an idiot!

I'll be OK, Nicole. I really do understand you, better than anyone else, except for God. So I'm not upset. I wish you could see how much I am helping you already, but I do also understand it may not feel like it right now. It will in the long run. You'll see.

Well the "long run" seems like a long time from now, maybe way too long. I know it's not your fault things happened the way they did. I know intellectually that it's not God's fault either. But it feels like it sometimes. Either that, or God is so pathetically inept that if he can't follow through with his promises, he shouldn't be making them. I mean if God wants people to be happy you'd think he could help out a little more, don't you think?

I can't help it, Nicole. I have to give you an angel-lesson.

I knew it!

Well, you asked for it with your insults and sarcasm about God.

Just send me to hell, why don't you? Go ahead, make my day!

No. That would be too easy for you. Listen. God is way different than that. It may seem too subtle at times or even hidden, but way underneath all these crazy happenings and confusion there is a loving, caring Force.

Oh. Here we go again!

No, listen. God didn't promise you anything except that you can receive God's LOVE, with a capital L, and the peace and happiness that come with LOVE. And whatever happens to you on the outside doesn't have to ruin what happens on the inside. What happens inside can blossom and grow and keep on growing, and yes, live happily ever after forever.

Stop! It's not doing it for me, GA! It's not helping. Just stop! I hear the words but they're empty. It's bull. Life absolutely sucks. And I know that God doesn't hate people, and doesn't hurt people, and doesn't take away gifts and doesn't set us up to be disappointed down the road. I know that, GA. But I still feel screwed over. I still feel like it could have been different. And right now even if there is some deep-seated way of understanding and with it some incredible sense of connection to God and the universe, and all that crap, it just isn't working for me.

Yes. But—

No. Just this once, let me sit with this. That's all for today.

Witch's Brew

Double, double, toil and trouble,
Into the witches brew:
A bucket of vomit,
Mixed with hate,
A dagger o' the devil's crew.
Add a few drops
Of hope mixed with pain,
To keep her coming back again,
And gallons of fear
And a single tear
Will fill it to the brim.
Now run and snatch her
And bring her here,

And thrust her into this stew,
Hold her under.
Hold her tight,
Beneath the witches brew.
When she wiggles no more
Not even a twitch
Dump the rest of her into the pot.
Heat it up ten times more than before,
And then we'll see what we've got.
Out of the boiling above the flames,
You'll witness her sad face appear.
Then we tell her full of sheer glee,
"There is no God, my dear."

N. M. B.

Saturday, October 13
Afternoon

I finally had a chance to talk with Luke. I tried. That's what you wanted me to do, right?

Yes. How did it go?

I walked into his room. More like I stumbled into his room. His room is piled with dirty clothes, empty boxes of computer parts he's ordered, tools, food, and junk. I don't know how he lives in that place. I made my way to his desk, his true home in front of his computer. I tried to get him to stop playing but he wouldn't.

So what did you do?

The only thing I could do was start talking while he played on the computer. I told him that I loved him, and that I was concerned about him getting in trouble, and wanted to know how he was doing.

What did he say?

He said, "Shut up!"

Creative. Then what?

I kept talking. "No Luke, you need to listen, because I may not always be here to help you, and you're going to have to stand up on your own. You're going to have to go to Dad and demand he straighten up and pay attention to you, and you are going to have to live your life for yourself and make it. You have to make it!"

What did he say?

"Shut up!"

Interesting . . .

So I said, "I'm not going to shut up, Luke. I love you. I want you to hear me. I love you, and want you to make it."

And he said?

"Shut up and get out of my room!"

Assertiveness: a good sign.

So I just kept talking. He stopped telling me to shut up. He just kept playing his game, shut me right out. When I said all I wanted to say, I kissed his head and left.

What did he do?

Nothing. Just kept playing.

I'm sure it got in. I'm sure he heard you. You did the right thing. You showed you care.

I can't say I know that's true, but I watched him from the hallway for a few moments after I had left, and saw him wipe his nose. I don't think he has a cold, or allergies. But maybe. It may be that he was doing a little crying.

What do you want to believe?

I want to believe that the runny nose was an indication that deep in his heart he was touched by what I had to say and that someday it will make a big difference for him. On the other hand, I'm so sad for him. I really want him to pull through this. I want to be there for him. I am OK with me dying, I guess, but him being left alone with just Dad? That's not fair. Why does he have to suffer? He didn't do anything. It's like he never got a chance. He never had a chance.

A chance at what?

At happiness, at experiencing comfort, love, security, at making something of his life instead of having it rip and tear him to pieces, or beat him into the corner of his room, silent, afraid. His bruises are a lot worse than mine, because they are on the inside.

Would you trade places with him?

Could I?

No. I'm only asking the question to make a point.

In one way I would, to take away his pain and loneliness. My heart breaks for him every day. It's breaking right now. I would take that from him. But I wouldn't trade places with him. I don't want him to die.

Why not?

Because at least he has a chance to make it, and better to have that chance than to have it all taken away.

Exactly. And guess what? There is a God up there who is caring for him even now, and angels who are with him now and all his life, and you would be amazed to see how many people come out of terrible circumstances and make something of their lives, and yes, learn to be happy.

I hope so.

I won't apologize for being optimistic or putting a positive spin on what looks like an impossible situation. That's my job, and it's who I am as an angel, and I've seen many people come out of hard places and live happy lives. The losses in life often end up being the driving force for good in people's later years. Hard times are often transformational times for people. Times when God feels absent are often followed by a stronger sense of God's presence and power for good than ever before. What do you say to that?

Yada, yada, yada.

That's not nice.

Whatever. Thanks for sharing. I do appreciate the positive angle. Without it I'd be lost. It's hard to believe those things in the middle of the hard times. You were saying that Luke has had angels with him all his life. I know that, but it occurred to me as you were talking that you probably know his guardian angels, since you work at the same street address.

I do. There is one who especially cares for him. She only comes when he calls her.

Does he call her?

He does. And she comes. He can't see her, but he can feel her, and sometimes in the darkest times when he calls to her she comes and he senses, almost knows for certain, that everything is going to be OK.

Can I meet her? Can you introduce me?

No. That's against the rules. But you can see her when you get here.

Do you think I will?

Oh, I think there is a very good chance you two will meet. I'd like that.

Sunday, October 14
Time Stands Still

Angel. I need to talk. I know it's late and I need sleep for the operation tomorrow, but I need to talk.

OK. Wait a minute. Let me get my wits about me. I dozed off a bit. Hang on.

Take your time.

OK. Here I am. Ready to go. What's happening?

Aunt Melinda came to see me tonight.

She did?

Yes. She knocked on my door. I didn't want to open it, but I knew I had to.

Why?

Because she knew I was going in for this preliminary operation and I was sure she wanted to wish me luck, and I thought it would be the charitable thing to let her do that.

That was brave of you, Nicole.

Thanks. I did let her in, and she had a really loving look on her face, and I saw Dad at the bottom of the stairs giving me that cheering-on look. You know, like a smiling, "Here she is! Don't blow it!" look. I was so nervous I thought I had already covered my head with my scarf but I forgot. She took one look at my bald head and winced, turned away, and swallowed, as if she was purposely swallowing whatever comment must have been heading toward her lips. She then stepped in and closed the door behind her and sat on my bed. She was very composed, and she smiled.

Did that creep you out?

A little. But she seemed sincere. She asked me how I was doing and I told her that I was actually hurting in a lot of ways. I mean it was obvious I wasn't going to say, "Fine. How are you?" So I told her about my numbness, and the headaches, and how sometimes I had to drop everything and throw up. I also made sure to tell her that Dad would help me every time I asked, and that I was being cared for by him in such a special way. That was really something of a lie, or maybe a big lie, but I didn't want her to start in on how bad Dad is and why I shouldn't be with him.

I understand.

After that she told me that she had brought something for me. She produced a chocolate shake from Stewart's down the street. It was the kind Mom liked and the kind she brought to Mom the day before she died.

Did you drink it?

I took one look at it and thought I was going to throw up. I pushed it away and said, "No thank you. I feel sick. But thanks for your kindness."

You said that?

Yes I did. And she seemed to understand and actually asked if I minded if she drank it. I said I didn't mind and so she started sucking on the straw, which actually made me feel sicker because they are supposed to stick a straw in my head tomorrow and suck out a piece of my brain. But I managed to overlook it and ignore her loud sucking noises.

Awful!

Really! And yet I felt sorry for her that I couldn't take her gift. It was a nice gesture. But then she started talking about how she was worried that Dad wouldn't be able to take care of me as I got sicker, and that perhaps I could understand that I might need live-in help, and that she would be willing to take time off, move in, and care for me.

No!

Yes! She did say, "Only if you want me to. I am not looking to do anything you wouldn't want me to do. I just want to help. Can you understand that? I'm looking to help."

What did you say?

I wish I had more time to be polite, but was about to throw up, so I just said, "NO. I—" And then I threw up.

You've got to be kidding me. You're joking, right?

I'm not. I said, "No. I—" and then threw up on her foot, and then continued, "I'll be fine. Really."

My goodness!

And then I said, "But thank you all the same, and can I get you a towel?" I suppose because of the shock of the sudden change in circumstances, she simply accepted my answer and my offer to get her a towel. We ended up laughing together as she cleaned off her foot in the bathroom, and then cleaned the floor joking about the whole thing. She did ask again, "Are you sure?" I smiled and said, "I'll be fine. Come visit and see." I had to add that last part in or she would probably not take "no" for an answer. That seemed to satisfy her. Then she asked, "Do you want me there tomorrow?" And again, I just looked at her and said, "No."

And?

And she looked back and said, "OK." That was it. She kissed me on the forehead, wished me the best, and walked down the stairs. She and Dad had a few civilized words—I didn't think that was possible for them —and then she left. Dad smiled and winked at me from the bottom of the stairs, and as I turned to go back in my room I caught a glimpse of Luke, at his computer as usual, but his head was shaking back and forth like, "I can't believe you just did that!" It was beautiful.

So you faced old Aunt Melinda.

She wasn't so bad. I mean, she means well. I can see that.

She sure does. Now you better get some sleep for the operation tomorrow.

No. No. There's more to the story. Seeing Dad wink at me and walk off I got this rush of energy, like some sort of holy rage. Is there such a thing?

Righteous anger? Zeal? Not sure. Tell me more.

This overwhelming sense of self-confidence came over me, like I was holding all the cards in a good game of poker, and Dad didn't have a chance at bluffing me out. I had him at my mercy after throwing Aunt Melinda off-track like that.

I'm not sure what you mean but I think I'm following.

Put it this way, after lying about how Dad was taking such good care of me and getting Aunt Melinda to buy it, I felt like he owed me big time. So right after I saw her drive away I walked downstairs and here's what happened, word for word:

"Dad?"

"Yes."

"So. Don't get mad at me and stuff. But I told Aunt Melinda that you were taking good care of me. That's a lie, Dad. I lied to her."

"Nicole! Don't talk like that!"

"I didn't tell her about how late you come home, or about how you don't even check on us, or about how you blow both Luke and me off regularly, and he probably is going to turn into a juvenile delinquent, and I could have died upstairs and it would have taken you two or three days to figure that out after you smelled my rotting body . . ."

"Nicole. You amaze me with how ungrateful you are."

"Dad!"

"No, you listen to me."

"No, Dad, you listen."

"I will not."

"Dad! I'm going to die and you are going to listen to me."

"You . . ." He stopped in his tracks.

"Dad. I lied to Aunt Melinda because I love you."

"Stop it."

"I don't want us to be taken away from you."

"That won't happen."

"It will, Dad. It will because your drinking is out of control."

"That's none of your business."

"It is, Dad. You smashed up the car. Ran from the cops. You passed out."

"You are really out of line. That's my issue, not yours."

"You drank yourself unconscious and wet your pants. I cleaned it up!"

"I'm leaving." He grabbed his coat.

"Dad. I'm dying. Stay. Listen to me!"

"I don't have to put up with this, Nicole! This is rude, disrespectful, and you are out of control."

"I'm dying, Dad. And you need to stop drinking now. You need to stop and never start again, for me, so I can have my dad with me when I go through all this, and for Luke, because no matter what you went through, and it's been a lot, and no matter what pain you may be feeling, he needs you. We need you."

"Don't be ridiculous!" he shouted. And then he walked out the door.

He left? Just like he did the time he had that argument with Aunt Melinda at your mother's deathbed. That's terrible of him. How could he leave you?

Don't worry. He came back. I knew he would.

Did he say anything to you? Did he apologize? Did he say he'd stop drinking?

No. He didn't say anything. I was up here in my room. He just went to bed. But it doesn't matter right now. I feel good. I feel shaky from all that yelling, but I feel good on the inside.

I know why.

Yeah. I did it. I put it all on him, all the pressure and stuff.

And you did it with so much love, Nicole. Tough love, but love.

I did. Tonight it feels like time has stood still. Just for a moment now I feel so light and at peace. Now I think I should try to get some sleep. This operation is said to be routine. I'm not worried at all. I am feeling upbeat about life at the moment. Maybe I can have some peaceful rest tonight.

You deserve it. May you have a peaceful rest tonight, and I'll see you in the morning.

Goodnight, Angel. Oh. I won't be writing to you for a few days, until I get home. I'll be in the hospital for at least overnight, maybe longer. Look. I know this isn't supposed to be a big deal tomorrow, but I'm counting on you to be with me through this. OK?

Of course. All the time. I promise.

OK. Goodnight.

Goodnight.

Wednesday, October 17
Afternoon

Dear Angel,

I'm home.

Welcome back!

They hurt me.

I know. I'm sorry.

They hurt me so much! I wanted to die.

I know you did. I'm glad you're alive.

It was worse than a nightmare. I was totally awake this time! I was wheeled into the operating room. There were four or five doctors and nurses. They put this thing over my head, and kept talking and paying no attention to me, to what was happening.

The thing they put on you is called a halo.

I know. There's nothing angelic about it besides the name. OMG! They put this halo on and then they started to turn each screw. First came screw number one, right into my temple. I screamed. They didn't seem to notice or to care. Dad came forward and they pulled him away. He argued with them. I screamed and screamed. The pain was horrible. Just think about a screw going into your head!

It didn't really go into your head. The halo was being fastened to your head. I'm sure they didn't mean to hurt you.

Screw two. Excruciating pain. I flailed on the table. I remember them grabbing my arms and holding me down. It was horrible. They shut the doors to the operating room because I was disturbing the whole floor. I must have been. "Stop! You're hurting me! Stop! Stop!" They didn't seem to care at all. They just went about their business. They acted like I wasn't there.

What about your dad?

He tried to come to me but they stopped him. Next thing I knew he was gone. They made him wait outside. I was all alone. Then screw three. I wanted to die. I prayed to die. "Dear God please take me now. Please kill me!" Then I could hear some woman say, "Please." I think one of the nurses was talking to another one, maybe felt bad for me. But they gave me something, in the IV, which worked very quickly.

I'm sure it was only seconds of pain but it must have seemed like an eternity. I'm sorry you had to go through that. I'm not sure why they would let you be in such pain. It's got to be unusual. That's not supposed to happen.

It was something out of a modern-day horror movie. Maybe I was hallucinating from whatever was in the IV, but that was my experience. It's what I remember, the turn of every screw into my head. But after the nurse said, "Please" the pain in my head went away instantly. Then I felt this huge weight on my chest, like someone was sitting on my chest. It felt like I was sinking into death, right there, like I was being smothered to death, falling into darkness.

Then what happened?

I went unconscious.

Good! Best thing I've heard all day!

I woke up in the ICU. It was all over. But it was awful up to that point, like a creepy horror movie, really!

I hear you.

Now that it's over, I feel like I have been to visit death.

What do you mean?

That scary part, the dark, ugly, empty part—I was there. I was part of the emptiness, the nothingness. Beyond all the pain, fear, there is this still place, or rather no place at all. It's hard to describe.

Do you think that's what is waiting for you when you die? Is that it?

No. This is the place between life and the life after. I think it's the door between the two worlds.

Like a hallway?

Not really, because a hallway is a place. Even a door is the wrong image, because this place in-between is empty space, nothingness, that nothingness people fear. That's death. I am not afraid. A few more weeks and I am outta here!

That doesn't sound right. Do you want to die?

I'm sorry. I don't mean that I am necessarily going to die. I'm hoping the operation will be such a success when they take the tumor out that I'll be free of all this sickness and pain. But I'm not afraid of dying. I'm afraid for Luke if I die, and for Dad and the people who will miss me, but not of death itself. In that place where I was, there is no pain or anything else.

And?

And through that place there is another place, full of light and love.

Did you see it? Why do you hesitate? Did you see the light?
No. But I know it's there. I just know it.

Thursday, October 18
Bad News

No school for me this week. Still got a pile of homework dropped off. I don't care. Mrs. Fischer says not to worry and just do what I can. I'm going to let it pile up.

Sounds like a plan.

Dad told me some bad news today. First of all, the tumor is malignant. I know I told you that they called it malignant from the beginning because it was near my nerves and stuff but they say it's also that bad kind, and it has spread further inside the brain, not in a nice line but here and there, "like a spattering of paint."

I'm sorry, Nicole.

Don't be sorry. It's not your fault. Dad also said that they are going to operate in two weeks and that this might just be the first operation.

Oh. There may be more?

It depends on how successful they are at the first one, but it sounds like they already know that it won't be easy to get the whole thing. And then Dad also said—and this is worse than any news about the operation—he said that probably I'm going to have to keep on getting the chemo and radiation after the surgery.

That's fairly normal.

Maybe for two more years!

Two more years?

That's what Dad said, but I think I'd die from the chemo way before that.

Let's hope the operation gets it all and you don't have to do that. In fact, I'm going to put in a word for you upstairs that this won't happen to you.

Will you do that for me?

Do you want me to?

Yes.

Then I will.

Friday, October 19
Hospital and Home

I went in for my usual treatments. Dad took me!!! Dad impressed me in the hospital. I remember so well the way he tried to get to me when I was screaming in pain. He argued with them to help me.

He loves you very much.

His face. He had this—grimace? Is that the right word?

I'll look it up for you. Dictionary says, "A sharp contortion of the face expressive of pain . . ."

Yes, that's it. And this was mixed with a huge amount of concern, and a bit of panic. He looked like Braveheart trying to break through the soldiers to save me. He was there when I woke up in the ICU. He still had something of that look on his face, but I could also see the relief.

It's a good thing.

I could cry.

What do you mean you could cry? I see you.

Yep. Um . . . I feel dumb acting the way I did, so inconsiderate, so bratty, so unloving.

It's good to see you softening up. I think what you did, though, was the right thing. Has he been drinking?

I can't find a drop in the house. I haven't smelled anything on his breath either.

No car bashing or bed-wetting?

Not yet. Mind you it's only been a few days. He still doesn't talk to me. And he's still a geek.

I think he'll always be a nerd. You can't change that, but it's so great to see him responding to your plea. Have you told him how impressed you were with him in the hospital? Does he know how appreciative you are of him?

I'm not sure. I think he knows. He knows I love him.

But to hear you tell him that you recognize how hard his journey has been . . . that would be another incredible conversation.

Hey! I've done enough!

Sorry, but to show your appreciation would be a wonderful gift for him.

On the one hand I really want to do that. On the other hand, I'm afraid. So many times I felt rejected by him, or blown off and ignored. Even if some of this was my own imagination, I don't want to go through one more rejection. Worse, if I die I don't want to be rejected just before the end. I have such a good opinion of him at the moment. I want to revel in it. Is that the right word? I want to splash around in it, drink it up, let it soothe and refresh me. I'm so happy he cares. I haven't felt this good in weeks. It feels good to feel good, even if it's only for a moment.

I have an idea. Write him a note. Maybe not to be delivered today, but it could be delivered to him before you go in for the operation.

Um. You call ME dramatic? It sounds good on the surface, but I'm afraid if I write something it will have to be perfect, like the perfect note saying goodbye.

How about trying to write something here? Then if it's good you can copy it and deliver it. It doesn't have to be the note to end all notes. You can write a short note and tack it to his door tomorrow.

OK. Let's see what happens.

Dear Dad . . .

Jeez. Can't do it. I have to just write a REALLY short note or I'll be stuck forever.

Then write a REALLY short note.

Dear Dad,
I'm sorry I was so mean to you. I know you tried your best. I love you.
Love,
Nicole

Not bad. Not bad.

October 20
Dear Dad,
I don't know if I will ever be able to give you this letter, but I hope to. If not, you will find it here when you discover this diary. I want you to know that I realize it hasn't been

easy being my father. I have not made your life easy. In fact, at times I made you very miserable by the way I acted. When Mom died I wanted you to be everything she was and when you couldn't be I got bratty and gave you such a hard time. There were times when I hated you and I know sometimes my words hurt you. I want you to know that I am sorry for those times. In those hard times when I tried to hurt you I was reaching out for love, and as misguided as it may have been, I was desperately telling you I love you, and need you so much.

I am sorry that Mom died, not only for Luke and myself, but also so much for you. I know you two didn't always get along, but who has a perfect marriage? I do know that you loved her and she loved you. There wasn't a day I didn't see that, especially when she got sick. You were there for her 'til the end, and I can see from how you have acted in the last six years that you miss her so very badly, and that your love for her has in many ways only grown stronger.

I want to thank you for all you have been and done for me. I thank you for teaching me to ride a bike, and for sneaking me coffee in the morning when Mom said I shouldn't have any. I thank you for painting my room pink, and treating me like a little girl, like your little girl. I noticed. I'm so proud of you as a father, as my father.

Thank you for making me strong just by being who you are, and for caring about good things and doing the right thing. You could have fallen apart and done all kinds of stupid things when Mom died, but you didn't, and you did continue to care for both Luke and me, especially making sure we had a good home, food, comfort, and security. These are not small things.

I realize that sometimes the pain must have been so great that you had to find a way to make it go away, and drinking seemed to be the way you tried to do that. I saw how you stopped, or slowed way down after Mom had been gone for a few years and how it started again when I got sick. I know me getting cancer too must have been like a nightmare for you. If I were you I'd drink too. But you stopped drinking just for me, for Luke, for all of us. What courage that took! What love! That's my dad who did that for me! You are a great dad!

I will remember your scruffy face when you kissed my cheek, and the smell of your aftershave wafting through the house after your shower, and your songs you sang to yourself. Yeah, we could hear them. I will remember forever your strong arms holding me, and those times you ruined dinner and didn't make us eat it. Thanks for so many trips to McDonald's and Taco Bell.

I also want to thank you for trying to help me in the hospital when I cried out in pain. I will never forget the look on your face. I saw your love for me, and I know that this will always be there, regardless of whether I live here in this world with you or move on to the other to be with Mom.

I'm sure I'll be OK. But if not, I know you will take care of Luke and pay even more attention to him, and double your efforts to help him grow up with some kind of sense that life doesn't have to be this crazy, and that some people really do live to a ripe old age. And if I die, please have the choir sing "Amazing Grace" with a lot of harmonies, and don't tell any revealing or embarrassing stories about me at the party after the service. Please? And DON'T DRINK! Thanks.

Now what can I say? Thank you for all. I love you more than anything in the world. And I know that you love me, and that gives me so much comfort and the feeling that life is worth living every moment. God bless you. May your journey find some peace and the good life away from so much death and sadness, and if I die I know we will meet again. Mom and I will be waiting for you on the path just across the street. I promise. It will seem like only a few moments until we meet again. I really believe that.

Love you,

Nicole

Sunday, October 21

Guess what?

Tammy came and visited you today.

You're just no fun. I can never surprise you! Yes, Tammy came over. Can you believe it?

How did it go?

Why don't YOU tell me? I'm sure you were hanging around.

Nope. When I saw her I said to myself, "This can only mean one thing—girl talk." I don't need to be around that. I knew you'd fill me in.

I feel good. Maybe not so much physically, like not at all physically, but really good on the inside today. I know everything isn't totally smoothed out with Tammy and me but it feels like it is! I'm soooo glad to be talking with her again and she's being so sweet, and seems to be really sincere, which is really new for her.

Tell me about it.

So you want to hear the girl talk?

With a minor translation here and there, that would be nice.

OK, I want to make it as real as I can for you so you can capture what I was going through, like word for word, with some editing so you can withstand the "uncomfortable" part. I finally got up the nerve to call her like you suggested, and I asked her to come over. She seemed delighted and we set up a time right away. But even though I knew she was coming, I was more nervous waiting for her than I was when Aunt Melinda came over. But I suppose that's because Aunt Melinda surprised me so I didn't have a chance to get nervous, and I had like an hour and a half to think about Tammy coming over. I put on my black jeans, white tank top with a purple blouse over top, and my favorite purple scarf over my head. She's such a style-conscious person I wanted to make sure I didn't like push her away unconsciously by wearing something drab. Do you think I was taking things too far?

Hey, I like you going with your instincts.

Dad left before she came. Someone stopped by and picked him up, and I really think he was going to an AA meeting! I saw a meeting schedule on his dresser when I was snooping in there yesterday. I couldn't find any hidden booze!

That's great.

Yeah. The best proof that he hasn't been drinking is that he got up at 9:00 a.m. this morning, which is early for him, and he snores a lot less when he hasn't been drinking. He did some chores, believe it or not, and then went out. We still don't talk much but it's way apparent that he's here for me like he wasn't before.

Did he read your letter?

I didn't deliver it. I'm not ready to do that yet. And you know, he's not a talker. He's just not. So if he shows me he cares about me that's good enough for me. Really. Anyway, she came over right on time and she gave me a long hug when I opened the door. That felt amazingly healing. We sat and talked about lots of things, like what she's been doing with her life and who she's interested in, and all about other friends of ours, and I hope you see I'm shortening this part just for you.

I appreciate it.

She even mentioned I looked great and that my scarf was beautiful and matched the blouse. See? I knew she'd notice that. And then she even asked me how I was feeling and what was going on with the sickness. I thought that was really kind of her because, like I said, she usually talks about herself and hardly pauses to let you get a word in.

"How are you?" she asked. "I think you look great! But I hear you've been really sick and that you had an operation."

"I'm sick because of the medication mostly, and the operation was just a routine thing to get a better idea about what's going on, so it was no big deal. The big one is coming up soon. Now they're talking a few weeks away."

"Do you want me to be there with you?" she asked. It was like nothing bad had ever happened between us.

"If you want to be. I'd like that. It's a long operation and you'd be in the waiting room for a really long time, maybe all day! You don't have to do that. But if you want to come over that would be great."

"I'll come for the whole thing! Don't worry. I heard you and Rick . . ."

"Yeah. It's the best thing. I'm soooo sorry Tammy. It was a mistake."

"You don't have to say that. I know it was." She's so confident! She continued, "I mean in the way that both of us thought it was totally over for me and Rick, and it just showed me that, and don't tell ANYONE this, promise?"

"Promise."

"It showed me that I wasn't over him yet, and that hurt, and I just couldn't be around you, and I did feel betrayed but that was just as much my fault, and now I really am OVER Rick after all that. I mean we're still friends but this time that really is all we are. And I don't know exactly what happened with you two but I do know that our friendship is more important than any boy, and it took me a while to see that. So I'm sorry too, and let's get over it and get right back to where our friendship left off."

My emotions are so not in control, GA, so I cried like usual. I felt really vulnerable crying in front of her, but she hugged me and it was a real hug, which made me cry even more. She trusted me so much, confessing that she still wasn't over him, and then what she said about our relationship being more important than any boy? It might not really be true but it was a wonderful thing to say! Don't you think?

It might even be true, Nicole. Friendship runs deep, and I can see how deep that friendship is with you two.

I don't know. She really likes boys. But let me tell you the last part of our visit. We talked for long time and I told her everything about Dad and Luke, except for the wetting his pants part. Everyone needs a little dignity reserved, don't you think? But we didn't talk about what happened with Rick. I think she knows a lot of it from him. Well, she might. . . .

I don't know. But I just told her it didn't work out and that we're supposed to be just friends, but I hadn't seen him at all and I was fine with that. Before she left she got quiet and emotional. She's like that. I love that about her.

"Nicole," she said, "Even though I can see that you're sick and the sickness has changed your face some, you still look beautiful. You really do."

"Thanks. I was planning on not going to school anymore because I'm feeling so ugly and people are staring at me. Actually, I'm not going back to school for a lot of reasons, like I just don't have the energy and I'm trying to simplify my life 'til after the operation."

"If you don't come to school I'll come see you. I could easily get lots of girls to come over if you want."

"No. I'm too tired for that. But if you want to come over, or if someone else asks about me and wants to come sometime, that would be really cool." It was awkward being torn between wanting to see a lot of people and also feeling exhausted by the idea of lots of loud, hyper conversation. Then she asked me something which seemed weird and out of place.

"Can I see you without your scarf?"

I looked back at her speechless.

"Trust me. I want to see the whole you."

"OK. But don't tell anyone how ugly I am. Promise?"

"Promise."

I stood up and unwrapped my beautiful purple scarf and it fell from my head. I smiled at Tammy and she smiled, and then we started giggling, and then laughing!!!!!!

"Nicole. It's beautiful! Your head is a perfect shape. You're beautiful."

Monday, October 22
Home Forever

I'm not going back to school. Not 'til this is over. I'm so out of it this morning, and even though I haven't gone to school in a week, I feel guilty because today is the first day I probably could go back and push myself through at least one more week.

Get real, Nicole! You're way too weak to go back. Resting is the best thing for you. You know that! You're taking care of yourself and there's nothing selfish about that.

I'm blank inside. This must be the tumor. Blank. Empty. Quiet. I'm going to take a nap.

Good. Take care of yourself.

Oh. I wanted to tell you that yesterday when Tammy was here, Luke came through the living room to get a soda from the kitchen and he saw me unwrap my scarf.

Is that unusual? He's seen you plenty of times without it.

I know, but he stopped just out of sight of Tammy and stared for a moment, then looked down like he was sad for me or in deep thought about it, and then he left. . . . I need to check in with him. Remind me later. Gotta take a nap. Tammy is coming over after school.

Tuesday, October 23
Afternoon

Checking in after another round of doctor visits. OK, so everyone's getting serious, like the doctor and Dad, and they set a date for November 9 for the operation. This is the first operation. There will be another probably. Like they are going to take out as much as they can and then do more chemo and radiation, but they may need to do another operation. I'm glad it's all happening, but it's scary. And, yes, I feel as sick as ever but I'm tired of talking about it. I'm sick of being sick!!!!!!!!! GA?

Yes.

Is there any way to change this?

What do you mean?

Is it possible to change this, even right now, into a happy ending?

Depends.

Depends on what?

You tell me.

You know how much I hate it when you say that. Can I get out of this predicament? Is there any way? In all the books I've read and shows and movies I've watched about guardian angels they always come in and save the day. So, is there a chance? Can you save the day?

Oh Nicole. You make me cry. I really love you so much. You know that. I would do anything for you. I'd turn your house to gold if given the chance, and I'd protect you from a hundred demons, carry you through any storm, and serve you in every way for a thousand years and more. I would do all those things. But I can't change this.

I appreciate it. I really do know you care. But what the hell? If you can do all that, you'd think you could cure some tiny brain. Mind you it's a good brain, but not that big of a deal, if you know what I'm getting at.

I would, Nicole, I would if that were the right thing to do. Sometimes healing someone at the last minute or creating a miracle that pulls them out of danger is exactly the right thing to do. It happens all the time. It has happened with you, many times, when you weren't even looking, that I jumped in and saved your butt. Sorry. But that's when it is called for and fits into the bigger plan and all that. This isn't one of those times. I wish it was, but it's not.

That sucks.

Yeah. It does.

I feel sick. The worst of it is waves of nausea every hour. I can't wait for it to go away.

I'm sorry.

Hey! Wait! From what you just said, it sounds like you know something I don't know. Like you know I'm going to die. I am going to die, aren't I? You just gave it away by that answer of yours. You said you can't save me so that must mean I'm going to die. And all this time you've been cheering me up for nothing!

Not true. Not at all true! I don't know if you are going to die! I told you that before and I promise you I am telling you the truth! I don't know what will happen in the future. Do you believe me? You must believe me.

Fine. I believe you. So what's up with the "I can't save you" line?

All I know is that me jumping in right now and reversing the natural course of these events is not part of the plan. I can't act on my own. I can't just decide to instantly cure you. If angels could do that then everyone would be cured of all diseases instantly.

What's wrong with that?

Really? Think about it. If angels could do whatever they wanted, any time they wanted, then no one would get sick, no one would get hurt, no one would die, no one would ever hurt anyone else, nothing bad would ever happen anywhere.

Sounds perfect.

Duh. We're back to the same old discussion we had before. If God can't step in and change things every time something went wrong, then why would angels be able to do that? It would make life a big joke. It would take away people's freedom. People would become angels' cute little playthings, like dolls, whom they'd manipulate in their make-believe dollhouse angel games.

OK, so I don't mean to get biblical on you, but my life is on the line here. God healed all kinds of people in the Bible. Hundreds got healed all at once. Jesus healed sick kids, blind people, lepers, and even raised people from the dead. Right?

Right.

So, why not me? Why not now?

I don't know.

Ouch!

Really. Maybe you will wake up tomorrow and be all better. More likely they will operate on you and remove that tumor and you will have a speedy and natural recovery. Isn't that a miracle in some ways?

I suppose. "The miracle of modern science." However, it does make you wonder why some people get to be healed and some people don't. Now I'm wondering why some people are born in poverty or are born into abusive families and so on, and some people are born with basically good homes and all their needs provided for. Even if you say it's all part of keeping people free, and making life a mystery for people, it still sucks for those who get the raw end of the deal.

Think of eternity. It's only a brief moment in this world compared to an eternity of happiness in heaven.

Right. The person who made that line up should have copyrighted it. He'd be a millionaire. I'm sure he was some monk with a great idea to help all those people dying from the Black Plague feel better. Believe me, I'm not falling back into some dark lapse of faith, rather I'm struggling to get it. Got that? The point is, and you can't argue with this, the point is that no matter how logical it is that God set it up this way, and even if people live happily ever after in some other dimension after death, and even if every person deals with pain and suffering in their own way and some can still find happiness even in their suffering, even with all that, it still sucks for the person going through it.

You have a point.

I knew it! I knew I'd get the best of you someday! OK. Now I can die. Cause you aren't going to save me, right? "Eat crap and then you die!" It's true. I bet no one made any money off of that one either.

You are losing your faith.

I am not! Just because I got you to agree with me doesn't mean you can start pointing fingers at me. I've never had more faith. I know you might find that hard to believe, but it's true.

Well, I'll take your word for it.

In fact, I think part of the reason I can't be miraculously saved is that if I were suddenly pulled out of this, all I've learned in the last months with you would be for nothing. It would make it all useless. All the insights, memories, treasures both old and new, would lose their value with the wave of a wand. Being cured like that would mock the world, me, you, God. It would be like a TV movie where at the end someone runs in from nowhere and saves the day. It would be like, "What? Why did I even watch that movie? That ending sucked!" So, um, thanks for not saving me? I don't know. I'd rather live than die, of course. Who wouldn't? But you know what I mean. I'm trying to be grateful no matter what happens, I suppose.

Look. I might get orders to save you, so don't get mad if that happens. On the other hand, after all we talked about, I hope you know that however it works out you are going to be just fine. Isn't that the point? You know it is. But let me do my job and you do yours. I don't know what that means anymore, but let's try. OK?

Maybe it means we should just be ourselves. I guess that's all we can be.

And my guess is if we do that, everything else will take care of itself.

And us.

Exactly.

I can't do that.

I'm not sure I can either. But let's try.

Tuesday, October 23
Late at Night

It's been a hard life. I think about the pain in the world and see that life is hard for everyone. Pain is easy when it's my pain, but unbearable when it's someone else's pain, I mean those I love so much.

You are a very loving person, Nicole. Your words sound angelic.

Maybe I'm getting ready to come to the other side. I hope not. But now that I'm here in this place I feel so much love and grief, and I can't stop crying. It's a hard life and a beautiful life. I am thinking mainly of Luke. I can't live with the pain he will go through. He's so innocent, so sensitive. It's hard. So hard.

In this place you must believe that he will be OK.

I just want to die right now. I can't hold his pain.

Believe that God is taking care of him, not just because that will make you feel better, but because it's the truth. It's the truth. God loves him. God is big and strong and great, and you know better than anyone that this life is just a brief moment in eternity, and it's a drop in the ocean compared to the eternity you will all experience and enjoy together. It's true, Nicole.

I'm trying to believe.

And to take that power away from God and somehow think that Luke is going to be on his own in some private hell apart from God's love is just robbing God of his greatness. It's a slap in his face. God has a plan for Luke, a big plan, if not soon, then soon enough; if not now, then in eternity.

Oh, I need to breathe and sigh and breathe. My nose is so stuffed up and my face is all wet. I'm locked in here hoping no one will come in and see me like this. I've got to stay in here 'til the tears dry, and my eyes aren't so red that everyone knows I've been bawling my eyes out.

If you must. Remember, God is in charge. You don't need to take on others' burdens. The Great Big Force of Love will do that. You love him so much no wonder you're crying, and it's really tender to see you cry like this. It's good. Don't get me wrong, it's good to cry, and it's because you love. But take it one step further, if possible, Nicole. Trust.

I'm having déjà vu. Weird.

Trust.

In what?

In LIFE. In the WAY life works. Trust in the vastness of the universe and its underlying currents bringing all to fulfillment.

Sounds very Eastern, dude.

What's wrong with that? There's a lot of truth in those religions. I could say, "Trust in providence." But that's such a buzz phrase.

You must be one of the most PC angels ever to do service in the heavens! What is your problem? Just tell it like it is! . . . Sorry.

I am! I see you're feeling a little better, if not a little pesky.

I suppose I am. So I feel sorry for interrupting you. It was good stuff. Trust in LIFE, and in the current of the universal love thingy. Right?

Close enough. There is an invisible current that leads to all things good, that leads to resolution, that leads to the Source of all that is, and all that is blessed. This is God. See? I said it before you had a chance to mock me.

Yeah.

Surrender to the Force.

Now you're sounding like Star Wars.

Let the current take you to the Source, and your brother, and all that you love. Let the current take you HOME.

I'd like to say that I'm very moved by your words. I'm actually feeling somewhat numb at the moment, no double-entendre intended.

Let's see, "double-entendre: a word or phrase having a double meaning, especially when the second meaning is risqué." I'd say that your use of that word is at the very best a stretch. But I get what you mean. Like emotionally numb and physically numb, right?

Yeah. Maybe even "Numb and Number." Or if we were in a movie together it could be called "Numb and Dumber."

I don't get it.

Exactly. Thanks for sharing today. I am again going to throw up, unfortunately. Comes with the territory. I think I'll appreciate your words when I come back and read them again, maybe tomorrow. 'Bye Angel.

'Bye Nicole.

Wednesday, October 24

Wow, GA! It gets boring not going to school! They make the homework easy, and things are terribly quiet here when Tammy isn't over. All this quiet time has given me a chance to reflect on what still needs to be done.

What do you mean?

What's left to do? Like, I'm getting too weak to do much of anything. I'm thinking, "what's left that I want to do while I can?" I wouldn't mind seeing the lake again. And I do want to go back down to the graveyard to see Mom's grave one more time. I have to do that for some reason. And I need to do that soon, like this weekend, or I might not be able to get down there by myself if I wait any longer than that.

Why don't you get someone to go down with you? Maybe your dad would drive you down?

Possible . . . but that is way too dramatic for Dad. Tammy would do it. She loves drama. It would be awesome if Luke came. I don't know if he's ever been there since Mom died.

Oh yeah. You wanted me to remind you to check in with him. How is he?

Same. Well, same old computer issues. He's stopped playing with Danny so he's home more. Yes, I did stop paying him to go out. That sort of backfired, didn't it? I do feel like there's something more I could be doing with him though. Every time I try to talk to him he blows me off. It would be wonderful if I could get him to go on a walk to the graveyard with me. But he'd never do that! Hmmm . . . What to do?

Why don't you write him a letter like you did for your Dad?

I still haven't given Dad that letter. I'm hesitant to make any waves because things have been going so well. But with Luke, I think it would be easier writing and giving him the letter right away. He might not read it, but I could do it just the same.

Could be good therapy for you whether he reads it or not. Right?

Oh. If he doesn't read it, I'll read it to him while he's chained there to his computer! I like the idea a lot. There's so much I want to say to him, and if I write it I can say it just the way I want. Let me think about this. . . .

October 24

Dear Luke,

I wanted to write to you in case anything happens to me and I don't get better. I know you know I love you, and I so very much know you love me, even though you may have a hard time expressing that when you are playing on your computer. Don't forget that I will always love you forever and ever.

Now, I want to share with you a few things. Take them or leave them. They are things I think are valuable to know, and will help you in time. This is your older sister's wisdom coming at you all at once, but it shouldn't be very hard to take because you can read it a bit at a time.

1. God. God is real and God is very loving. Believe in God, and God is pure love so that's not so hard to believe in. God wants you to do the right thing, always, as much as you can. And when you can't, don't worry, God will be there and take you back again. God never leaves. God is there even when bad things happen to you. Believe me. I know.

2. Angels. Angels are real. I have a guardian angel who talks to me. He's real. I hear you have a guardian angel too. Actually, I hear you have many, apparently. That's good, and I have heard from my guardian angel that one of them really does come to you when you call. That's cool. You probably already know this, but I wanted you to know that I know this.

3. Life. Life is a mystery. It's a beautiful mystery, an adventure. It doesn't matter how long you live as long as you live it to the fullest. One day of wonder and action can make for an eternity of happiness. I know this. Try to pull yourself away from that damned computer. Maybe you can't do that all the time, but

just once. Try it once. Turn it off and walk down to the lake. Open your eyes and see all that the Great Big Powerful Force of the Universe has put there for you to see. Drink it in, bathe in it. I'm not talking about the lake. I'm talking about the beauty of it all. And then go back and play your computer. And then . . . do it again. In fact, next time you go to school do the same thing with people. Open your eyes. See them. See all the wonderful kinds of people and all they have to offer. Imagine that God loves them just as much as you and me. Imagine how special it must be to be them. Now, do something good for these people. I don't mean just once. I mean get a job! Do something useful with your life! Do something that makes a difference! They will appreciate it, but even more than this, you will too. When you love others and show that love by helping people, it all comes together. That happiness returns back to you, and more than you started with. It just keeps growing. I know this. I'm standing at the door of heaven and I have seen this.

4. BTW heaven is real. And you know, it's not corny to believe in it. It's right here now, in all the goodness inside and around all of us. And after we die we don't just disappear. We may feel like we are going to, but we don't. We live. I know this. I've had many discussions with my guardian angel about this. Many of those discussions were debates. And I have concluded not only from our conversations, and not only from the fact that there must be a heaven if I'm talking to an angel, but also because I feel it in my soul (and you

can too, if you don't already) that we will never die. Love can never die. We will all be together in heaven. Believe this. It not only makes life easier, it's true. And when you get there, if I beat you there, I will say very proudly and very obnoxiously, "I told you so."

5. Everything has a reason and meaning behind it. I don't know what those reasons are all the time. Turns out no one does, not even angels. But there ARE reasons, and part of our adventure is to figure out what they are, and when we can't figure them out, to accept that there is something higher going on that we just don't understand with our little peon minds. Look at the stars. Feel small. And in that feeling know that you have a huge part in all of this. It's true. Welcome to the universe. You are akin to all that is. (That's actually a quote from somewhere.)

6. I could go on and on, but I am actually surprising myself at how deep I can get, and I think I sound very wise, so I don't want to blow that by going into detail about a lot of other things. As for sex, drugs, rock and roll: don't use people, or drugs, and rock the world as much as you can! OK. I'm already getting trite.

7. I have decided I am going to copy this note and give it to you now. Don't show it to anyone. If I die, share it with people, if you want.

Luke, I don't know how to close this letter. Maybe I'll close with a story about your favorite animals. I know you're too old for this anymore, but somehow I think this is an important thing for you to remember—how I told you those stories at night and helped you get to sleep. Remember me,

that just like then I will always be there when you need me.
Just pretend it's you and me a few years back. You're lying in
your bed, and I'm lying on the floor with my head propped
up on Tigger, and surrounded by his stuffed animal friends.
As we quiet down we can hear the crickets outside on a warm
summer night. We both breathe in the summer air, and I
begin the story. Here goes:

Tigger, Cutie, Linus, and Modie were sitting around playing with clay one day when suddenly this paper airplane fell
from the sky. It hit Cutie right in the head. "What the hell?"
exclaimed Cutie. "Cutie!" barked Tigger, "Don't swear! But
what on earth hit you in the head?" They all looked and saw
that it was a note, formed into a paper airplane, and it must
have come from miles away, because it was written in a different language. They had never seen that language before
so they took the note to Professor Pliposy. (Remember him?)
And he put on his big round glasses and looked at it and
looked at it, and said, "Oh . . ." and "I see." Modie asked
Professor Pliposy what he saw. And he replied, "I see you
have a piece of paper here, with writing on it." Cutie blurted
out, "Duh prof—" but was stopped in mid-sentence when
Linus stuffed a big apple in Cutie's mouth to shut him up.
"What's it about?" asked Modie. "It's written in ant language.
It's from your brother Freddy. He's been kidnapped by Gendor, and he says, 'I'm here with five princesses. Life isn't so
bad. In fact, it's kind of good being stuck in a tower with
these beautiful creatures.'" Before Cutie could say anything
Tigger stuffed another apple in his mouth. "The letter continues," said Professor Pliposy. "It says, 'Life wouldn't be so
bad if they weren't planning to ship us all off to the planet
Bop-bop-bop-petulia tomorrow.'" Well, Luke, you know

they got out that old magic carpet and headed off to Gendor Land. And you can guess what happened. Yep. They rescued Freddy, and the princesses, and they all got married and lived happily ever after. I know I cut to the end quickly and this story is shorter than it should be. But Luke, that's just how life is sometimes.

God bless you always. I love you with all my heart.

Nicole

Thursday, October 25
Morning

Luke read the letter I wrote him. I gave it to him last night and he put it by his computer and kept on playing. So I left and came back later, and I could see that he had opened it.

What happened next?

I asked him if he read it. He just kept playing computer.

Kids are like that. He's too young to understand.

No. He kept looking at the computer screen and didn't stop hitting the keys but he did say, "Thanks." And then I could see that he was smiling as he intently played his game.

See. He got it!

Wait. I turned to leave and he mumbled something to me. I turned back and asked him if he were saying something to me. He said, "I have a surprise for you tomorrow." He just kept playing. I asked him what it was several times, and he blew me off. He kept playing his game.

That sounds exciting. He probably made you something.

That's what I was thinking. He's really good at electronic stuff. He might have bought me something. I hope he didn't steal it.

He wouldn't do that.

No, he wouldn't. I can't think of what it would be. I really don't need anything. The only thing I can think of is he's going to clean his room and act like that's a big present for me.

Would it be?

It would be, actually. It would show me he was listening, and learning. That's too much to ask. I'm thinking more that he's going to make me a cake, or brownies, or get me breakfast in bed this morning. That's it! He's capable of doing that.

I suppose we will just have to wait.

Can't you sneak in there and see what he might be planning? I know. You'll say it's against the rules. But it would really help me see that you care and that you really do exist.

Oh, Nicole. You are so insulting to me. You have doubts I exist after all this time? I don't know what else to do.

Go find out what Luke is planning. Go on. That would make me happy.

I doubt that very much, but I will, just to show you I can.

Good. You gone yet?

No.

Why not?

Give me a second!

You're such a phony!

OK. That's it. I'm not going to do it because you called me a phony. Go find out yourself!

I'm sorry. You know I can't do that. Please?

No. You'll have to be surprised. That's the best thing anyway.

Please?

Learn patience, Nicole, patience.

Thursday, October 25
Afternoon

So, no surprise from Luke but I had a weird conversation with Tammy.

Yeah?

She asked me if I'd go to a Halloween party with her on Wednesday.

She's being nice.

I know, but I said like, "No way!" And she seemed like she really wanted me to go even if I felt funny about it because it would be good to see people.

Yep. Very true.

I said to her, "What would I dress up as? Myself?" I was making a joke but she said that would be a good idea, that I could just go as myself and didn't have to dress up. I guess I took that as an insult, but maybe she didn't mean I didn't need to dress up because I already look like a freak. That's how I felt when she said it, but I think she was just saying I didn't even need to dress up if I didn't want to.

Are you going to go?

No way!!!!!!!! I told her even if I wanted to I would feel overwhelmed going to a party like that. She seemed really disappointed but she accepted it. She was just trying to be helpful, right?

I really believe that's all she was doing. She's gotten so nice.

I know. So I did ask her if she'd go to the cemetery with me on Saturday and help me get back if I was having trouble, or we could call for a ride. She seemed kind of perturbed that

I would want to do that, but not go to the party. But I said it was something I promised myself I would do before I had the operation, and that she would be helping me get down there in case I got tired or too dizzy and ended up walking in circles because of the brain tumor. Ha ha!

And?

She said she would.

Thursday, October 25
Evening

Guess what? Guess what?

What?

You are not going to believe this! I can't believe it!

Tell me.

I can't believe he did it! And he did it for me!!!!!!!

OK, I give up. What happened?

Luke shaved his head!

He shaved his head?

He did, for me.

He shaved his head for you?

He said, "You shouldn't have to look like that all by your-self. Wait 'til you see what I'm going to do." Then he came back and his head was shaved!

That's the sweetest thing I've ever heard!

It really shows that even if he spent the last three years in front of a computer he must have been thinking of me at least some. It must mean some of my caring about him and pestering him got through! Don't you think?

Yes. Definitely.

And he said that when he saw me unwrapping my scar and showing my bald head to Tammy, he felt like that was brave of me. I think that's because he knows Tammy really well because of all the time she's spent over here since we were children, and that she could have embarrassed me by making some rude fashion statement about my head and hurt my feelings. But I showed her anyway.

I agree with him. It was brave of you and it's brave of him as well. And it shows how much he really does care for you.

I know. (Smile)

How does your dad feel about it?

He doesn't know yet. Ha ha. Luke is so cool! I love him.

Friday, October 26
Evening

Been recovering all day from treatments. Dad helps me back to the car after chemo. I get really weak and it seems like I'm dizzy all the time now. But with all that I was wrong about how everything would turn to hell before the operation.

What do you mean?

I thought I'd feel worse and worse. But I don't. I'm sick but it's not getting to me like it did before. Not today, anyway.

Wonderful!

I feel better than I did two weeks ago! I'm getting a short reprieve. Is that the right word? Don't bother looking it up. At this moment I feel only a little pain, and for a Friday not as nauseous as some Fridays. I can move my neck more than yesterday, and the fog has lifted for the moment. Still some numbness, dizziness comes and goes. Oh, now I notice my

ll screwed up, but you can't have everything. I

py for you.

dn't yell at Luke. He did a double take when Luke
d in. LOL. He asked Luke, "What's up with the shaved
ad?" Luke said, "I'm supporting Nicole."

And?

Dad just said, "Oh. OK." And then he asked if they were
OK with it at school. Luke said, "I don't really care." And
Dad left it at that. I think Luke must have talked to someone
because they wouldn't have ignored him. The school can get
very uptight. I think they gave their consent to him doing this
or we'd know about it. That's so cool! I'm cold. That's good.
It's good to feel anything.

I'll get you a blanket.

Don't bother. I'll get one myself. But I would have loved
to see you lift your finger just once for me before I die.

Nicole.

I'm just being a pest. I always get this way when I feel
good. I wish every day was like this. I cornered Luke and
asked him to help me get down to the graveyard with Tammy
tomorrow. He said OK. Then I told him I wanted to go to
Mom's grave and he just looked at me, like a double take, and
then said OK again and that was it. Dad was sitting at the
kitchen table when I mentioned this to Luke.

What did he say?

"Pass me the salt"? JK. He said, "If you get too tired to
walk back give me a call and I'll come pick you up." I don't
know what's going to happen when I get down there but I
can't wait. Even if we were going somewhere else like to a

park or something, I'd still be thrilled because both Tamm
and Luke are going with me!

<hr>

Saturday, October 27
Evening

<hr>

I dropped the letter I wrote to Dad on his dresser before
the three of us—Luke, Tammy and I—left for the cemetery. I
wanted him to get that letter, or at least have that letter before
I talked to Mom at the graveyard. He was downstairs watching TV. I thought he might have seen me sneak in there.

Tammy came on time at 1:00 p.m., and she said that she
wanted to see that Barry Stevens grave I had told her about,
and that her dad told her she had some relatives down there
too, near the old part of the graveyard. So she was going to
check that out. I think that was her way of telling me that
she would leave me alone if I wanted her to when we got to
Mom's grave.

When we went in to get Luke out of his room I was surprised that he wasn't sitting in front of his computer. He had
his jacket on, with his hood over his head, ha ha, and was just
standing in his room like ready to go. So we went. On the
way out the door Dad reminded us that if we needed a ride
to call and said, "Don't push it, Nicole." I liked that. See?
He cares.

He does. Very much!

It was a crisp day today but not really cold. It felt good to
get outside, and not just see the colorful leaves falling from
my observation post at the window, but experience them falling all around as we walked down the road toward the lake

...d right to walk around. The lake was peaceful, ...e, and I felt it was greeting me and giving me ...nfort just feeling its peace. It's hard to explain. ...cired as we walked by the familiar spot where I ...wade and watch the fishermen, and we rested there a ...ment, and rested several times on our trip. I expected that Luke would be fairly patient with me but Tammy was even more caring and would ask again and again if I needed to rest as we approached our destination.

She's grown so much.

When we cleared the first grove of trees and the graveyard appeared before us Luke stopped and asked, "Where's Mom's grave?" It was still a distance away, but with the many leaves fallen from the trees I could see it clearly through the bare branches. I said, "It's down there," and pointed toward the lower half of the cemetery. Tammy asked about where the older part of the graveyard was, and I pointed to the right and told her it was down there, and that's where she'd find that little boy's grave as well. Everyone hesitated at that point and looked at me. "Do you want us to go down there with you?" Tammy asked. I looked over at Luke. He said, "Yeah. I wanna see it." So I nodded and we made our way down there.

Luke is so brave.

I can't believe how different I felt this time than the last time when I couldn't go to Mom's grave. I was really tired already, like usual, but I felt so much support. I didn't feel that loneliness I felt the first time. I was there with a team, a family! WE were going there. We walked right to it and stared quietly for what seemed like a long time. The gravesite was covered with a blanket of yellow and reddish leaves from the large maple standing right next to it. All the graves were covered in this magnificent blanket. After a few moments Luke walked up and started pushing the leaves away. At first he used his feet like two rakes, pushing the leaves from side to side. But then I got down on my knees and started clearing the leaves away with my hands, and he got down and joined me immediately. Tammy watched. I don't know why we cleared the leaves off because they were quite beautiful, but there was something about brushing everything away from around the stone that felt important and healing. I could tell Luke felt the same way.

When we were finished Luke stood up again. Tammy broke the silence with a little more than a whisper and said she was going to go check out the old graves and look for her relatives. Luke looked at her, and then Luke looked at me, sort of like he didn't know what to do at this point and was looking for direction. Tammy asked, "Wanna come?" He smiled and nodded, and just before they walked away he glanced back one more time at the stone, and then at me, and then they both turned and walked away toward the older graves about a hundred yards away.

I knelt there and just listened to the silence. Someone was using a leaf blower on the other side of the creek in the development not too far away, but the distant noise of the blower contrasted with the silence of the graveyard and somehow made it even seem more still and silent where I knelt. At first I thought about Mom when she was alive, and some great memories flashed over me, most of them I've told you about in this journal. Her wonderful smell came back to me and mixed with the slight pungent smell of the rotting pieces of wood and fallen leaves all around. Breathing that and the fresh air in felt like breathing in all the good things of both heaven and earth at the same time. I blurted out in a whisper without even thinking, "Thanks Mom." I don't even know why I was thanking her, but it felt right.

I finally just sat on the ground in front of her stone because my legs were tired of kneeling and I just let all the thoughts and feelings I had inside come and go in this place of peace. I felt no sadness. Just peace, and a little fear still. I reflected on the fact that Mom wasn't really there but at the same time knew that I had come here for a reason, and perhaps that reason was to get in touch with both the Mom we left behind at this place and the one I wanted so much to see in heaven. Sensing that fear inside made me realize that I had come to ask Mom for help in making that fear go away. She had gotten through it, so she could help me get through it. Even if I have to go through that door of death I could do it if she helped me. Somehow because she had died, death could be easier for me. I know that doesn't make a lot of sense. It's hard to explain. Maybe all I'm saying is that as I sat there I realized how much I still needed my mom.

So . . . let me wipe my tears . . . thanks . . . So I started talking to her.

"Mom. I need your help. You were always strong. I believe you are even stronger now in heaven. I need that from you. I know I must have it in me somewhere, because I'm your daughter. I came from you. I don't understand all that's happening. I can't. It doesn't make sense. So I just need to be able to be strong, and be brave, and to believe! I need help . . . to believe in me!"

Did she answer you?

Yes. From that cold earth below my broken body I got the sense that everything that happens here is small and insignificant compared to . . . what's really important. And I'm not sure how to describe what that is. But the quietness around the grave just made me feel like these problems I've been facing are nothing compared to the vastness of heaven, earth, everything! And then I heard her speak, not from the grave, but from deep inside of me. It wasn't you or some other angel, because it came from inside the core of my soul. I could feel it right down here. "Be strong!" That's what she said. "Be strong!" Even though it was a simple reply I knew what she meant, and I knew I could do that. So I said, "Thanks." I took a big breath and got up. I went to leave but I felt like there was one more thing I had to do. I wanted to leave her something, some tribute. I didn't know what. I didn't have anything in my pockets but my cell phone. I wasn't going to leave that. Then it came to me. So I did it.

What did you do?

I dug a little hole with my hands, just a little two-inch-deep hole on top of her grave. I brushed off my hands, reached up and unraveled my scarf, kissed it, and set it in the hole and buried it there.

I'm crying.

Me too. I stood up and walked away. I was finished there. As I made my way over to Luke and Tammy, I saw out of the corner of my eye that someone was standing at the top of the hill at the edge of the graveyard. My eyes are so bad now I couldn't see who it was, but Luke shouted, "Dad!" And then Dad started down the incline and as he approached I saw a piece of paper in his hand. I knew it was my letter.

I thought so.

He came right down and picked me up off my feet with the biggest hug I have ever experienced in my life! He didn't say anything. He didn't need to. His warm tears down my neck told me all I needed to know. Luke and Tammy came running over and he hugged them too. I thought Tammy would die, but she seemed to be OK with it. Then he sighed and looked at Mom's grave and smiled, and then we walked up the hill to Dad's car.

What happened next? I'm dying to know. What happened?
We went to Taco Bell.

❊   ❊   ❊

OK, it didn't happen quite like this. But I wanted to write the poem anyway, and use a little creative license. I can do that! It's my story!

Reunion

My father found me today.
He found me sitting on the grass
One more time by the water.
This time he didn't call out.
He didn't talk.
He picked me up
As if I were a baby once again,
His baby.
And he hugged me
As if there would be no tomorrow.
His tears wet my ear and cheek
And the warm water from his face
Trickled down my neck and back.

He said nothing
As he carried me on his shoulder
All the way through the woods
And fields, and roadway
To his house, to our house, our home.
Dad did that today.
I'm not waking from a dream!
Dad did that today,
He carried his little girl all the way home.

There are no words to end this poem, or to express even a small portion of the gratitude in my heart. I have lived for this day. I have lived.

N. M. B.

Sunday, October 28
Morning

They're all asleep.

It's 7:20 a.m.! Of course they're asleep! It's Sunday! Why are you awake?

Can't sleep. Woke up and can't go back to sleep. Angel?

Yes?

It's Sunday. How about a little church? Can you sing me another verse of "Amazing Grace"? Any verse will do.

My pleasure.
The Lord has promised good to me.
His word my hope secures.
He will my shield and portion be,
As long as life endures.

Monday, October 29
Evening

I was watching Luke play his computer game today. It's a game that people play together on the Internet. Thousands of people all play at the same time.

Tell me more.

I don't know a whole lot about it, but I know that you work hard and get magic powers, and you are part of a community of real people, and Luke is like some big shot in this game.

Really?

Yeah. He plays all the time. I mean *all* the time!

How do you feel about that?

I've been really concerned, as you know. But the more I watched I saw that there is a lot of interaction in this game, and you can be a bad person or a good person, and you can help people or hurt them. Luke's one of the good people. He's a leader. Can you believe it? At his age, like all these people follow him in this game!

Hmmmm.

Yeah. Exactly. So I was thinking, what is reality anyway? Like, in the real world Luke is just another kid stuck on the computer. But in this world, he's a hero. Ha ha. Maybe that's really pathetic. But . . .

But somehow that brings you comfort? Doesn't it?

I don't know why, but it does. He may be a computer geek, but at least in this world of geeks he's a hero. My hope is someday he'll turn off the computer and do something in this world. Actually, it's more than a hope. But I have to let go. I guess watching him helped me see there's something good in it. I don't know. I mean what is reality? Really? If everyone ends up in a different world playing out life together, working together, making choices, becoming a villain or a hero . . . then, does it really matter what world we're in?

Interesting thoughts.

Ha ha. I'm crazy.

Sometimes.

Tuesday, October 30
Night

I told Luke about my theory. He said I was delusional, that people who spend all their time on the computer need to have real lives and do something useful. He's so smart.

He takes after you.

Thanks. When he stops playing computer I'll believe you.

How are you?

I'm sick.

I know.

Yeah. But happy. What other choice do I have?

Um . . .

OK, I mean, I'm happy. What else would I ever want to be? Really. That's what I mean.

I hear you.

Yep. Sick and happy.

I'm proud of you for that. It didn't just happen. You did that.

You know, between the barfing and diarrhea, life isn't so bad. I can't wait to get better. I think I might get better. I'm going to play this like it's the end, but I think you are going to pull off that miracle in that operating room.

I'm glad that you have hope. Hope can bring miracles. But why do you have to play it, as you say, like it's the end? You mean you need to go in there thinking you won't come out? Why?

I don't know, GA. I don't know why. I don't want to be fooled, I guess. I'd rather be surprised. I'm tired. I'm so tired. *And sick.*

So very sick . . . It won't be long now.

Wedne∂day, October 31
Halloween — Late

Oh, Angel! I'm so stunned!!!!! I can't believe it!!!!! So, remember when Tammy invited me to that Halloween party?

Yep. That would have been tonight.

That's right. And I said I didn't want to go, and she looked disappointed and like she had something up her sleeve, or was hiding something, because she really wanted me there way more than normal and all that?

I remember something like that.

Guess what??????

What??????

At about ten o'clock she banged on the door and led in a group of friends. She had a scarf over her head! All at once she took it off and started jumping up and down and hugging me and screaming with excitement. She had shaved her head!!!!!!!!!!

NO!!!!!!!!!!

Yes!!!! And then Rick, yes RICK, and Lauren and Skye, and Lianne, and Pete, and Ruthie, and even Emily all dropped their hoods and towels from their heads and they had all shaved their heads too!!!!!

Really?

And everyone was screaming and jumping up and down and hugging me like we had just won the Super Bowl!!!!!!!!

Oh, Nicole! What does that tell you?

You can see right now what that tells me. Look at me. I'm a wreck! In a good way! I'm speechless. I didn't know. I didn't know people would do that for me!

Yes. They did it for you.

It changes everything! Everything! I'm not going try to figure this one out. It's something I just want to feel. I just want to let it in. I do have friends and they do get it! They get it and I didn't think they did! I didn't think they cared. But they do! A lot of people really do! I am loved! I truly am loved!

Friday, November 2
Evening

I'm hoping this will be the last time I have to go through this.

What do you mean? You know you're going to have chemo for a long time after the operation.

Just imagining, hoping, praying.

Sunday, November 4

Hi GA. It's Sunday and you know what that means?

"Amazing Grace"? Which verse? I can never remember the middle verses of that song.

Um, let me look it up on the Internet. . . . Back. This is next:

> *Yea, when this flesh and heart shall fail,*
> *And mortal life shall cease,*
> *I shall possess within the veil,*
> *A life of joy and peace.*

OK. Let's do it together.

> *Yea, when this flesh and heart shall fail,*
> *And mortal life shall cease,*
> *I shall possess within the veil,*
> *A life of joy and peace.*

Thank you.

Anytime.

Sort of hits home today.

Yes. It does.

Sunday, November 4
Evening

I'm feeling much better tonight, which isn't that great, but I do feel like talking. The operation is Friday and I have a little more to chat about before then.

Sounds good. I love to talk.

Something you said has been sticking with me. It was about going with the flow. I like that idea. Even if all things seem to fall apart, it's there, pulling things together again.

The flow.

Yeah. I've seen that, GA. I'm envisioning a wreck after a storm, or massive destruction after a flood, and trying to picture how it can flow into something good. . . . Not sure

I can see it anymore. . . . It's funny how life is. I feel sometimes I can find myself climbing through the dark clouds and getting a glimpse of the light, and then just when I think I understand, it's back into the clouds. Like sometimes I just about get it, and then there's some part that doesn't make any sense at all.

I know what you mean. It can feel that way sometimes.

The closer I get to understanding life, the more I realize I don't understand it at all. It can't be put in a box, or made into a formula, or explained in an equation. I want it to make sense, and it just about does, but then . . . I know. It's like a puzzle. I feel like I've been able to put so many pieces together to see the whole picture, but now when I get down to the last two puzzle pieces, they don't fit. They definitely belong to the puzzle but they don't fit anywhere! Like I've squeezed some other puzzle piece in somewhere it doesn't go. I have to take the whole thing apart and start again.

So what does that tell you?

Not sure. Life is a puzzle and it can't be solved? That may be the first thing I've learned. Thinking that over, I don't believe that though. It must be solvable. Life is a puzzle too big for anyone to solve on their own?

That certainly is true. It's been so heartwarming to see you so close to Luke and your father, and Tammy too. And look at all the support you've gotten!

Believe me, I'm so content and so grateful for that, but there's still so much I don't understand, and even that connection with the people I care about doesn't seem to completely solve the puzzle.

What is the puzzle, Nicole?

Life. I said that, didn't I?

But what is the question you need answered right now?

You mean, before I go? Before I die?

What do you need to know? What's the question deep inside?

The question? Will everything be alright?

Oh. Will you live?

No. Will everything be alright for all of us, forever?

Deep.

Will everything make sense one day? Will everything fit together in some grand plan in time? Is there a grand plan?

Know what I'm thinking? The way you're looking at it there is no answer. You're right. The puzzle doesn't fit together that way. There is another way, which has to do with that flow. It's not in any formula or equation, but it's just as real.

I'm thinking about what you're saying and you're on to something. It could be that the answer to the puzzle is to accept the puzzle. In order to understand I must accept that there is a mystery to my life, and I must accept the mystery.

There's magic in that.

I feel it. So, built right into this world is a part that will never be fully comprehended or understood, or solved like a puzzle.

That's what makes life special.

It's very against how I think. I want to understand everything. I want to believe it can all be mapped out and explained. But there are parts on the map that will always remain blank, or apparently what the Pirates of the Caribbean call the "world's end." There really is a place like that. . . . There always will be.

So what do you need to do?

Accept the mystery. Let the understood float away at the end, and allow myself to be lifted up into the mystery, to be carried away.

To fly?

To fly without effort, without mapping the skies. Now I get it when people look into the starry night and feel so small, but that feeling so small feels good, because it's all about how much we don't know. And somehow, teetering on the edge of the world, that's a comfort.

Monday, November 5

So, GA. What will you do if I die?

Retire.

Can angels really retire?

Well, we can switch jobs. There are plenty of other jobs to do. This one wears on you after a while. If you die, I will definitely take a huge vacation to show you around and get better acquainted.

You better! But really GA, this might be one of the last times I write you. And I want to confess something to you, and also thank you.

OK. Do whatever you need to do, but remember, I'm in this for the long haul, and I'll be here with you forever.

Somehow I know that's true, deep inside. I know. And maybe that's why I have to say this. I confess sometimes I wondered, and I'm sorry, if you really ever helped me. I've heard so much about guardian angels and seen so many movies where the angel comes in and changes things and saves the day and all that, and there were many times I thought you might do that. And I was at first disappointed that you didn't and then kind of pissed.

Yeah. I know.

Like I used to think, "What kind of angel is this? He's not doing anything!"

I know. Sometimes I could hear you thinking that, even though you didn't say it. It's OK. It really is.

No it's not. Because it's not true. What I realized, Angel, is that you may not have come running in and waved your hand over my cancer and cured me, or taken a magic wand and turned Aunt Melinda into a toad, or picked up Luke and Dad and dropped them into a therapy session together, or slapped Rick upside the head when he slept and got him to come over and apologize to me, or make Tammy see her part in our troubles or what else?

Oh, I'm sure there are many more things I didn't do.

Yeah, but I realized even though you didn't do those things, you did.

I did?

OK. You didn't cure me but you gave me a life, by helping me figure out how to live. You got Rick and Tammy and Aunt Melinda and who knows who else, maybe Luke and Dad, HEY . . . and ME, and everyone to wake up and grow up. But you did it somehow without anyone knowing or seeing, or pushing them, or making some miracle happen that would force them to do the right thing, to care, to love.

Why do you think I did that?

Because they all changed. I've seen it. I have experienced it. I'm living it. Even if I do die I have lived to see this. That's a miracle for me, because you got me to see and feel all this at sixteen years old! And you did this in a matter of weeks! OK, maybe months, but that's got to be a record! Don't you think? So, for all that, I just want to say . . . thank you.

Nicole. I want to thank you.

Oh, don't be such an angel! I'm thanking *you*!

OK. I accept your thanks. And you're right. I did play a big part in helping you and all these people grow. I hope that's OK to say. I did, but do you know how? I helped you make all these things happen. I listened to you, encouraged you, prodded you, and even yelled at you sometimes.

Did you?

Well, maybe not yell. But what I'm saying is that I was there to support you, and you are most welcome for thanking me. But there's a bigger truth here. You are the one who decided not to give up, who decided you were going to grab on to life and not let go until you could understand and make something of it. You have grown so much, Nicole, and you have that strength that your mother whispered about inside of you when she said, "Be strong." Your body's been growing weak, but the real you on the inside has been growing stronger every day, and even though you may feel ugly on the outside, inside you've become more and more beautiful.

Really?

I can see it! Yes. It's true! And if you look at the people in your life and how much they've woken up from a place of numbness or hurt, or just being asleep inside, and how they've grown, you helped them do that. Luke basically even confessed that he could be brave because you were brave. I think that goes a lot deeper than shaving his head. You've shown him that he can face the world. You've shown him that if you can face death then he can face life. I know that. I can see that in him.

Really?

Yes! You showed your dad that you were not going to lie down and die emotionally like he had been doing, that you weren't going to stay in some fantasy that everything was OK when things were turning awful and out of control with his drinking and all the selfish, irresponsible, and irrational stuff that comes with it. You said, "NO! I won't let that happen." You told him you loved him and would not let it all end in a horrible mess of waste. And he heard you.

He did!

Yeah, and he woke up from his misery and all that self-pity and he saw the real you. He saw his daughter for who she is, the one who would not give up, and he woke up and loved her. In fact, he always loved her, but you broke his shell, and then he chose to let that love pour out through those cracks and finally break open and burst forth for you, and Luke! And do I have to go on? Look back at what you wrote yourself, about Tammy and Rick. Loverboy had to stop his hormonal high and consider the big picture, higher things, more important things, because you showed him how important those things are to you. Tammy went from a stuck-up little priss—

Are you allowed to say stuff like that?

Not sure but it feels good. So, she went from that to . . . well, being a lot less of a stuck-up little priss.

No, she changed a lot. She's been so loving.

I know. It's true. And I'm not saying you made her like that any more than I'm saying I made you what you've become for yourself, but I am saying that you showed her what a deeper person looks like. You didn't give up on her. You called her. You showed her so bravely that you wanted and needed her friendship, her love, and she stepped in and started letting that part of her come through and gave it to you. And who knows how much more this whole good thing you've started will spread through her and her friends, through Luke, your Dad, even Aunt Melinda!

Don't forget Aunt Ellen. She's always been an angel.

And you've become one too, and helped a lot of other people on the way. Be strong, Nicole, just like your mom said, and believe in yourself. You did that. And no, you didn't do it alone. I helped, and that great big creative force for love and all that's good and right with the world, all worlds, helped too.

You mean God.

Whatever. God is working through you.

And through you.

And through everyone, as much as they're willing.

It's true. But GA, I have an important question. You talked about how much I helped everyone else, and you've made me feel so good about that. And I know and appreciate and love how much you've helped me. But what about you? Have I helped you? Can people do that? Have I helped you at all, GA?

Yes. Nicole, you taught me so many things I'm not even going to list them. OK, I'll list a few: patience, trust, even faith. Nicole, you showed me that I can believe everything will work out in the end if I keep on hoping and believing. Dreams can come true. And they have for me. Nicole, being with you has taught me all about love, true love.

The kind that never dies?

Yeah, that kind.

I wish I could hug you.

Feel it. We're hugging right now. And I don't want you to talk anymore. Just listen. Don't answer me. I get the last word. I, your guardian angel, promise I will never leave you. Whether you write to me or sit in the stillness by the lake, whether you live for another eighty years or come see me in a few days, I will always be with you. I know now that you and I are in this together, for the long haul, and that, my beautiful angel Nicole, is a very long time.

GA?

I said no more talking!

Yeah. But you're a pushover.

Really! What do you want? Don't spoil the moment. I'm on a roll!

I won't. I just want you to sing to me one more time.

OK, we've come to the last verse. I'm happy to sing it to you. But be quiet and listen, and no comments!

> *When we've been here ten thousand years*
> *Bright shining as the sun.*
> *We've no less days to sing God's praise*
> *Than when we've first begun.*

That kind of fits with things nowadays too.

It does.

SHHHHHH!

Tuesday, November 6

Aunt Melinda came to see me today.

She was nice.

That's all I have to say.

Wednesday, November 7
Afternoon

It's me again. That is to say, me, Nicole, is writing this entry. This is it. It's been so good. Will you be with me? I know you will. I have nothing left to say. No more questions to ask. No profound words to leave to the world. I only have me, and that's good enough. In fact, that's a miracle in itself. Really, because that's one thing I know, and everything else is faith, and love, and the countless possibilities that follow.

Standing Tall

The leaves are all dropping now.
Color gone,
Brittle,
They fall away.
I am the naked tree.
I shiver in the wind.
No longer shade to hide me
My bones arch here and there:
Twisted branches broken.
Winter's darkness comes.
Will I live this night?
Will the heavy snow of winter break me?
Will I fall silently in the forest?
I have stood the test some one hundred times.
I will see the dawn.
I will witness the spring.
I will live 'til these leaves
Grow green again.

N. M. B.

Nicole here. This is my last entry. After this entry I'm going to give this to Mr. Schnarr to hold for me. He can make it into a book. I would like that. If I'm dead that is, otherwise it would be really embarrassing!

Oh, GA, this is the last time I write to you. I know deep inside that I won't be writing to you again. Shhhh. Don't answer me today. I know you will be with me. I am frightened but I am STRONG, and still amazingly calm. It is all fading now, like the shock of a loud noise ringing in the ears, it slowly passes away and fades to quiet within. All is quiet now. So quiet . . .

My heart is grateful. I thank you my beautiful angel for helping me get to this place, and be who I am. I know I have become something, perhaps everything I ever wanted to be, even though my body and brain fail me. You gave me that chance. You walked with me every step of this path, and even carried me when I couldn't walk anymore. I love you.

I love my father for who he is and what he has lived through, and he has listened to me and cared for me and has grown in the last few months. I will hold no anger toward him, but only love and compassion as he loses his only daughter born of the only woman he ever loved. I pray that he continues to grow and to be there for Luke. And I am still filled with sadness about Luke. But I just have to let him go, as he must let me go. I am glad that he knows he has a sister who loves him, and who never gave up on him. You were right, GA. He will be better for that. And I rest in comfort believing, as you say, that love never dies.

To my friends: Smiles! Wonder! I know I am loved. That's baffling to me, in a good way. Their love is like a surprise gift to me. I wish them all the best, until we meet again. I send them angelic breath of blessings and love.

So, what now? Shhhh. Don't talk. I know what. I will write the end of this story before I go.

I want to pull through, and what is there to say about this story of pulling through? I live! I get better! I continue writing to my angel, and we all grow up, ha ha, you included, GA, and we all live happily ever after. But that's easy to write, and so simple. And if I don't pull through? Who will finish this story? How will it end? What good would sharing any of this diary be if I did die and this journal didn't have an ending written here? I will tell whoever may read this what will happen if I die. And it's a happy ending. It really is. Here goes. . . .

And so Nicole came to the hospital early that November morning. A large crowd of family and friends accompanied her, so many people the hospital didn't know what to do with them. They waited in the waiting room, and her father and brother stood by her side as she was carted across the hospital floors to the operating room. When they reached the door they each kissed her with words of "good luck," while the tears they could not hide bespoke their quiet goodbyes. They held each other in the lobby as she was led away from them, and she took one last long look as the closing doors separated her from her family. That image of father and son hugging each other gave her such hope, knowing they had each other to hold, and having the courage to hold each other and to share their sadness, comfort, and love. Would there be any other picture by which to remember them? Not one so sweet.

As she was scooted onto the operating table she was amazed at how small it actually was. And yet the equipment surrounding her stood up like mountains of dials, meters, tubes, electronics, and flashing lights. "Luke would love this place," she thought to herself. "All these gadgets." As she lay on the table so many faces appeared over her, garbed with caps and masks. They introduced themselves to her one by one, as if they were going to be good friends, and they asked her several times who she was and why she was there. She found this amusing, because though they were only trying to verify that she was the right patient for the right operation, she did happen to have a brain tumor, and might have just as easily told them she was there for a root canal. They worked steadily, preparing all sorts of machines and tools, and they stuck a needle in her arm in a very businesslike fashion, but with the care of experience and expertise. Not long after this she felt herself slipping into the deep, as if she had been cut free from whatever held her fast to this conscious world. They asked her to count to . . . Well, she didn't even hear what number they wanted her to count to. All went silent, dark. It was a familiar place, empty, peaceful, so still. She was not afraid.

Nicole did not know how much time had passed. She could not see but she could hear. What she heard was not the sound of spitting monitors, conversations in the hallways, or the hum of bright fluorescent lights. She heard the sound of singing birds. Like birds which sing in early morning before the dawn and then grow silent as the day breaks, these birds broke the silence of the night. They called to one another and from tree to tree carried on their conversations. Nicole somehow knew that the birds were talking about her, as if in excited anticipation of her awakening. She lay there in the darkness listening, resting, for what seemed like a few moments mixed with eternity. She lay there until the birds, each in their own time, grew silent, content with the rising of the sun and the birth of day.

As she felt more energy filling her body and spirit, she also noticed the light. As if a veil were gently lifted off her face, the light softly filled her face and eyes. The light became bright around her but did not hurt her eyes. She noticed she was lying in a forest, the light shining through the leaves of the trees as they fluttered in the faint breath of a warm wind. An occasional bird would sing, but she also heard a sound more constant and enlivening. It was the sound of trickling water. She sat up to see before her a winding stream with the clearest water she had ever seen. And right away she noticed that the sound of the waters came from three directions, upstream, downstream, and the busy ripples of a current right in front of her. She smiled. This was too cool.

Though she saw no one there in the woods, she felt that she was not alone, as if there were very tender and caring invisible beings who helped her, comforted her, lifted her to her feet as soon as she felt ready. She also noticed that the forest was alive with little creatures. Several little reddish-brown chipmunks scooted here and there amidst the leaves, rocks, earth, and moss. Occasional squirrels leapt from tree to tree above, and those birds! The birds were adorned in a variety of colors she had never seen before. Some were of the bluest blue, and several little birds stood proudly with yellow beaks and heads, and the most gorgeous lavender tummies, with darker wings of a color not recognized. The reds of the cardinals were a brighter red than she had ever seen. They were so many and so varied, and dotted the brownish-green forest with explosive reds, blues, purples, and yellows here, there, and everywhere!

As she stood there and gained her bearings, she noticed that something even more dramatic had happened. She had stood up with no dizziness, and no pain. She reached for her face and felt cheek to cheek the soft, tight skin of her earlier youth. The numbness completely gone, her cheeks welcomed the hot tears that spilled from her eyes. Stepping toward the water and then into the stream, skipping from stone to stone, she spied a quiet pool between the rushing waters and leaned over toward the water to find her reflection. What she saw was the most beautiful young woman she had ever seen, with wide and bright hazel eyes, golden flowing hair, vibrant face and smile. Her tears grew even steadier until they fell into the still water and blurred the image within. Standing up, she felt the weight of days, months, and years drop off of her, with all of its heaviness, sadness, and pain. Gratitude and wonder now bursting forth in her heart, she gazed upward. Though the branches of the trees seemed to part and fill her face with the sun's full light, it was her spirit which had opened fully and now filled her whole being with joy.

She composed herself the best she could. It took some time because she was really quite overwhelmed with excitement and all this new beauty. She realized that beside the stream was a well-trodden path that looked like it led to an opening into clear sky. She almost felt that something or someone had given her a little nudge and said, "Go on." But she saw and heard nothing. It was just a feeling. So she did take a few steps and then began to walk briskly through the forest path as it wound here and there with the stream, and then crossed over the stream by means of a wooden bridge made of logs and branches tightly wound together. The path continued up a slight embankment and toward an opening at the top of the hill.

When she reached the opening she gasped with amazement. There, it seemed, was the end of her road. Literally, it was Cherry Lane just as she remembered it as a child. What could this mean? Was she home? Had she somehow forgotten all that had happened after the operation and now had awakened back where she started? She walked up the road toward her home. As she came closer to the end of the road, as it met up with the pike, she saw that her own house was just a bit different than when she had left it. It didn't seem quite real.

Just then she noticed her father and brother coming out of the house, talking and laughing. She ran and threw herself into her father's arms, but passed right through. She reached out for her brother's hand but her hands just slipped right through his. They both jumped in the family car and drove off. It all happened so quickly she didn't have time even to react, to try to get into the car with them, or chase them down the road. As she walked toward the road where the car had disappeared, it dawned on her that something really different was going on. She was a smart girl, and had seen all those ghost movies. She said, "I knew it. I'm dead!" Though this was not a shock to her, as much as just a realization, she did keep repeating to herself quite loudly, "I'm dead. I'm dead. I'm really dead!"

Just then a voice called to her from across the street. The voice replied, "No you're not. You're not dead. No one ever really dies." She looked up to see that it was her mother! She looked beautiful, vibrant, and young, and she was beaming with happiness.

"MOM!" Nicole cried as she launched herself across the street, looking both ways before she crossed. They fell into each other's arms and cried and laughed and cried, and then laughed some more.

"Mom, Mom, Mom!"

"Nicole! Oh, Nicole! You're not dead. Love never dies."

As they hugged and between hugs held each other's hands, the entire scene across the street faded away, all the homes with the picket fences, patios, and pools, everything disappeared. In its place the beautiful forest she had left behind stood before the both of them. And there was the path she had followed. She then knew without a doubt that she was no longer on earth.

"Yes. You are in heaven!" her mother blurted out with such humanity and tearful joy.

"Heaven!" Nicole repeated it several times. "Heaven! Heaven, Mom!"

They walked and talked for a few hours it seemed, but they never got tired. They talked about all the old memories and about Dad and Luke. Her mother said that she thought of them every moment of the day, and sometimes she even got to look in on them to see that all would be just fine. She had comforted Luke many times, and was always there when he called. She said she was so sad that Nicole had to suffer, but she had known that Nicole would soon be with her.

"Can we stay together forever, Mom?"

"I think that might be part of the plan. We'll always be able to see each other. In heaven you're only as far away as you want to be and as close as 'Hello.' But you will have your own life, Nicole, and I'm sure it will be full of love and good times. It just gets better and better here. When your father comes, I'm going to show him everything!"

Nicole took a few moments to breathe it all in. But those last words of her mother had brought the strangest feeling to Nicole's stomach.

"Butterflies!" she said as she put her hands over her stomach.

"Yes. There are all sorts of butterflies here," replied her mother.

Nicole didn't even hear her mother's reply. She knew these butterflies were caused by something else. A realization? Anticipation? Or was it that deep intuition of love that shot through her body as she turned and looked to the top of the hill?

There he was, smiling brightly and opening his arms toward her. Each ran to the other and embraced passionately. They looked into each other's eyes with a full love never experienced or witnessed on earth.

"I've been waiting so long for you. Now we are together for a very long time," he said.

"How long?" Nicole asked.

"Remember, Nicole. Love never dies. It lasts forever."

Nicole asked her guardian angel to take her on one of those flights again, over the forest and fields and water below. She turned to her mother and said, "We'll be back in a while." She took his hand and he pulled her into his arms. They lifted off the ground together, flying high over the trees.

"By the way, GA," Nicole asked, "What *is* your name?"

They flew off into the morning sun together.

For many people on earth it may look like the end for Nicole and her secret guardian angel. But this was just the beginning.

Yep. That's how it will happen.

Nicole Meredith Bealert

Addendum

Be forewarned. If you are content with the way Nicole concluded her diary at this point, feel free to go no further. What you have just finished reading is, indeed, the way Nicole imagined her story would end. But if you wish to know more about the details of what actually occurred the day of her operation, read on.

It could be said . . . No, it should be said right away that on the day of the surgery, Friday, November 9, Nicole Meredith Bealert died during the operation. This was, after all, an extremely difficult procedure, because the cancer had grown around some nerves and parts of the brain directly in charge of her vital systems. After a very long and difficult operation lasting some seven-and-a-half hours, on removing what looked like all but a tiny piece of the tumor wedged underneath the cerebellum, the surgeon pushed his scalpel a tiny fraction of a centimeter too far into the deep gray tissue and apparently "nicked" something he shouldn't have nicked. Nicole's vitals shut down immediately; the monitors went flat, her heart stopped. My beautiful girl died.

And so it is only fair and appropriate that I tell my part of the story, not to interfere with the way Nicole wanted it to end, but to tell you how I saw it end, because, well, because I must. Here is my story and the way I see hers.

When Nicole was asked to count to ten as she lay on the table, she only remembers a huge gap opening up between the numbers three and four, which turned into a space of infinite expanse. At that point everything went dark.

The operation was going better than expected; the crack surgical team worked methodically to remove the tumor, and paid close attention to any change in Nicole's vitals. In the end, though, it only took a tiny mistake to turn a successful operation into a nightmare. The conversation in the O.R. went something like this, starting with the surgeon, and then it seemed everyone had something to say in the chaos that followed:

"Oh, God."

"Did you?"

"Get the sutures!"

"Doctor! Something's wrong."

"I know, I know!"

"Sutures?"

"Everything's flat."

"Is it plugged in? Did you pull something?"

"No, no, Jesus, I hit something."

"She's gone."

"Prepare the defib."

"You're kidding!"

"It's flat."

"What happened?"

"I must have nicked something. Let's go!"

When that monitor went flat, and buzzed that stinging alarm to the team, warning that Nicole's functions had ceased, everyone knew that meant she was clinically, medically, scientifically, and unequivocally dead. And in that instant when, excuse me, but all hell broke loose in the operating room, Nicole suddenly awakened to find herself flying through that vast darkness toward a growing light, as if being shot through the barrel of a cosmic gun into some other realm of life.

"Clear."

Boom!

"Nothing."

Instantly Nicole stood on the brim of a grassy hill gently sloping upward, and all around her was the light of a morning brighter than anything she'd seen. Everywhere she looked from this lofty vantage point, she spied majestic mountains blending into graceful valleys, grassy fields stretching into green forests of every kind, and the clearest and most exquisite array of rivers and streams she'd ever seen. Here and there small towns popped up in the distance, and the buildings and houses seemed to be twinkling, glittering, and glistening, like some ornamental Christmas scene. A very warm wind blew through her hair.

"Hair?" she suddenly wondered to herself.

Yes, it was hair, her hair, long, beautiful, glistening in the morning light, and as it brushed across her face in the wind she noticed it smelled like spring.

"Whatever this shampoo is, I've gotta get more!" she spoke out loud to herself.

As she became more aware of her circumstances, she noticed she was wearing a beautiful dress, a type of silky material with a variety of colors and depth, almost like it was layered with different portrayals of reality, and when she looked closer, she could only think of a garden, that she was clothed in the most beautifully made and decorated dress she had ever seen. And instantly she knew, as she raised her arms, that instead of the gaunt, bony, bruised, and needle-marked limbs of her dying body, that she was whole again. She had the arms, legs, face, and body of a healthy, strong, beautiful, vibrant, sixteen-year-old girl! A flush of tears filled her eyes.

"Clear!"

Boom!

"Nothing. Doctor!"

Nicole suddenly found herself on the top of the hill. As she raised her head she saw in the distance a man walking toward her. Not only did he look exactly like she had imagined, but something inside of her just knew, all the way down to her soul, that this was her angel. She ran to him like she had never run before, without effort, as if flying toward him. As she reached him he smiled so wide as he raised his arms to receive her, tears in both their eyes. They embraced.

"Clear!"

Boom! Things just went dark for a moment, like a lightning blast temporarily blanking out a TV, or some longer-than-usual black blip on a movie screen. In the blackness voices, disconsolate voices, spoke.

"It's no use. Someone call it."

"Four fifty-five p.m."

"That's it."

"No."

"Yes. She's gone."

Lost for a moment, she awoke to the warmth of their embrace, realizing that the two of them melded together as if one person. All time and any sense of place disappeared; God, heaven, life, love, all worlds, the universe and everything blended into one. She knew without any doubt where she was—heaven.

As Nicole pulled her head back far enough to look into her angel's face, their eyes met, and to them their minds seemed as one. No words needed to be spoken. His eyes spoke to her of his love for her, and she could even see into his soul, could see that he knew how deeply she loved him. In a wave of passion she moved to kiss him, but lifting his hand, he gently placed his finger on her lips. He raised his eyebrows just enough to ask a question without words, something that must be asked before anything else could happen in this new world. As she paused, startled a bit by his reaction, she saw a very slight and somewhat coy grin form on his mouth. She knew. She instantly knew what he was asking. He didn't need words, or pictures, or some long review of her life. They didn't need to delve into one of their lengthy philosophical discussions, or duel about who or what was right, or even make any gesture of any kind. His silent gaze held the most important question she had ever been asked up to this point in her life, and for that matter, up to this point in her death as well!

What was the question? If you asked Nicole she'd say it was beyond words. It was so many things brought together at once. In a flash she saw her brother, father, family, and friends. She saw she had eternity before her, and infinite possibilities. She knew the question was about whether she wanted to stay here in this new place or go back, whether she had learned enough about the world, or loved enough, and even whether she believed enough. Did she believe? Did she believe in miracles, and at this point, what did the word "miracle" mean, anyhow? And while all this was happening inside of her, a new question formed, directed toward her angel. Without words her eyes meekly met his, and the question didn't need to be asked out loud. Would he really save her? Would he break all the rules? Was it possible that he loved her so much that . . . he took his finger off her lips and placed it on his own, as if to say, "Shhhhh. This is our secret."

Suddenly every machine lit up in the operating room. Doctors and nurses who had been bent over in bewilderment jumped and gazed at the monitors, which now pulsed their messages loud and clear—LIFE!

"What the hell is going on?"

"Let's get this thing going again."

"I've never in my entire life . . ."

"A miracle!"

"She's got one hell of a guardian angel working overtime."

"Enough of that. Let's do this thing."

Nicole came back to life. She lived. That's the end of my story.

❊   ❊   ❊

Is that how it happened, GA? I like that.

Yep. That's how I saw it. Now the rest of the story, I mean your life, well, that's up to you.

I know.

The End
or rather

The Beginning

Nicole Meredith Bealert

Thank you, Nicole, for sharing your journal,
your life, and your guardian angel with the rest
of the world. I'm proud of you.

G. R. S.